ENDERING

MIRA'S JOURNEY

T.L.HUTCHINSON

Agrenon
From the Royal Library Of
Agrenon

DEDICATION

To the me who read books by moonlight as a child.

To the me who wrote stories in all her school notebooks.

To the me who took
'I can't wait to watch you fail'
As a challenge

We fucking did it.

TRIGGER WARNINGS

Gore, loss of a loved one, blood, sickness, murder, trafficking, kidnapping, political unrest, tight enclosed spaces, being drugged, physical abuse, torture, asphyxiation, graphic violence, grief, mourning, loss, corpses, assault mentions, incarceration, flashbacks, ptsd, and near death experiences.

Please take care of yourself <3

"Mira, you have to be faster than that." I ignored the woman at the edge of the forest clearing. Rolling hard as my attacker crashed toward me, leaping to my feet as he landed, a mass of brown fur and metal plating. I took three quick steps back, still facing him as the sand settled, giving me a clearer view of his form. He turned, moving his hind legs away from me. Barbarza have weaker hind legs. Yes, she had told me that. I had to get behind him.

"Aww, what's wrong Arlo?" I teased him as he lowered his head between his shoulders, snarling at me. "Is the little human too quick for—" He lunged, and I pivoted, moving to his side and slamming my back against his hind leg, moving with him as he tried to turn to snap at me, my maneuver leaving me barely out of his reach.

"Get back here, you pain in the ass," his voice sounded in my head, half laughing, his green eyes alight with faux frustration.

"Naw, you see, I don't want to," I said, before his weight shifted. I didn't need to think. He was going to roll on me. I ducked, moving to the space under his legs as he toppled to the side. Coming out in front of him, I reached for the knife that was supposed to be at my hip, only to find nothing there.

"What's the matter, little Endering? Looking for your knife?" His voice dripped with sarcasm. I tore my eyes from his, listening to his steps as I looked for the bright gray-white handle, spotting it in the sand behind him. I met his fierce gaze as he stalked forward.

"Yeah, you disarmed me, but at least I don't look like a hyena that lost a fight with a hair dryer." He lunged, and I leaped beneath him, bypassing his attack. I had to be quick. I had to keep myself from those front legs of his. My hands found the handle of the blade as I landed, hearing him pivot from his new spot on the training field where I had been a moment before, kicking up sand. He lunged again before I could get up. Rolling onto my back, each of his front paws landed on each side of my head, his bared teeth lunging toward me as I pushed the sharp edge of the blade against the plate armor at his throat. His teeth gently came to a rest against my temples as the knife caught on his armor.

"That's enough for today," Sil said from her place at the edge of the clearing. "You don't want to be too tired for tomorrow,"

"Tomorrow?," I asked, as Arlo snorted, lifting his teeth up off my of my head.

"You didn't tell her?" He looked at Sil, who shook her head.

"She'll be fine,"

"Silvia…"

"She. Will. Be. Fine." Arlo stepped off of me, turning to glare at my grandmother at the edge of the clearing. Her salt-and-pepper straight black hair stopped before her shoulders, those mossy eyes sharp as she glared back.

"Wait, I'm going in tomorrow?" I got to my feet, trying to dust off the sand that covered me.

"Yes."

"Holy shit, finally!" I said, turning to hug Arlo around the neck. "We're going in! You're going home! Oh, do I get to see the eggs? Are they cool? What power am I gonna get? Is it going to be awesome?"

"Calm down."

"I'm calm, I'm totally calm. Who's not calm?" I heard Arlo chuckle in my head.

"You're about as calm as a tornado."

"Shh…"

"Don't you shush me." Sil pursed her lips into a thin line waiting for our bickering to stop. Arlo jerked his body a little, shaking me slightly to get his revenge.

"Jerk."

"You love it when I'm a jerk."

"Anyway," Sil said, interrupting us. "You won't know the power you get, until you get there, you get to see the eggs tonight, and don't forget that you have to actually act like an Endering of Agrenon," Sil said firmly before leading the way toward the cabin. Arlo helped me scramble onto his back, his plates clanking as he followed her.

"Fine, fine. Whose idea was it for the eggs to hang out on Earth, anyway? Seems like a terrible decision."

"The Echalon, their eggs, their plan," Sil said. "And you better not question it unless you want to be proven wrong." I rolled my eyes, letting the silence fall in as we got to the back porch of the cabin. I slid off Arlo, knowing he wouldn't need help with his plates of armor, and followed Sil inside, bouncing on my feet.

"Where are they? Are they cool?" Sil waved, gesturing for me to follow her into her study. The small square room was lined with poster-sized drawings, a few weapons were mounted against the wall, and a trunk sat in the corner behind the large, heavy oak desk. A small cabinet resting in front of the desk held the eggs, tucked away from prying eyes. Sil grabbed a bag, unzipping it as she nodded to the cabinet. I rushed over and opened it, revealing the two small orbs inside. They were each a little smaller than a soccer ball, one a deep amber color, the light bouncing around inside the egg like it would on the multiple faces of a crystal. The other was a deeper gray, but it still caught the light like the first, though the light looked softer, almost weak, as it bounded through the rougher egg.

"Wow," I said, touching the amber egg.

"Wow, is a good way to describe them," Sil said, holding out the bag. "Remember, they're the last of their kind, at least in Agrenon."

"What about everywhere else?" I asked, pointing to a map on the wall.

"As far as we can be sure, this is it in all five kingdoms, the others might have secret stashes of them, but we don't really have the authority to barge into their castles and ask about it," she said as I carefully picked up each egg, placing them in the bag. She zipped it shut and let me take it from her, sliding it over my shoulder. It fit like a messenger bag against me.

"Why are they being hunted again?"

"Their hearts are boiled down into a drug that can take an Endering out of a fight, or molded into pretty jewelry. So, in short, people suck. Remember, leaders will rip their kingdoms apart, just to get their hands on an Echalon's heart," I shifted the bag. The eggs weren't heavy, but their presence weighed on my shoulders.

"This was my dad's mission, right, before he disappeared?" I asked, and she nodded.

"It's yours now though, considering he isn't around to follow through with it and those two are getting closer to hatching every day." she pointed to the eggs. "Saha might know what happened to him, if we're lucky. Just remember, she's probably going to have a bunch of shit for you to do when you get there,"

"Yeah, no kidding…. and what about my mom?" Sil's eyes narrowed, and I quickly changed the subject to a less explosive subject.

"Queen Saha won't take advantage of them, right?" Sil closed her eyes, sighing heavily. The queen wasn't her fondest subject of conversation, but it was better than getting her to talk about my mom.

"No. Thankfully, she's not *that* horrible," she said before standing. "You can keep my blade for when you go in." She pointed to the knife at my side still. "Let's get some food and get some sleep," she said, walking past me to lead the way out of the room. I glimpsed the twisting banishment mark at the back of her neck, but tried to shove it out of my mind before following her to the kitchen. We sat and ate in relative silence.

"Sil, why were you banished?" I knew better than to ask too many questions of her, especially about the banishment, but here I was pushing buttons even I knew I shouldn't be pushing. She couldn't even step through the portal. I needed to know, so I didn't make the same mistake, but she didn't answer me, just picked up her plate before getting up and going back to her study. I had tread dangerous waters.

It was going to be me and Arlo out there in this fray, but we were ready. Ready to take on the world on the other side of the portal. After I finished eating, Sil still hadn't come out of her study. I left her alone, knowing better than to push her any further. I held the egg bag close and slipped into my room, the night already descending upon us as I changed and slid the bag back on, tucking myself around the precious cargo inside. Arlo would be waiting for me tomorrow, waiting for me to bring him back home. Waiting to introduce me to the wonderful world I had been promised. A world of dragons, and adventure, and joy; a hell of a lot better than any school or job on Earth could be. I was an Endering of Agrenon, and it was my job to guard the Echalon with my life. I was ready. I held them close to me, pulling a blanket over us, and took a breath, trying to calm myself. I was going into the Otherworld. Even if it was a terrible name.

"It's alright, I'll get you home. We're going on an adventure."

2

"Get up, Mira,"

"Don't want to," I said, rolling over. The egg bag shifted against me as I moved and remembered the events from the day before. I tried not to fall out of bed as my blankets tangled against my leg. "I'm up!"

"Remember what you're doing today?" Sil asked, standing in the doorway. She had a hoodie draped over one arm, a drink for each of us in each hand.

"Yup," I said, untangling myself and the bag from the blankets. I pulled the bag over my shoulder and moved to take a cup of hot chocolate from her.

"Easy," she said, shaking her head. "I'm surprised you got any sleep."

"I got a little," I said, drinking the hot chocolate as she turned and led me to the kitchen.

"Hurry, Arlo's getting antsy,"

"You would be too if you finally got to go home," I said, finishing the last of the piping hot liquid before passing the cup to her.

"*Hurry, Mira!*" I could imagine him in my head, pacing back and forth.

"Alright, alright," I said, returning to my room. I grabbed my favorite undergarments and a pair of jeans that fit well, along with a comfortable dark-blue tee shirt, before heading back through the kitchen and into the bathroom. I left the egg bag at the door as I showered and dressed quickly. Picking the bag back up on my way out as I walked to the kitchen, where a plate of eggs and sausage sat on the table.

"Spoiling me now, huh?"

"There is nothing wrong with feeding you well," Sil said, sitting down with her plate. We ate in silence, but every few minutes, a sharp, high-pitched noise resounded through the open windows in the living room.

"Oh, you're fine, be patient," Sil said, looking towards the back door to where Arlo was undoubtedly waiting as we finished. I passed my plate to her, and she took it to the sink.

"It's like he's dying or something," I said, and she rolled her eyes.

"*Come on!*" Arlo said, the whine sounding again.

"Hurrying up." I went back to my room, pulled on socks and boots, and returned to the kitchen, where Sil passed me the bag she had packed the night before. I checked that the egg bag was at my hip again and slung the pack over my shoulders.

"Ready?"

"I better be. Otherwise, he's gonna start growing thumbs, and then we're all screwed." I shrugged, and she managed a smirk, gesturing to the back door. I led the way.

"Your nonchalant attitude really isn't helping my anxiety about all of this." She reached past me to open the back door.

"You'll be fine," I said, seeing Arlo shifting in place next to his saddle. "Did you get that out?" I asked. Sil nodded.

"*Come on!*" Sil took the time to get the saddle in place and secure before I put my foot in the stirrup, slinging my leg over and settling onto his back.

"You be careful," Sil said, resting a hand on my hand.

"I've got this, don't worry; I'll be back before you know it."

"I hope so. Be safe. I love you," she said before stepping back.

"Love you too, and I will."

"I won't let anything happen to her," Arlo said. *"Now, can we go?"*

"Go," Sil said. "Just—"

"Be safe. Got it. A hundred percent safe, I promise," I said, giving her a thumbs-up as Arlo walked toward the forest. I looked back at Sil, standing in the doorway now, watching us go on our way.

"Arlo?"

"Yeah?"

"How long is this trip going to be?"

"Don't worry, Sil can handle herself," he said, knowing the real question I wanted to ask without me even having to ask it.

"I know she'll be fine, but will we?"

"We'll be fine."

"At least tell me we're close to the portal..." His laugh sounded in my head. The cool twilight air raised goosebumps on my arms, and I leaned over onto Arlo's back, my arms laying in the dip between his shoulders as we traveled the hour-long journey to the portal. "Is that it?" I asked, seeing the stone arch as we approached.

"Yup."

"It looks like shit." The arch was a dark gray, and it looked like someone had tried to glue a bunch of rocks and boulders together. Almost as if it had once been a unified thing and was gradually crumbling.

"Mira, it's so old we don't even know how old it is; of course, it looks like shit." He shook his head, approaching the arch steadily before stopping in front of it.

"Ready?" I asked

"Only if you are." He turned his head to look at me, and I nodded. He faced the portal again and started forward.

"Last moment on Earth," I said before holding my breath and closing my eyes at the last minute. A tingling sensation rose over my whole body; a static-like feeling washed over me, like when a limb falls asleep from lying on it for too long, but over every inch of my being. It wasn't until it faded that Arlo spoke.

"Home..." I opened my eyes and the sting of tears threatened to overwhelm me. In twenty years, Arlo hadn't been here, his home, and now he danced in place. I leaned back in the saddle, grabbed the handles at the top, and pressed my feet hard into the stirrups.

"Well, go on." I didn't want to be tossed to the ground, but Arlo needed a moment. He jumped and trotted to the nearest tree, rubbing his face and neck against it.

"It smells like freedom!"

"It smells like the woods."

"That's the smell of freedom!" he said, and I rolled my eyes. He shook out his fur and started through the trees at a gentle trot, tail wagging, ears perked.

"Where are we going now? Besides, toward the castle," I asked, keeping my head low as we went through some thick branches.

"Well, the first landmark is the Sky Fields, if that's what you meant."

"Sky Fields?"

"Oh, I can't wait to see your face when you see them; they're stunning! Dangerous, but stunning."

"Oh, don't bother going into any of the details." I reached down to rub his flank, and he tossed his head.

"I won't. It'll be much better to see you surprised; I think that's the best part of escorting a new Endering. You all seem to think everything is wondrous and new and shiny," he said. *"And once we're done with this, I will finally get to go see Tamaj again."*

"Your mate, right?"

"That's right, it's been a long time."

"Do you think she moved on?"

"Barbarza mate for life, and she knew what I was doing. She wouldn't have even tried unless she had undeniable proof I was dead,"

he explained, tail wagging gently as he wove through the ever-thickening trees.

"I can't wait to meet her; she sounds pretty great. How do people choose mates, though?"

"She is. You make your partner a trinket, usually something small that they wear to signify that they're taken. I made her an earring, beaded with feathers. Your dad actually had to help me since I don't have thumbs."

"Damn thumbs." I shifted in the saddle before another question came to mind. "What's Saha like?"

"Glass."

"Well, that's shitty."

"Why?"

"She's fragile?"

"Photomyran are all fragile; they're plant people and easy to physically break, Mira. I think you'll like her, though."

"Considering she will not be boiling the hearts of unborn children to get high, she sounds pretty awesome," I said, patting the egg bag at my side to ensure it was still there. "How long does this trip usually take?"

"Bored already?" he asked, and I rolled my eyes.

"Fine, don't answer," I said, letting the conversation stretch into comfortable silence until the sun graced the horizon. "Can I ask you about something Sil wouldn't tell me about?"

"Sounds like dangerous territory…but ask," he said

"My parents, she said they got lost here…is it really that dangerous?"

"Mira, we don't know what really happened to them…all we know is your father went to check on his brother, and when he didn't come back, your mother went after him. You know as much as we do."

"They would have come back, right? If they could?"

"Your father would have, for sure."

"And mom?"

"Your mother…was a complicated woman. I don't know for sure if she would have, and that has nothing to do with you."

"Sil wouldn't even tell me her name."

"That's because if you leave the two of them alone together for any serious length of time, they'd probably try to rip each other's throats out with their teeth," he said, snorting and shaking his head.

"They hated each other that much?"

"Oh, yeah. They were always there for each other, though, when the going got tough, but those two couldn't stand each other otherwise."

"Great," I said as Arlo came to a stop.

"We should bed down here for the night."

"Fine, we're not going to be cold, right?"

"No, we're not going to be cold," he said as I dismounted and pulled my bags close. The sun dipped behind the horizon soon after I got a campfire started, the darkness descending on us.

"Tell me a story?" I asked.

"Aren't you a little old for stories?"

"You're never too old for stories."

"I'm tired. If you forgot, I did all the walking today."

"I'll carry you tomorrow." He laughed from where he lay near the fire and rested his head on his paws.

"Good luck with that."

"Please?"

"There will be time for stories tomorrow. Now sleep."

"I don't think I'll be able to sleep; there's a whole world to explore."

"The world isn't going anywhere, Mira," he said as I sat down and leaned against his side.

"Fine, but you're telling me a story tomorrow night."

"Deal."

"Mira, get up!" I leaped up, one hand on the egg bag. The smell of blood lingered in the air, but I couldn't see through the thick darkness of the night. I reached out to where I had left my backpack and unfastened it.

"Arlo?" I pulled out Sil's knife. The sound of a snapping twig made me turn and quiet laughter filled the night. The laughter of a child. "Arlo?" My eyes adjusted to the darkness before a Barbarza stormed through some nearby brush.

"Get on!"

"What's going on?" I said.

"Get on!" I stumbled toward him, the laughter getting louder. I scrambled onto his bare back, grabbing the fur of his mane as he sped off, almost pitching me to the ground.

"What's going on? What are they? Why do I smell blood? What's happening?"

"I went out to check a perimeter I made once you were asleep and was attacked. I had to come back for you. Just hold on."

"What? Are you alright?"

"Hold on!" He charged forward, and I hung on tighter.

"Where are we even going?" Only panting met my ears. He didn't know. He did not know which direction we were heading. I could almost feel the frantic nature of each movement until he collapsed beneath me, pitching me over his head and onto the ground. I could feel the skin of my arms tearing as I skidded across the ground. Blood crept down my arms as I pulled myself up. Everything ached, but nothing was broken.

"Arlo, come on, we gotta get goi—" My heart leapt into my throat as tears stung my eyes. "Arlo?" his stomach was torn open, blood streaking his belly and back legs. The rest of his intestines hung out of his open belly. "You didn't say it was this bad!" I said, dropping the knife and rushing to push my hands against his stomach.

"Mira, don't do that."

"I have to stop the bleeding!"

"Mira…" There was too much bleeding, and we both knew it.

"I can't let you…you should have told me!" Hot tears slid down my cheeks as I pressed harder on the open intestines.

"You would have tried to stop me. We didn't have time; they were coming, and they're still coming." He hadn't tried to get up. His

breathing was heavy. *"I had to give you a chance. There's something wrong with them; they don't smell right, they don't look right,"*

"I'm not leaving you," I said as dawn broke sending streaks of light across the sky as the sound of laughter approached.

"You have to. Don't let them bite you, lick you, anything. Follow the sunrise, sleep in the trees."

"I'm not leaving. I can't do this alone!" I pulled my hands from his belly and went to his head, pulling it into my lap and stroking his fur.

"You can because you have too," he said, coughing blood onto my lap. I shook my head, wrapping my fingers in his mane.

"Shh, it's going to be okay. You're going to be fine. We're going to get to the castle, then we're going to see Tamaj, and then —" He breathed out, his body shuddering. His eyes dilated as they glazed over, his chest no longer moving. The laughter grew closer, but I pulled his head as close to my chest as I could, hugging him tightly. "I'm so sorry," I said before getting up and resting his head carefully on the ground as the mottled brown creatures came into view. They looked like medium-sized dogs, their teeth sticking out of their bottom jaws, their short floppy ears torn, and their eyes glazed white.

I turned, bolting to the closest tree as they picked up speed, barreling toward me. I scrambled upward, feeling a tug on my pants. Looking down, I saw one had grabbed hold of the hem of my jeans. I kicked out, landing a blow to its head, my pants tearing as I scrambled up and out of their reach. I turned my head as I settled on a branch stable enough to hold my weight and pressed my hands to my ears. But not before hearing the shrill laughter as they started to eat the corpse of my best friend.

3

The laughter didn't stop for hours. The sound of the creatures on the forest floor made it hard to think as hot tears slid down my cheeks. I rested my hand on the egg bag, pulling it close to me. I had left Sil's knife near Arlo and would have to make a break for it once daylight came. My heart pounded as my eyes adjusted to the darkness. Which way did we come from? Where was the portal? I couldn't do this myself. I had to go back and get Sil. I had to ask her what I should do. Arlo was supposed to be my guide; he was supposed to have my back. They didn't expect the dog creatures. No, that wasn't it; Arlo said they were different. Sil and Arlo had known those creatures existed, but something wasn't right with them. This wasn't the world they had left.

I unzipped the egg bag, reaching in to run my hands over the two Echalon eggs. I had to do this for them, but how was I supposed to keep going when I didn't know what to do?

"Follow the sunrise, sleep in the trees," I said, more to myself than anyone, before zipping the bag back up. Arlo had tried so hard in his last moments to help me, to get me away from danger, to give me the directions I'd need. I couldn't let him down now. He couldn't die for nothing. I closed my eyes tight, trying to wipe the tears away as the darkness faded. Leaning up against the tree trunk, I waited, trying not to think of the soft giggles in the brush. It wasn't until the light broke through the trees that the laughter vanished. Was it safe to come down? Every rustling leaf and shifting branch made me think I was going to die. Was there a chance it was quiet only so I would come down? Were they smart enough to plan like that?

I waited longer, until the sun's heat had warmed my back, before slowly climbing down, listening closely for snapping twigs or laughter. All that met me was silence as I slid onto the forest floor. Turning, I looked back to where Arlo's body lay, not much more than scraps of flesh clinging to scattered bones. My stomach twisted, threatening to toss the remnants of my last meal, but I swallowed hard, trying to keep it down as I spotted movement.

A person was slowly approaching Arlo's body through the trees. His tawny brown skin had cool undertones and his posture was cautious, his sword drawn in one hand as he approached, slowly, knees slightly bent, quickly looking back and forth as he approached Arlo. I couldn't let him get to Arlo; who knew what he would do? I scanned the area, spotting the knife I had left near Arlo's body, and ran for it. My legs trembled and my cheeks were still sore from crying the night before. I heard him scramble as I got to the knife, my foot slipping. I took a knee, looking up to meet his eyes. He had raised his sword a few yards away, holding it with both hands now, but his face had gone pale. His eyes were wide and the floppy mess of dark brown hair on his head almost obstructed his gilded brown eyes.

"Back up," I said, returning to my feet. He immediately stepped back, even though I was in the most prone position. He blinked hard and took a few steadying breaths before looking me over, and his eyes flickered to Arlo and back to me. "Don't even think about it."

"Think about what?" he asked. His accent was thick and clearly didn't originate from Earth. He lowered his sword a little.

"Whatever you were thinking about doing with him," I said.

"He was your friend." It wasn't a question.

"If you so much as touch him—"

"I won't, but he's gone,"

"Doesn't matter." He tilted his head, slowly lowering his sword even more while I spoke.

"You're...very new here, aren't you?"

"What's it to you?" I asked, a smirk tugging at the corner of his mouth, but it didn't last as he ultimately lowered his sword completely. Slowly, he took a knee, lowering his head and holding each arm out to the side.

"I'm no threat to you, Endering," he said, holding the position. I recognized it from Sil's lessons. It was a common pose, one of vulnerability and trust. Used for a slew of different things, from convincing a frightened person you don't want to fight, to proposing and marrying, which occurred at once.

This was clearly the former.

"Damn straight you're not," I said, letting go a breath. He held the position for a moment before I finally lowered my knife. "I won't hurt you either...so long as you don't mess with him."

"Deal," he said, getting back to his feet. "For the record, though, I wasn't planning on it."

"You're an Empathic Maraung, aren't you?" I asked, keeping my eyes on him, firstly because I didn't trust him, and second, because Arlo's remains were the only other thing to look at.

"Yes...what do you know of Empathic Maraung?" he asked, slightly lowering his head and looking up at me from beneath his eyebrows.

"I know enough," I said, but honestly, I didn't know shit. I really should have paid more attention to Sil's lessons. He smirked as if he knew I was lying.

"Almost everyone in my village felt what happened out here; they sent me out to see what it was," he said, gesturing to Arlo's body. "Were you bitten?"

"No, I wasn't bitten. Why didn't you come to help us? You could have saved him." He was already shaking his head.

"It would have been...like asking to die," he said, as if looking for a word he didn't remember.

"Suicide."

"Right, that's the word," he said, shifting his sword a little. "Are you sure you weren't bitten?"

"I'm sure...what would you do if I was?" I asked, looking him over. He couldn't be much older than me, but he was muscular, agile-looking. Could I take him in a fight?

"Thankfully, you won't have to know; I'm Anza."

"Mira," I said. "You would have killed me." The answer was clear.

"I probably would not have been able to, but The Fever is hard to stop; it would have been the only way," he said.

"The Fever, like, a fever? Arlo, my friend, said there was something wrong with the animals from last night. Is that what's wrong?"

"Yes. The sickness has claimed many lives; we don't know how far it has spread, just that once you're bitten, you're infected. It begins with a fierce fever as the first symptom—"

"And you kill the infected to keep the sickness from spreading," I interrupted, and he nodded.

"Some of us do, others...hope for someone who is bitten that does not become ill."

"Are you one of those people?" He went quiet again, not meeting my eyes. "Do I scare you or something?" He almost laughed.

"You're an Endering. Even those who will inevitably try to harm you will be afraid of you," he said. "No other species has the kind of power that you have."

"Not like I know what my power is." I almost immediately regretted the words once they left my mouth.

"Never tell anyone that," he said firmly. "If they know you don't know it, it makes you an easier target."

"Right."

"You...look like you can use a meal...and maybe a chance to clean up?" he said.

"Follow a strange man I've barely met through the forest for food and a bath? Yeah, no."

"What other option do you have?" he asked, letting the question linger. I didn't answer. "If I was really going to hurt you, I wouldn't have told you to keep the power thing to yourself. You've been through a lot, you're in pain, and you deserve to rest."

"Will we be safe?"

"There's no such thing as safety here."

"Safer then?" I asked, and he nodded again.

"I suggest one thing."

"What?" I asked

"Take a piece of his bone with you...we can craft it into a weapon so he can still fight by your side." My stomach flipped and twisted as he spoke.

"Do I have to?"

"No...but where do you think that knife in your hand came from?" I looked down at the white blade, and suddenly the white hue and deep marks made sense. This knife was Sil's, one of Sil's fallen friends.

"I can't."

"I can do it for you if you'll let me." I nodded, trying not to look at him as he moved to the scraps of Arlo's remains. It took him a few moments to select a piece of bone, but he returned to me, holding a long, sturdy-looking bone with a large section on the end. It had to have been a part of Arlo's leg.

"Let's go get you cleaned up," he said.

"You first," I said, anxious of the idea of him behind me. He hadn't tried anything yet, but after all I'd been through already, there was no way I was going to let him walk behind me. I also didn't know where we were going. He didn't challenge me, but nodded and walked toward where I had seen him the first time. I took a deep breath, my hand going to the egg bag at my hip, and followed him. It didn't take long to realize how eerily quiet he was, his feet barely making noise as he moved, picking through the forest carefully. I tried to copy him to keep my mind off the leg bone he was carrying, but I ended up making more noise.

It only took thirty or forty minutes before Anza led me through a swath of ferns, and suddenly, the forest broke open a little. I almost didn't notice the houses; they stood on stilts above my head. As I turned and looked up at them, it was clear we had already passed a few, which hid in the swaths of trees and brush to a point where if you didn't know what to look for, you would miss them. They were all different, tucked in treehouses with glints of colored bits that almost looked like glass carved and woven into the well-structured wooden homes.

"This is your village?"

"Yes, the village of Arkaley," he said, parting another set of ferns.

I stepped through, hearing the soft bustling of people moving as we left the trees behind. There, in the middle of this forest, was a small but bustling village. Maraung, like Anza, and a handful of Photomyran bustling about, tending to children, conversing, washing clothes, and making food. A child tried to wander from its mother but someone else redirected them right back to her. Everyone was doing something until I walked in. At once, most of the people stopped, eyes turning to Anza and me. I took a small step back.

"That's kind of creepy," I said.

"It's okay, stay still." Panic rose inside me, but for a moment, no one moved. Then their eyes dropped, looking away from me.

"What the fuck?" I whispered, looking to Anza, who managed that slight, almost sad smirk again.

"You really are new. Empathic Maraung are open to the emotions of others; they can feel your pain, your discomfort, your fear, and they could feel your emotions last night."

"And anyone can develop that skill? Is it only Maraung?" I asked, as he waved me forward into Arkaley.

"Not everyone, but not just Maraung. Some people find it hard to gain the skill, others master it quickly, but at least two-thirds of Arkaley can do it." I stepped forward to follow him, but he stayed quiet, not meeting my gaze.

"They fear me too."

"Remember what I said earlier. Most of us here are well-meaning, but there are a few that...well."

"I got it," I said as he led me through Arkaley. We only made it a few yards before a child approached me and grabbed my pants. I turned to them. They had a tousle of hair on their head, resting in hues of olive and brown, but it was their eyes; those eyes, the color of well-watered moss, made me stop.

"So sorry." It was tough to breathe, and tears welled up in my eyes again as the community started to shift around me. Hushed whispers were exchanged quickly as they approached. Slowly, one by one, the community surrounded me. Anza leaned closer, hugging me carefully, slowly, giving me all the time in the world to pull away, as if to protect me from too much at once. Someone hugged him. Someone hugged them. Before I knew it, I was in the center of a giant circle; a few Maraung and Photomyran hugged me, and those that couldn't hug me hugged those around me, a giant circle of grief.

They didn't know me. They might even be terrified of me. They didn't know Arlo either. That didn't matter. Grief was grief as far as they were concerned, and though Anza had warned me that not everyone in Arkaley was a good person, it was nice to see that I was not alone. The moment passed, and slowly, they separated from me. The last person to walk away was the child, their hand leaving my pant leg, looking back at me for a moment as they fumbled back to their parents.

"Are you alright?" Anza asked.

I shifted the egg bag to make sure they were both there; they were.

"Y-yeah, can we, um…" I reached up to wipe the tears out of my eyes. "Can we keep going?"

"Of course," he said, leading me toward a small home. Two people were already standing at the base of the ladder that led up into the home; one had a change of clothes and the other had a bucket of hot water. Anza said something to them I didn't understand, nodding his head. They nodded in return and the Maraung holding the clothes passed them to me as Anza took the bucket of hot water.

The two people scrambled off and Anza led the way up, using one hand to traverse the ladder, the other carefully balancing the water as he climbed. I waited until he was at the top before climbing up. The home was built into the growing trees, a small porch on the outside, with well crafted wooden walls, and a roof made of arranged clay shingles. Small depictions of growing vines had been neatly carved into the outside, green stones tucked and molded to complete the elegant and swirling pattern. Anza sat the hot bucket of water on the porch and slipped into the home for a moment before returning and passing me a cloth.

"Thanks," I said.

"Don't forget to clean out those scrapes on your arm; they'll get infected," he said before moving to the edge of the porch where the ladder was. He sat, swinging his legs off, dangling them and waiting for me to be done. I set the egg bag on the porch and plunged the cloth into the hot water. I don't know how long I scrubbed to get the blood off me and clean my wounds, but the water grew pink as I finished. Anza waited until I was done before he spoke again. "If you want to change, you can pop inside for privacy,"

"Right…can I ask you a question?"

"I have a feeling you're the kind of person that would ask anyway," he said, shifting to look at me.

"Yeah, probably; I wondered why…you came for me?"

"I see it like this: if I can help, then I must. It's my duty to do what I can, I have a responsibility, an ability to respond, so I must."

"If only we could all be like that," I said before slipping into the home. It was a completely open floor plan, with some foldable walls made of wooden slats that could be moved. In the center was a round table; round woven mats stood as placeholders. A foldable wall walled off a corner with furs spilling out of it. Something shifted in the corner, but I tried to ignore it. I quickly dressed in clean clothes before carrying the bloody clothes back to the porch with me.

"I can get those washed."

"I can do it; you guys shouldn't have to cater to me."

"We aren't; it's called compassion," he said, holding his hand out. I hesitated momentarily before passing him my bloodied clothes. "Come on, let's get this to the weapon smith, unless you want to make one yourself?" he asked, gesturing to Arlo's leg bone.

"Oh, no, I don't think I could stomach that," I said.

"Alright, anything you want him to craft it into?" he asked.

"Maybe…a small axe? Something I can throw?"

"I think he can handle that," he said, hesitating momentarily before sighing. "Why don't you rest?"

"It's mid-morning."

"And you look like you fell out of that tree you likely slept in."

"How did you know I slept in a tree?"

"It's one of the few ways to avoid Hazzal that doesn't result in immediate bodily harm."

"It wouldn't be fair to you."

He scoffed and shook his head. "You still don't get it."

"Get what?"

"You need help, whether you like it or not. You need rest to keep going with whatever mission you're on, so rest. They won't stop me from helping you," he said, gesturing toward the entrance to the home again.

"You don't mind helping me?"

"No."

"And them?" I asked, jerking my head toward the center of Arkaley.

"They are only afraid of what you can do."

I thought for a long, hard moment.

"Alright; I'll rest."

"Good."

"Anza?"

"Hmm?"

"Thank you."

"Oh, what is that Endering saying…potato potahto?"

"I don't think that's it," I said.

"Meh." He shrugged before slipping down the ladder.

"Night," I said to the space he had been in a moment before slipping back into the windowless home. It was clear where people had slept before; each area was a bundle of furs settled on a bed framed in wood hidden behind a foldable wooden wall. I picked the closest one to the door and pulled the egg bag to my stomach. I pushed the wooden slat wall away, giving me a better view of the home. I climbed into bed wrapping my knees up and over the bag, as close to my chest as I could before pulling a large fur over myself. I tried to convince myself it was Arlo's fur as sleep dropped over me like a heavy cloud.

4

The light filtering through the open door, spilling over the furs and across my eyes, woke me. I held the egg bag a little tighter as I opened my eyes.

"Shit."

"Oh, you live?" Anza said. I sat up, turning to look at where he sat at the table with his legs crossed, carefully sharpening a small but elegant white throwing axe.

"Nope, super dead. On another note, that is *not* Arlo's leg bone."

"Ahh, but it is," he said, twisting it in his hand to admire it. "Hungry?"

I didn't realize I was hungry until I saw the two bowls on the table. My stomach snarled, and I scrambled out of bed. Anza shook his head as I tucked into the warm meal there. I didn't even care what it was; rolls were covered in a thick sweet red sauce which bubbled with meat and vegetables. I plucked a piece of the bread and shoved it into my mouth. The flavor made my mouth water, sweet and savory and very hot. For a moment, the fact that Arlo wasn't here to see me shove food into my face like an idiot made my chest tight. He would have thought it was funny.

"Don't choke."

"Don't tell me what to do." He rolled his eyes as I scarfed down another lump of sweet bread, nearly choking on it as I swallowed. "How long have I been out?"

"Out?" he asked, furrowing his brow.

"Asleep."

"Ah," he said, nodding. "All day."

"Why do I still feel tired?" I asked, my body aching with every bite of the food.

"Probably because you got your hind end handed to you this morning."

"I thought I might feel better after that much rest." I didn't. Every inch of my body still ached, and I still had Arlo's body in the back of my mind, swirling in the laughter of children. A child's laugh would never be the same. For a moment, the red sauce on my plate was hard to swallow. I reached out my hand toward Anza; he didn't hesitate to hand the axe to me, handle first.

"May he stay with you, even in death." His words almost sounded like a prayer as I wrapped my fingers around the handle. The axe was perfectly balanced, a tattered scrap of leather around the handle forming a loop so I could keep a firm hold on it. The end of the handle had a round hole through it, as if designed for adding in some sort of gem; two more holes rested near the top of the blade, on the dull side. Right before the bone spiked out on the opposite side of the blade.

"What are the holes for?"

"Some Endering like to adorn their weapons. They pick what they want, and I thought maybe you would want to because you didn't make it," he said, turning to his bowl of food, finishing whatever was left of it. I rubbed my thumb across the leather before setting it down on the table again.

"Come on," he said, getting up from the table. I shoved the last roll into my face, getting up.

"Where are we going?" I choked out from around the roll.

"To get some air," he said, and I followed him out into the night, sitting a foot from him as he slid his legs through the edge of the railing. The sun had dipped low under the horizon, the night ready to crash down upon this small town.

"Only to get some air?" I asked as he started looking through the forest, watching for something.

"No, there they are," he said. It took me a moment to spot movement, a small group carrying supplies back to the village. "They went out earlier,"

"You were making sure they got back."

"I'm not the only one," he said, and I looked up to some of the other houses, a handful of people were slipping into their homes, their worry for the safety of their friends settled.

"It's nice, seeing so many people care about each other."

"Not something you're used to?"

"No," I said quietly. Sil had always been caring, but fierce. Some subjects you just didn't bring up to her, but Anza cared, and the people here seemed to care for one another without a second thought.

"I'm going to head in; I have to feed Rania."

"Who?"

"My sister."

"She's in there?"

"Yeah, you take your time out here," he said.

"Alright, I'll be in, in a bit." I turned my eyes to the sky, remembering Sil telling me that some people in this realm believed their fallen family was studded in that night sky, glittering back at them.

"Arlo, if you're up there, I really hope you're with me," I said into the empty night. I waited for a response, but the wind didn't even stir. I got up and slipped back inside to find the home was as dark as the night. I fumbled to the table, got my axe, and slipped into bed, ensuring the egg bag was still securely fastened to my waist. I settled into the furs, trying to imagine they were Arlo yet again as I let the collecting warmth take me.

It wasn't long before I started to dream. I knew instantly I was dreaming, standing in that small clearing in the forest where Arlo's body had been. Instead of a mangled, tattered corpse, Arlo lay there, turning to look at me. I met his eyes, soft, patient, and kind, before he spoke. There wasn't any blood in the field; it was peaceful, calm, a welcome comfort in the darkness.

"You need to wake up."

"What?"

"Wake. Up." The crushing weight on my body shocked me awake, and I shoved hard against whatever was after me. A low growl sounded as the creature hit the floor of the home too close to me for comfort. I didn't even know what shape it was, but I pulled the axe up as I got to my feet.

"Anza!" I got out before I could finally make the creature out, the white eyes making my stomach twist. It lunged. I swung. With a cracking noise, it collapsed onto the floor of the home.

"What the hell was that?"

"I think it was a Hazzal. It must have gotten in."

"Hazzal can't climb." I stepped back, pulling the axe out of the creature.

"Anza?" I heard him get up, scrambling over to the corner we hadn't occupied, the one with the folded wooden divider and furs spilled out of the edges. The one that something, no, someone, had moved against when I first changed.

"No, no, no!" My throat grew tight as Anza's voice cracked the space and I backpedaled toward the door. "Rania!"

Anza's cry rattled my bones. What had I done? She had been infected; she was trying to kill me. I turned and ran out the door, almost falling off the edge of the balcony before turning hard and feeling for the ladder, my eyes finally adjusting as I scrambled down, axe in one hand, the other on the egg bag as I slipped into the thick of the night, eyes from the dozens of homes around me following my every move.

I'm not sure how long I ran before the laughter started up; my eyes could barely make out the silhouettes of trees as I stumbled my way through the forest. I scrambled up the first tree I saw, knowing I could climb quickly. It wasn't long before the Hazzal showed up, but they didn't stay long, unable to locate me from the ground. I had to keep moving, but how? It wouldn't take them long to catch my scent again. It wouldn't take much for Anza to find me now, too.

"Why do you have to keep messing everything up?" I said to myself before slipping back to the forest floor. Even though I knew it was dangerous to be on the ground, I couldn't stay there; Anza and the other villagers would find me once daylight broke. I ran through what had happened in my head again and again. How could I have avoided hurting her? Was she dead? She hadn't been moving when I ran. I tried to move more quietly, but I could barely see the trees in front of me, never mind the rest of the forest. Something could come for me and I wouldn't even know it. Branches slapped my head and legs as I moved, laughter bubbled up to my left, and I broke right, running as fast as my tired legs could carry me. More laughter. I kept running, but I could hear them close behind me, to my left, to my right.

Suddenly, they all stopped, and the ground vanished beneath me. I realized I must have run off of a ledge as I free fell. I only barely recognized the sound of running water before I hit the surface. Shock ran up my legs and arms as I slammed into the ground, water rushing around me, about a foot deep. I could hear the laughter coming closer, but before I could get up, it turned to a soft snapping sound. I looked up, spotting the white eyes of the infected Hazzal on the bank of the creek I was now in. They weren't coming closer.

The water was so cold it bit through my clothes, burning against my skin, but I knew the moment I left the stinging embrace of the banks, I was as good as dead. I stayed in the creek, picking my way forward, hoping the Hazzal wouldn't suddenly become brave enough to come after me. I kept going, stumbling over the rocks and logs I couldn't see, using the softest glint from the light of the almost nonexistent moon to make sure I kept myself in the water.

Still holding my axe in one hand, my other hand on the egg bag, the Hazzal followed me along the creek's edge, creeping with me until daylight broke. They vanished into the forest, yelping as if the daylight hurt, and I climbed up out of the water. All of my limbs were heavy and aching as I climbed the rocky bank onto the creek's edge, my feet pulsing with pain at the change of temperature as I sat down on a fallen log to take off my shoes and socks. Blisters bubbled up on my heel and even my toes felt tender and sore. Pin-pricking agony roared over my feet.

I needed a fire. I needed warmth. I needed to keep going. I set my pack down, resting the axe against the fallen log, before there was suddenly a hand against my mouth and I was being dragged backward.

"Are you out of your mind? That's an Endering!" I opened my mouth, slathering my tongue against the inside of the Maraung's hand. He dropped me and I didn't hesitate to run; I got back to my bag and grabbed my axe, but hands grabbed my leg and pulled me down. Pinning me beneath them.

"Yeah, the best thing about Endering? The ones who know their powers don't run." I didn't think my body could feel colder than it did, but the look in the man's eyes as I turned my head made me feel far colder than the creek ever did. I turned a little more and saw that there was a man and a woman. I tried to thrash against them and pitched one off of me for a moment, but my limbs were still slow and sore from the cold and they got right back on top of me, pinning me back to the cold ground before tossing my axe away from us.

"Korrewen?" the woman asked.

"Oh, yeah. They're always hurting for Endering."

"Get off of me, or so help me, I am going to end you!" I said, trying to thrash against them again, but I didn't get anywhere. I was running on a few hours of sleep and my feet were still cold from the water. I kept trying to fight against them, even as they tied my hands behind my back.

"You're not going to end anything," the man said.

"Korrewen might not even want her; they need males."

"Genetic diversity is always important."

As they bickered, I lay still, collecting my strength; I needed to move. In one big burst upward, I managed to throw them off their balance and stumble to my feet, running, barefooted, into the woods.

"Now look what you did!" I kept running, even though I could hear them right behind me. My feet and lungs burned, aching with each step I took before a subtle thudding sound rang out.

"No!" one of them roared before a hand grabbed at my shirt, all but strangling me as he slammed me against a tree, his hand finding my throat.

"You call your friend off right now!"

"What?" I barely realized that the noise had been an arrow and that his partner, the woman, was shrieking, her hand pinned to a tree several yards back.

"Don't you play with me! Tell whoever it is to st—" Another thud as a rush of brown slammed into the side of the man. Relief washed through me, but it was short-lived. Slowly, the figure got back to his feet, his back to me, arrow nocked in his bow, a short sword strapped to his side, and a heavy-looking backpack on his back. Over one shoulder was my egg bag, my axe and Sil's knife hanging from a belt loop.

"Anza..." He didn't respond to me, approaching the other Maraung slowly. The man who had been trying to trap me, kill me, sell me, whatever was most convenient, scrambled backward toward his partner, who was still trying to escape the tree.

"Back off," he said, trying to get Anza to back down.

"You're going to forget that you saw her. Forget that an Endering even graced this forest. She's mine. If you don't forget, I will hunt you down and filet the skin off of each of you, slowly, one by one." It hurt to breathe as the two Maraung men glared at each other for a long moment before the other Maraung and his partner looked at each other and nodded. "Go." They didn't need to be told twice. The man helped rip the arrow from the woman's hand and they vanished together into the forest. I needed to move. Anza was going to kill me. I had hurt his sister, probably killed her, but even as he turned to stand directly in front of me, I couldn't move. He lowered his bow, my heart slamming in my chest.

"I'm so sorry. I didn't know it was her; I never would have —" He put a hand over my mouth, tears stinging my eyes as I quickly came to terms with the circumstances of my demise. Tugging on the rope that bound my hands as I closed my eyes, I expected to feel pain. I expected my blood to spill on the forest floor. I expected death. I didn't expect a sharp knife to pass along my hands, cutting away the rope that bound me. He lowered his hand from my mouth as I opened my eyes again to see him take my bag off his shoulder and offer it to me. "But...I—"

"Did what I couldn't," he said simply. I took the bag slowly, afraid to move too quickly, slinging it over my shoulder.

"She...she was infected, wasn't she?"

"Yes...I was hoping for a cure. I couldn't do what I should have. You did."

"And they banished you?" He nodded, passing me Sil's knife and my axe. "I'm so sorry."

"It doesn't matter; my sister was gone a long time ago."

"Why...and don't take this the wrong way," I started as he set his bag down, taking out a pair of dry socks and passing them to me. I took them, unable to express my gratitude. "Why did you save me? I'm not your problem."

"If I can help, I must," he said.

"Right."

"Do you even know where you're going?" Anza asked, pulling my wet shoes out of his bag too. He passed them to me.

"Not really. I was told to follow the sunrise. I don't know if that's really the right way, though."

Anza sighed, shaking his head. "Can I come with you?"

"You want...to come with me? I thought you'd want to kill me."

"I'm not happy with how Rania's story ended. I want my sister back, but she's gone. Going with you and making sure you don't die is a lot better than wandering into the woods to let the Hazzal take me, at least until we get you to the castle," he said, finally standing upright again and slinging his bag back over his shoulder.

"Alright...I really am sorry." He raised a hand as if he could stop the words from coming out.

"You have nothing to be sorry about," he said, his voice tight. I noticed how puffy the area around his eyes were, but tears didn't fall; he had already cried all the tears he could. "What's done is done."

"Okay," I said, and silence descended between us. I wanted to ask him why he let those two Maraung go, why he didn't kill them, but I had already pushed too far. Killing wasn't in his nature. Anza made a fire, and I put my shoes near it before he passed me some dried meat. I didn't ask what it was; I just ate it. It tasted plain and salty, but I didn't dare complain.

"It was smart."

"What?"

"Sticking to the creek, it was smart."

"Oh...thanks." The silence returned, stretching on. I got as close to the fire as I dared, letting the heat help dry off my clothes.

"What'd you mean...when you said I'm yours?"

He hesitated, watching my shoes dry but not looking at me.

"Many people believe Endering are less like people and more like pets, beings to be owned; by saying that, it made them feel like they had infringed upon property that wasn't theirs. They are unaware of the idea that you are your own person," he said.

"And you're not?" He met my gaze as I asked him that, but only for a moment.

"No, and I'd prefer you didn't rip me limb from limb when your power manifests."

I let the silence stretch out. The day crept on and we sat in silence, watching the fire until, eventually, my shoes were dry enough to keep going. I put the socks and shoes on and adjusted my egg bag, ensuring it was still there. I had almost lost them. I had almost lost my life. It didn't really hit me until Anza stamped out the fire that I had been very close to dying.

"We'll make our way to the Sky Fields and rest on an island. We'll have to cross the field after."

"An island?" I asked, his lips tugging a little at the corner of his mouth.

"You've never seen the Sky Fields before." It wasn't a question, but almost as if he was reminding himself. As he led the way into the forest, I breathed out, rolling the tension out of my shoulders. My heart had stopped slamming in my chest, and even though my limbs still ached with the weight of the cold, like they were made of lead, I knew that following him wasn't the *worst* decision I had made in the last few days.

5

<hr>

"What's wrong?" Anza had stopped out of nowhere, still a few yards ahead of me, holding back a broad fern. He didn't answer until I got to his side.

"Nothing, I like to see people's faces when they see the Sky Fields for the first time." He swept back a row of thick ferns, revealing the cliff face we were on. My breath caught in my throat momentarily as I saw the bounding plateau before us. Rising into the sky were dozens upon dozens of floating islands covered in swaths of vegetation. Trees reached for the sky from each island, vines dropped from their sides, and some only had thick bushes and small trees, but far below, an expansive plateau reached out toward the horizon, void of greenery. As I stepped forward, Anza grabbed my wrist, his hand gentle and careful. It wasn't a controlling movement. No, it was a suggestion, a warning. I stopped.

"It's amazing." I barely saw him nod as an island drifted up from somewhere below us, slowly slipping past us. I touched the smooth dirt as it slid past, feeling a tingling in my fingertips, almost like the dirt was singing. I let it slip past, looking out at the expanse. The islands shifted in the light of day and I almost forgot how tired I was as Anza let my wrist go.

"Beauty can be a dangerous thing," he said. "We need to be careful." I turned to him, nodding. We carefully picked our way down a narrow path from the cliff's edge to the plateau's bottom. Anza pointed at a small island still tethered to the ground by a vine tied to a tree. I followed him over to the island, trying not to stare out at the shifting islands, admiring the light dappling the foliage. I barely noticed the dozens of holes on the plain brown plateau floor. "Alright, the night's coming; we can climb up and rest on the island until morning" he said, holding a vine out to me.

"We'll be safe up there?"

"Safer."

I took the vine and tried to steady my breath, my legs and arms reminding me how tired I was before I started to climb. Crossing my feet and maneuvering the vine carefully, hand over hand, inch by inch, I moved up the vine.

Taking deep breaths and refusing to look down as I moved. I had to have been nearly halfway when I slipped, but I dug my fingers into the vine, catching myself before climbing up again, my throat dry from the fear of falling. I didn't think I would make it to the top for a moment, but finally, I collapsed on the thick grass that covered the top of the floating island, Anza right behind me.

"Everything hurts."

Anza cracked a smile, dipping his head as if trying to conceal it from me.

"Yeah, that will happen when you run headlong into the night," he said, offering me a hand, and I took it, letting him pull me to my feet. "We can't camp out right on the edge; a piece could break off easily," he said.

"Right...this place it's magic, right?" I asked, and he snorted, leading the way into the thick foliage.

"No, only Endering can do magic. I don't know why they float, but I bet if Echalon were around, they'd have some sort of explanation for you; they had a nasty habit of getting to the bottom of things."

"A nasty habit of getting to the bottom of things?"

"Apparently, they liked to...what's the phrase, something with rain?"

"Rain on your parade?"

"That's it."

"If it's not magic, why does it feel alive?" I asked, and he looked back at me. "The whole plateau, it feels like it's buzzing, singing, breathing," I said. He furrowed his brow.

"Maybe because it is?" he said, but didn't sound sure. "There are a lot of dangerous things here; this place is very fertile, a great place for animals to live and thrive if you can get onto an island," he said.

"And if you can't?"

"You're dead," he said, shrugging. "We need to rest, though. Tomorrow will be a hard day."

"Today was a hard day."

"I promise it will not get any easier," he said.

"Great," I said, letting him lead me into the brush, his hand dropping mine after a moment.

"Someone there?" The voice came from the trees. Anza and I immediately drew our weapons, expecting an attack. The confrontation in the forest was still fresh in our minds. What was the chance we'd be attacked again a handful of hours later? I didn't want to think about it, but if someone was going to attack us, would they call out like that?

"Here," Anza said, slowly creeping toward the voice.

The foliage broke into a small clearing, and at the center, a fire pit sat, ash and logs edged with rocks to keep the fire contained. On the other side of the pit, a Barbarza stood low to the ground, hackles raised, ready to attack. Beside her, a Photomyra stood. Greens and reds fell in layers around him; his individual petals and leaves had been styled into a shirt and pants combo that sat on his body.

I remembered Sil's lesson on Photomyra, that they didn't actually wear clothes, that every fold and curve of what looked like clothes was a flat prehensile limb. His hair was bundled back with his floral blooms, which looked like two short vines that slid out from his hair. His clothes and hair were both styled to be symmetrical. Dark green eyes looked us over as he pressed his back against the Barbarza.

"Friendly?" he asked, his hand resting on the hilt of a short sword strapped tightly to his hip. His Barbarza companion didn't move her eyes from us. She was ready to move if she had to.

"Friendly," Anza said.

"Great…want to…maybe lower your sword?" the Photomyra said. Anza looked at me and I met his eyes; he nodded once, and we lowered our weapons together. As we did, the Barbarza relaxed a little, she was still defensive, but her teeth were no longer bared.

"It's unusual to see an Endering in these parts." My stomach flipped as her soft, subtle voice touched my mind. No one had reached out to me mentally since Arlo had passed.

"That doesn't mean she can be taken advantage of," Anza said while I struggled to find my mental footing.

"Oh, of course not. No one wants to piss off an Endering."

"No," I said after a moment. "They just want to sell me or steal from me." Anza flashed me a look of approval, the corner of his mouth twitching, almost as if he was suppressing a smile as discomfort settled around us.

"Well…that is pretty unfortunate. We were going to build a fire tonight if you want to sleep around it with us?"

Anza hesitated for a moment.

"It's fine," I said, looking at him. "If they do anything funny, I'll zap them with my laser eyes." He and I both knew I had no idea what my power might be, but these two didn't know that. It was totally workable. I could have laser eyes. I could zap them with a single thought. They didn't need to know it was something I saw on television once. They probably didn't even know what a television was. I held his gaze, trying to get him to go along. He blinked slowly, nodding as he did. To them, it must have looked like I was trying to comfort him, but I knew differently. He was telling me I had made the right choice. Told the right lie.

"Yeah…no one wants to get zapped," the Photomyra said nervously, wringing at his wrists. "I'm Sanji."

"*Jinera*," the Barbarza said, stepping back to settle onto a patch of flattened grass.

"Mira," I said. "This is Anza." I sat down outside the ashen area the fire would occupy and took off my shoes, rubbing my feet as Sanji and Anza lit the fire. Everything hurt so much more than I had realized while trying to get onto the island. As my muscles rested, I realized how much I had been through these last few days; so much had changed. This world had already ripped me to pieces on a fundamental level. Jinera and Sanji kept to their side of the fire and didn't probe about where we were going or why. They peacefully settled in and cooked something for dinner, a stew. It wasn't until my stomach growled that I realized how hungry I was.

"We're happy to share," Sanji said. I looked to Anza, who still seemed hesitant, but there had been no reason to dislike these two people. We needed food and a good night's sleep and they thought I had laser eyes. It would be so cool to have laser eyes.

"We'd really appreciate that," I spoke more from my stomach than my mouth. A hunger clawed at me like a creature had been released inside my stomach, and it wanted to get out. Sanji took his time finishing the stew, adding ingredients here and there as Anza repacked his bag, trying to make it easier to get supplies we would need in the next leg of the trip.

Food was served. I knew we couldn't trust these two, but Sanji's stew was so rich in flavor and warm, a warmth that spilled through me, radiating into my entire body, easing every muscle as we ate. Even Anza seemed to relax a little more.

Could these two be our friends? Could they be trusted to come with us? Was Anza wrong? Maybe, just maybe, he was paranoid. Maybe the people in this world were trying to get by, but good at heart. Resting finally, with a warm stomach, my eyes began growing heavy, drooping with the weight of sleep as I finished my stew. Sanji offered to take the bowl, and even Anza yawned. It had been a long day. I had almost no sleep the night before. The fire crackling was so warm. Anza and I got ready to sleep and tucked into bed, and even though I was exhausted, I was surprised by how fast sleep took me.

Until I woke up.

"Mira, get up!"

"Meh."

"They took everything." My eyes snapped open, and I scrambled to my feet, reaching for the egg bag I had on my waist the night before. Gone. My axe was gone, Sil's knife was gone, our bags were gone, everything was gone. Anza and I met each other's eyes.

"How?"

"They must have put something in that stew."

"Or our bowls."

"Right," Anza said before pointing at a Barbarza track in the dirt. "That's fresh."

"How fresh?"

"Very fresh," he said, following the paw prints. I followed him.

"They have a head start on us. Do you think we can catch them?" I asked as we got to the edge of the island, seeing that it was bobbing against the ground, no longer completely floating.

"Oh, yeah," he said. "If we're careful." He pointed out over the flat plain of land and my throat tightened. There in the distance were two small forms, a humanoid and a Barbarza.

Between us, islands touched down on the plain and dozens of thick, tendril-like creatures were reaching out of the dark holes that littered the plain. "They woke the Nazzir."

"That sounds bad," I said, but he didn't respond, looking at the edge of the island for a way down. "We can jump," I said, looking over the edge, it wasn't far down and we were losing time. If they got much farther ahead we would lose them, and the eggs, and everything else we had.

"No, we really can—" I didn't let him finish, inching myself to the edge and over it, dangling my legs as I prepared myself to drop. "Mira!"

"Come on," I said, letting go. I fell the few yards to the ground, bending my knees as I landed hard. My legs still hurt and I fell back on my backside, placing my hands firmly on the ground to support myself. The ground started to rumble and at first I thought something big was rushing through the forest behind us, but it only took a split second before I realized the rumbling was coming from beneath me. Anza landed beside me, a little more neatly, before reaching over and helping me up. We locked eyes. Fear rose in those deep gilded brown depths before he said a single word.

"Run."

6

I realized why Anza didn't want me to jump as we ran, the ground trembling below us. In the distance, Sanji and Jinera were battling the Nazzir, so the Nazzir couldn't have been near us. My lungs burned as we covered the ground quickly, running side by side, heading straight for the two thieves, and with every step, I could see more and more of the tendril-like creatures slipping out of their holes.

It wasn't long before one swung itself at me. I dropped, tasting dirt and sand as it swung clear over me, only to look up and see the edge of an island heading for me. I rolled, watching it crash against the ground I had lain on a moment ago. My stomach leapt up into my throat, eyes burning from the kicked up dust and sand as I spotted the hole next to my head. I jumped up as the Nazzir burst out of the hole, putting my back to it. I ran after Anza before it could lash out at me.

"Are you alright?" he yelled back at me, risking a glance.

"Yeah, keep going!" I said, waving at him. He was so much farther ahead of me now; he would get to them first. I dodged and wove around the tendrils, ducking as another tried to slam me to the ground. We were about halfway to the thieves when the ground gave out under my leg. A new hole opened up beneath me. Razor-sharp teeth dug into my ankle, hot, fiery pain ripping up my leg.

"Anza!" The Nazzir pulled me back into the hole, my hands scraping along the ground as I tried to hold on. He got to the hole in time to grab my hands, but my grip slipped. "Get my bag; get them safe!" I got out as the Nazzir dragged me into the darkness.

"Mira!" His voice was the last thing I heard. My chest was tight, and I only had enough space to kick with my other foot. Pain still shot up my leg as I scrambled around in the dark, feeling the creature inch its way up my leg. At my calf, my knee, digging in deep with teeth that were sure to leave a scar. If I lived.

"No, no, I'm not ready. I have to—" Something within me slid into place, warm and fierce, as my hands continued digging into the dirt of the fresh hole. Something shifted below me, far below me. Something had moved. Something besides the Nazzir. In an instant, I knew whatever it was had slammed through the space the Nazzir held. Slowly, its teeth loosened, its blood bubbling up in its mouth. Something had killed it and I didn't want to know what that something was. I kicked out, getting my leg free, and crawled upwards, following the sound of the wind and the screams. It was only a few moments before I saw the light at the end of the tunnel.

Scrambling upward, I finally got to the edge of the hole, hauling myself out. The fresh blood running down my leg and into my sock made my heart slam in my chest. I stretched my leg to ensure I could use it and looked up to find Anza and the thieves fighting. Sanji had Anza pinned against Jinera's flank, Sil's knife pressed against his throat. Against a Barbarza and Photomyra, he didn't have a chance alone. I clenched my fists and ran for them, slamming into Sanji at full speed, sending him sprawling. Anza pivoted, grabbed my axe from its place in Jinera's saddle, and threw it at me. I caught it as she slammed against Anza, knocking him to the ground.

"Get the knife!" I said to Anza, keeping my eyes locked on the Barbarza. She growled, her body low, stance wide. All the times I had fought Arlo came flooding back. Avoid the front; attack from the back. The hind legs are weak, but her forelegs were made for slamming and smashing. She inched forward, and so did I. There was a long moment of hesitation before she lunged at me, her teeth bared. I leaped toward her. I saw triumph flash in her eyes before I passed her. Under her. Passing completely under her and coming up behind her, as planned. She had never fought an Endering before. She had gone into this thinking she might have a chance at winning. Getting to my feet fast enough was the hard part, but I staggered up as she landed. I slammed my axe into the heel of her leg. Blood spewed out and her shriek filled both my mind and the surrounding air. It made my stomach twist as she crumpled into a pile. It took a moment for her to get back up. I spun my axe, twisting it in my hand, ready to hit her again if I had to.

"If we don't get out of here, we're all dead," Anza snapped.

"Your choice is simple," I said, keeping my eyes on Jinera. "Give me my stuff back and live or die here."

"You really think you can kill us, little Endering?" Jinera asked, snapping her teeth. They had the eggs. The kids. The kids that were *my* responsibility.

"Honestly, it's kind of funny that you think I can't." I laughed, keeping my eyes locked on hers. I didn't need to look away to know Anza and Sanji had finished fighting; the tension in the air spiked as a Nazzir came painfully close to us.

"Fine," Jinera said, turning to grab the bags with her jaws, and she tossed them toward me. I stepped forward, catching the egg bag by the strap, keeping my eyes on her as I grabbed the others as well. I held the egg bag close, opening it and glancing down long enough to verify that both eggs were still there.

"Mira, down!" I dropped, and the whooshing of a Nazzir sounded inches over my head. I lifted my head enough to see Anza taking his weapons out of Jinera's saddle.

"Anything else of ours?" I asked.

"No," Anza and Sanji, who already had quite the black eye, said at once. The Nazzir came back over my head. I got up and Anza waved for me to follow him. We turned our backs on Sanji and Jinera, letting them figure out what they would do about the Nazzir and their luck on their own, running headlong toward the forest in the distance. The Nazzir were the only factors keeping them from following us.

"You wait until he finds out what's in that bag, Endering! Do you think you are safe with him? Everyone will betray you for that!" Sanji's voice rang, cutting deep as we ran. I didn't care if they made it off the plains; they had almost ended a species. But what if he was right? I hadn't told Anza what my mission was. Sil had told me the Echalon were the most precious creatures known to this world. Could I really trust Anza not to fall into a mindset of greed? He could have been vengeful when I killed Rania; he could have come for me. What would he do when he realized he had been moments away from finding the most valuable thing in the world? I saw him steal a glance at me as we ran, finally getting to the safety of the forest from the flat, expansive Sky Fields. The sun was already dipping downwards.

"We must have been out most of the day," Anza said, forcing the last part of the sentence out through his panting as we finally stopped. "We need to keep going; there's a town nearby with a place we can rest."

"Can we make it?"

"By the grace of the stars, I hope so," Anza said, standing upright and looking into the woods. "Come on." I wondered what he was thinking about, what he wanted to say. There was no way he didn't hear Sanji, no way he was going to let it go. I could almost feel the tension rolling off of him. I didn't sheath my axe, in case I needed it. Darkness fell before we got to the town, laughter kicking up in the woods.

"We need to get in a tree," I said.

"It's not much farther." He pointed forward at a light in the distance.

My legs screamed with pain, my arms heavy, and even though my leg had probably stopped bleeding, I needed to at least clean the wound. I hated to admit it, but I couldn't do that in a tree. He was right. We hurried out of the forest and to the building. It was made of wood and positioned directly on the ground, longer than it was wide. It was one story with double doors at the front. Anza and I scrambled up to the doors, hurling ourselves inside as the Hazzal appeared at the edge of the forest we had left behind.

"Can they get in?" I asked as we closed the doors.

"Shh," he said, turning to look around the inside of the building. It reminded me of the churches I'd seen in movies, rows of pews on both sides, but the front was different. There was no space for someone to preach from. Instead, a statue kneeled on a platform, head bowed, hands in its lap.

"Who is that?" I asked.

"I swear by the stars, shut up. There could be people in here." Anza's eyes cut through the dark, glaring at me. I bit my tongue as he listened. "We go seat by seat, make sure we're alone," he said; I could barely hear him as he spoke, but nodded. Wordlessly, I took the right row, and he took the left. Walking from the back, we checked each pew for people, slowly working our way up to the statue. As I approached the statue, the moonlight streaming into the windows dappled the floor.

"Safe?" I asked as Anza joined me

"Safer," he said. "This statue is of Queen Sahaveya," he explained. The statue was carved of wood and was so large that her face was only about a foot from mine. The pedestal she sat on made her taller, but still, the Photomyran queen bowed. Her petals fell into a luxurious dress around her, her hair formed into a loose bun at the back of her head. The flower of her floral bloom lined the edge of a carefully carved mark on her face, her burn. Sil had told me about the queen, how needy she was, and how that neediness was only rivaled by her kindness and compassion. She was a true queen. The Queen of the People.

"What is the statue for?"

"This place is dedicated to the people of Baryn as penance for a mistake that was made."

"A mistake?" I asked, pulling the egg bag close.

"The queen failed to act quickly on a matter that developed quickly in Baryn; it's a fishing town on the other side of the kingdom," he started. "I don't know exactly what happened, but she could have acted sooner. They call her the bowing queen because when she came to set it right, to show that she was wrong, she bowed to her subjects."

"But queens don't bow, neither do kings; we bow to them," I said.

"She did," he said. "She did the things she needed to do to fix whatever was going on and built places like this across the kingdom in case people needed shelter and warmth."

"Thank goodness she did; I can't wait to tell her it helped."

"Mira…"

"Yeah?"

"She's not around anymore."

"What?"

"She died in childbirth years ago, as did her child. Her Royal Endering had to take up the throne to keep other nations from coming in and claiming Agrenon; he's been running the kingdom ever since."

"But…my uncle was her Royal Endering." That was why Olaf never went back home to visit. It was why I didn't have a single memory of him, and why I had only seen him in the few pictures Sil had let me see.

"And he has no children."

"Wait a minute," I said, tearing my eyes from the statue to look at him, taking a step back. "You're telling me that…Olaf wouldn't make me…"

"His heir is up to him," Anza said. "You also have to factor in whatever is in that bag." I could feel the color drain from my face. He hadn't moved, though, and only then did I realize I had stepped between two pews. I was as good as trapped. I tightened my grip on my axe.

"You're…not bringing me to the castle, are you?"

He turned to me, furrowing his eyebrows and sighing.

"Yes, I am. It would be easier if I knew what we were trying to do."

"Sanji and Jinera knew, and they tried to steal everything we had."

"I know, and whatever it is, it has to provide more riches than a young Endering. Enough riches to justify crossing an Endering that you think can shoot things from their eyes. It's unheard of, leaving an Endering alive and not taking them instead.

"If I tell you, you won't cross me?"

"I don't think I could if I tried," he said, stepping back to give me space before sinking into a pew on the other side of the aisle. I loosened my grip on my axe and sat it down on a pew on my side.

"Yeah…I'd shoot you with those laser eyes." He chuckled as I turned toward him, pulling the egg bag into my lap. "Promise me?"

"I promise you I will not cross you, kill you, betray you for anything you're about to show me," he said.

"Okay," I said, swallowing hard and unzipping the bag. Reaching in, I pulled out the dark gray egg, the light from the moon dashing through it as I held it up for Anza to see. Inside, in the moonlight, I could see the form of an unborn child, his head, arms, and legs curled up tightly in his little space. The light spiraled outward into the corners of the room like a disco ball might. Anza stared at the egg with wide eyes as he tried to process what he was actually looking at. For a moment, the silence crushed down on us like a wet blanket, but a few seconds later he spoke.

"Is that what I think that is?"

"Yeah…I have two…a boy and a girl," I said. "Sil said you could tell by their eggshells, they have genetic color markers or some shit; I don't understand it…I don't think she does either." Just keep talking, cut through the tension.

"That's an Echalon."

"Yeah," I said, putting the egg back in the bag. The silence stretched on, his eyes locked on me.

"You promised."

"I won't break my promise. Mira, if anyone finds out about them—"

"People already found out."

"We have to keep you out of towns and villages. Keep you out of sight. Sanji and Jinera, those two bandits from the woods…"

"The bandits didn't know."

"But if Sanji or Jinera do, anyone could come after them. It was already going to be hard enough to get to the castle being an Endering, but knowing you have Echalon with you?" He shook his head, finally turning his eyes back to the statue. "We're going to need supplies in the morning."

"Like?"

"A cloak to hide you, winter gear for the next leg of the journey," he said.

"Not until morning, though?"

"Right, we need rest, and the Hazzal won't let us get that far," he said. "We should also look at your leg." I looked down at my calf; the pants I had worn were in shreds, dried blood covering almost my entire leg. I could feel the wetness in my sock. I untied my shoe and pulled out my foot as Anza got up, heading toward a space behind the statue.

"What are you doing?"

"This place was built to help people," he said, walking back toward me with a bag. "That means the town stocks it with medical supplies." He set the bag down next to me before going to the space behind the statue again, then coming to my side with a clay pot of water. He took the time to clean my leg, ripping off the shreds of my pants that still dangled there, his hands working gently, carefully, against my blood-stained skin. We didn't speak as he cleaned out each tooth hole from the Nazzir, which spiraled around my leg like someone had let a garbage disposal rip me apart. I was thankful it didn't hit an artery.

"How bad is it?"

"It'll scar, but you'll live."

"Great," I said. "You know I could have done this, right?"

"I know."

"Why did you?" I asked as he started wrapping the final bandages around my leg.

"I thought you were dead."

"What?"

"When the Nazzir took you. Listen, I know we don't really know a lot about each other, but watching someone I'm trying to help vanish into the dark of a Nazzir hole isn't exactly fun."

"Oh."

"How did you even get out?"

"It let go." Even as I said the words, I knew it wasn't right; something else had happened in that hole.

"Let go? Nazzir don't let go."

"I don't know, Anza, one minute it was trying to eat me, and the next it...it was almost like it was dying, something moved under us, I think it killed it." He swallowed hard, carefully finishing the wrapping before he sighed.

"Well, thank goodness for whatever happened. I'll go in the morning to get the supplies we need," he said.

"Alright...we'll sleep on the pews?" I asked.

"Yeah," he said, going to the other side of the aisle and settling down on the pew he had sat on earlier.

"Anza?" I looked up at the statue of the queen, feeling my throat get tight.

"Hmm?"

"Do you think…that we even can make it to the castle?"

"What do you mean?"

"I feel like we haven't caught a whiff of a break. Is it going to be like this the whole time?"

"I think we should take it a day at a time," he said.

"Right." I rolled over, putting my back to the bowing figure of the queen, trying not to think of what was to come should I make it to the castle, trying not to think about all the things we may have to do to even get there, if this was the start of the journey, there was a chance I wouldn't get to finish it.

7

"It's morning."

"Go away," I said, burying my head into my arm. Anza's laugh filled the echoing space. I opened my eyes to see the sunlight streaming through the windows, dappling on the floor of the small sanctuary. I looked over to where he was sitting on his pew to see the light splashing across his face, turning his eyes from a deep brown into swirls of lighter brown and gold, flecked with darker specks like coffee grounds, but only for a moment.

"Is that your response to every sunrise?" he asked before locking eyes with me. "What?" he asked, turning to look behind him before turning back to me.

"Oh, nothing. We'd better get up, right?" I said, barely catching his smirk out of the corner of my eye. I stood, rubbing sleep from my eyes before stepping in front of Queen Saha's statue, looking up at her. He joined my side after only a moment. He was already dressed in thick, warm clothes, but the way he shifted made it almost seem uncomfortable, like they were too restricting for his liking. I reached down to get my socks and shoes but found my socks were missing.

"Hey, where are—" I looked up; he was already holding out a new clean pair of socks.

"How do you do that?"

"You soil a lot of socks." I snatched them from his hand as he smirked. I couldn't help but smile, but forced my eyebrows down to glare at him.

"Do not." He turned his eyes back to the statue as I got my new socks on, holding the egg bag tight against me, feeling the eggs' forms inside. "You already made a run to the town?"

"Yeah. There," he said, gesturing back to a pew with a set of warm-looking clothes, including a new pair of pants, a coat, and a cloak.

"How cold are the mountains going to be?"

"I don't want to think about it," he said, crossing his arms as if he could protect himself from the cold.

"Awesome, just fabulous," I said sarcastically before stepping back to change, keeping my eyes on him to ensure he didn't try to risk a glance my way. Carefully tying the cloak into place around me, I went back to grab my shoes and pulled them on, tying them up tightly. "Ready?"

"As ready as I can be. Hood up?" he asked, and I pulled the hood to my cloak up. Reaching in my pockets, I found gloves. Pulling them on, I realized the deep hood and gloves paired with the long, thick clothes hid almost every inch of my skin. I could pass as a Maraung. So long as no one looked at my face too long.

"Has anyone ever told you that you're a genius?" I asked.

"No. Usually, they tell me that there's a beetle where my brain should be."

"That must be a smart beetle piloting a meat suit like that," I said, glancing at him from under the hood. He grabbed the front of my hood and pulled it down, plunging me into darkness for a moment before heading toward the door.

"The smartest beetle on the planet," he said as I fixed the hood. He looked back, smirking. I couldn't help but return the smirk. It only took a few strides to catch up with him, and shoulder to shoulder, one hand on the egg bag, the other on my axe, we walked through the doors of that small sanctuary and back into the Agregonian wilds.

"We really can't go see the village?"

"They'll spot you."

"It can't always be a bad thing."

"We really shouldn't."

"Fine," I said, crossing my arms. I understood why, but I didn't want to see woods this whole trip to the castle. I wanted to see all of Agrenon. We skirted around the town in silence, stepping through thick groves of trees. It wasn't until the town was behind us that we heard a crying in the distance.

"What's that?" We waited, listened, and heard it again.

"That's a child." Anza's words made me feel cold, my stomach dropping as we, together, immediately started running headlong toward the noise. We only made it a few steps before we nearly crashed into a young Barbarza and Maraung together. I checked my hood, making sure it was low enough to not be seen.

"Are you alright?" Anza asked as they righted themselves, the Barbarza shaking his head as they looked up at us.

"Yeah...but our friend," the Maraung said, pointing back toward where the crying sounded; it was closer.

"Show us." The little Barbarza turned quickly, his friend clinging to his back, and they ran back from where they came. We followed. This could be a trap to lure us in and harm us; we could be beaten or killed here in these very woods. We had faced so many bandits and terrible things in the night. With so many infected by The Fever, this could easily be a quick way to get ourselves killed. Those thoughts vanished as I saw a Photomyran child at the bottom of a steep cliff face. Her arms and a leg were scraped, but her foot was trapped under a small boulder. How bad was it, though? Her leg was undoubtedly crushed and broken.

"Tell me you have a healer in town," Anza said, holding a hand to stop me from rushing to her.

"We do. We have to get her to him. He's old, and he can't get out here."

"We weren't even supposed to be in the woods."

"You can worry about how much trouble you may be in once your friend is alright. Come on, I'll push the stone, you two pull," Anza instructed.

"I can help."

"No."

"Anza—"

"We can't risk it." He flashed me a glance, and I knew he was right. I stood back as he stepped forward, pulling on the end of my hood again to ensure it was firmly down as he tried to move the boulder alone. I watched as he pushed and shoved. At one point, it rocked as if he almost had it, but he couldn't move it alone. Every time he rocked the boulder, trying to push it from this angle or that, I could hear the sickening shifting of bone as the child screamed. Her agony and tears dripped down her face. Her eyes were frantic as she searched for some sort of relief.

It was the fourth time that he tried when I decided it was enough. I moved to his side, pressing my hands firmly against the boulder, feeling the shifting and vibrant stone beneath my fingers as I pressed when he tried to move it again.

"Mira," he warned.

"Get over it," I said. He sighed but didn't protest again and together, we shoved. The boulder slid out of the way quickly, and the Barbarza and Maraung pulled the Photomyran girl from the rubble. "Alright, we've gotta get her into town,"

"Right," Anza said.

"You're an Endering." The voice was tiny and quiet and I noticed my hood had fallen back. I turned to look at the small Photomyran girl, who had managed to sit up, tears in her eyes. Silence filled the air for a moment.

"Yeah, I am, but you can't tell anyone. If you do—"

"They'll come for you," the Maraung said quietly.

"Right."

"The healer's home is just inside the village; we can get there through the south entrance. If we're careful, no one will see you," the little Barbarza said.

"And you wouldn't tell anyone we were here?" Anza asked. They shook their heads. Tears still streamed from the little girl's face. She was stronger than she looked.

"Alright," I said.

"We can't trust them."

"They're kids; look at them, they're terrified," I said.

Anza took a moment to look the kids over. He knew the only other option was to kill them, and even in the short time I knew him, I knew that wasn't an option he was going to consider. He sighed, the resignation of what we were about to do glimmering in his eyes.

"Lead the way," he said as I carefully, gently picked her up, trying to ignore the sounds of pain she made as I moved her. The Maraung jumped back on his Barbarza friend's back before leading us to the south entrance of the village. The little Photomyran clung to me, tears still dripping down her cheeks. I needed to distract her.

"What's your name?"

"Queira," she managed through her tense breaths.

"You're doing such a good job, Queira; I don't think I've ever met a Photomyra as strong as you."

"Really?"

"Oh, yes," I said. Anza caught on to what I was doing.

"Photomyra are special too; when you guys break your bones, they heal back stronger."

"They do?" she asked as the south entrance of the town came into view.

"Yep," I said, though I did not know if what Anza said was true. "You're going to be able to kick so many things."

"I like kicking things, like rocks."

"Well, you're going to kick so many rocks when your leg is all better," I said.

"You'll be the best rock kicker in the village," Anza said as her tears started to slow. Her friends had gotten to the entrance and opened the door. As we got to them, they pointed to a nearby home. Queira reached up to pull my hood down more for me as Anza rushed us into the home.

"Hello?"

"What in the stars do you think you're doing coming into my-Queira?" The older Maraung was settled at a table sorting leaves of different plants, but upon looking up, he scrambled to his feet, reaching for a walking stick. "To the bed, put her on the bed," he said, pointing to one of his few cots. Thank goodness the room was empty except for us, no other patients. I gently sat her down on a cot, stepping back as he came over, carefully looking over her leg.

"What did you get into now, child?"

"Trouble," Queira said without missing a beat.

"Clearly...it doesn't look like you severed anything important. I'll need to set your bones," he said before turning to me.

"Thank you..." his voice fell as he met my eyes. "You're a—"

"Not here. I'm not here, and I never was," I said quietly. He hesitated for a moment before nodding.

"Most people wouldn't think twice about leaving a child hurt in the woods these days. They're too busy doing unimportant things. Thank you." I felt Anza shift near me before Queira reached for me. I knelt beside her and she pulled a rock out of the folds of her petals, round and smooth, about the size of a baseball. It didn't look extraordinary, it was brown and pocked, but it was special to her.

"Here, I want you to have this."

"Oh, honey, I don't need to take your rock."

"It's a lucky rock. Please take it? It's the one I was trying to get when I fell. It'll get you to the castle; that's where you're going, right?" I bit my lip, looking at her little outstretched hand.

Those bright blue eyes, the yellow buds on the sides of her head, were already wilting with sadness. She looked like a trampled daffodil. It would break her heart if I didn't take the damn rock. I sighed, gently taking the rock from her.

"I'm putting my trust in your lucky rock to keep me safer," I said.

"It will; it kept me safer than I would have been without it." There was no way she could have known that, but she clearly believed it. Wasn't that enough?

"Well, this must be a mighty rock. Thank you so very much," I said, glancing at Anza, who stood with a small, sad smile at the door. We had to go, and we both knew it, but the storm in his eyes made it clear that he didn't want to. We had to help; it was his way. It was why he had run toward her screams without a second thought. I put the rock in my pocket. "We've gotta get going, but you remember how strong you are, alright? Kick all the things when you're better."

"Will I see you again?"

"Maybe, who knows?"

"May the stars guide your way," the older Maraung said as we stepped out.

"Thank you," Anza said as he closed the door. We slipped out of the village and headed toward the mountain as I turned over the rock in my pocket. It wasn't heavy, but it was extra weight. I could dump it here and keep going; she would never know. I turned it over in my pocket again, trying to ignore the ache in my chest. "You okay?"

"I just feel bad. We shouldn't have risked that, but she needed help."

"I know we shouldn't have risked it, but it's not in my nature to not help, and clearly, it's also not in yours."

"And that's why we did. What was it you said? We could, so we were required to or something? And bonus points, we didn't die," I said, shrugging.

"Right, now we have a mountain or two to climb," he said,

and I groaned, turning to look through the trees at the towering mountain not so far from us. Sarcasm dripped from my voice as I spoke.

"This is gonna be...so fun."

8

"I hate everything," I said as Anza laughed, reaching down from a sheer ledge. I reached up from my spot poised on the precarious path we walked on, taking his hand in mine, and scrambled up the side of the ledge, Anza pulling me up. I wasn't built for this shit. I was built to punch things, not scale rock faces, and I was furious that my hands couldn't find the right places to grab. Even when I tried to copy Anza, I slipped, so he had resorted to helping me up, irritation bubbling in my chest.

"I know, I know." I finally got to the top of the short ledge but the moment I got my footing, though, he lost his. I pivoted, his hand still in mine, and braced myself on the cold ground, catching him as he nearly fell back over the ledge we had scaled.

"I've got you," I said, shifting my weight to pull him back up, my feet almost slipping as he got his footing. Sliding against him to rock slightly before he let me go.

"Good save, thanks."

"Yeah, of course," I said, stepping back quickly, so I was no longer pressed against him. "How far do we have to go again?" I asked, trying not to feel like a penguin as I walked. The cliff face was covered in ice and patches of stone. Every few steps, I slid, a little unstable, like I was about to slip, and I fucking hated it.

"Just a little farther; the first Hold is up ahead."

"That's what you said at least an hour ago, and I still don't know what a 'Hold' is."

He laughed. "You'll know it when you see it."

"I would really appreciate a different answer than the one I've been hearing for the last billion hours." I kept following him up the narrow, winding path toward the top of the cliff face, the wind battering us in every direction. He didn't respond as he graced the top of the cliff, standing up tall as he surveyed what was before him. It took me a few more moments of scrambling, climbing, and sliding before I got to his side. Occasionally, he glanced back, watching me to ensure I didn't fall. A few yards away stood a small cabin, fashioned on the ground with mounds of snow all around it. It was large enough for about four to six people. A small window and door were visible, but the snow had buried in the door.

"Please tell me this is the Hold you were talking about."

"This is, in fact, the Hold I was talking about."

"Great," I said, trudging toward the door. Anza followed, and for a few moments, we had to dig at the base of the door together to clear it enough to move it. We pulled hard on the handle, hard enough to open the frozen shut door. Anza wedged between the door and the frame, pushing it from inside. I pulled, and together we made enough room to get into the Hold.

"Wow." Through the small window, enough light filtered in to see the room before us. On the far wall, a fireplace sat unlit, with a pile of cut wood nearby. A single small bed was centered in the middle of the cabin, and to the right of it was a set of shelves with bundles of something inside. The cold had crept into every inch of the Hold, but it was dry. Anza shuffled quickly toward the fireplace.

"Those bundles on the shelf should hold food," he said, pointing to the side of the bed. He worked at getting a fire started as I grabbed and unraveled a few of the bundles. The first had dried meat wrapped inside, and the second a wooden box full of hard crackers. The third had small rounds of cheese that had been sealed with wax. I opened another to find a clay pot of leaves.

"What's this?" I asked, holding out the leaves to show Anza. He had started the fire and came to my side, leaning in to sniff the leaves.

"Mmmm, tea."

"Tea?"

"That's gonna be so good," he said before looking underneath the bed. He reached down and pulled out a soft wooden crate, which had a variety of supplies in it, including a teapot and a strainer.

"Nice," I said, taking the teapot. "Water?" I asked, and he seemed to know exactly what I meant.

"Snow."

I shivered but went to the door and trudged to a clean splash of snow, heading away from the cliff, scooping as much as I could inside. It was quiet, calm, and peaceful, snowflakes lazily drifting downward as I worked to get the water we'd need for tea. I had finally finished packing the snow when I felt something hit my head, icy, cold, and sharp, but not painful; an explosion of snow on the back of my head.

"You...did not just—" I turned to Anza, who had already made another snowball.

"What are you gonna do about it?" I couldn't help but smile; that crooked grin and the color of his eyes, as the light hit them, made it alright, but there was no way I wouldn't get revenge. I bent down, gathering snow together to make my own snowball.

"Easy, Mira..."

I thought about going easy on him for a second, but only a second.

"Nah," I said before pelting him with my snowball. He tried to duck, but I got him right in the shoulder, only for him to throw his second one at me. As it hit me, I got down on my knees to scrape up another, but he rushed me, picking me up and spinning me around, laughter erupting from the both of us as we spun. I patted his back to be put down, and he gently set me back on my feet.

"I win."

"Never. One of these days, I'll get you back."

"We'll see about that," he said before letting me go and reaching out to grab the teapot. "Let's get some food inside of us." My stomach snarled at the thought of dinner.

"Before my stomach eats itself? Yes, please." He had started toward the cabin as I spoke but looked back at me with that still-present smile before leading me back to the cabin. We took off our winter wear when we stepped in and hung it all near the fireplace. I ran my fingers through my tangled curls as Anza put the teapot near the fire to warm up. My fingers quickly got tangled in a mess and I sighed before taking them back out of my hair and pulling what little I could see over my shoulder so I could see the knots.

"What's wrong?" Anza asked as he checked for and found a bundle of dishes, getting out two cups. I grabbed a piece of dried meat and put it in my mouth before gesturing to the hair knot.

"I don't have a brush," I said, before swallowing and sighing, sitting on the floor, my back to the bed as he prepared the tea. I watched him stoke the fire, the teapot heating up. Once the teapot whistled, he scooped some tea into it and set it aside to steep before moving to the bed, shifting so one leg fell on each side of my body.

"What are you doing?" I asked, turning to look up at him.

"Your hair?" he asked. "May I?" I bit my lip but nodded, turning back around to watch the fire as his fingers slipped into my hair, careful as he began to untangle the mess. I slid the egg bag around and onto my lap, unzipping it as he worked and setting both the eggs on my lap.

"Thanks," I said as he got up.

"Oh, I'm only half done," he said, pouring the tea into the

cups and passing one to me. I took it as he returned to the bed and started on the other half of my hair.

"Well, thanks anyway."

"It seemed like you were getting frustrated with it."

"Yeah, a little; the hood makes it all tangly and terrible."

"I can braid it back for you if you'd like?"

"You know how to braid hair?"

"I had a little sister, and she was quite insistent."

"Right." I couldn't help but feel bad, taking a sip of the tea. It was warm, fruity and sweet, but not too sweet. Anza passed me a cracker before continuing with my hair.

"I didn't...mean to make you feel bad," he said quietly.

"Tell me about her?" I didn't want to talk about how I felt or should have been better, smarter, faster, or anything but who I was.

"Mira, I don't think—"

"Please?" I asked, and he settled in before starting to braid back my hair into one centered braid.

"She was so irritating in all the best ways," he said. "She always took the last roll at dinner, even when I wanted it, and she did this thing if I wanted to hunt where she would hide each of my arrows individually around the village, she'd delay me for hours because she didn't want me to go."

"Yeah?"

"Oh, yeah, it was so frustrating, but now...now I understand why she did it."

"She didn't want The Fever to get you."

"Yeah, so she delayed me until it was too late to go out, and I'd have to go out the next morning instead."

"Are they out here? The Hazzal?"

"Oh, no. It's too cold out here for many animals, but people come through here all the time."

"People are a problem, though, right?"

"People are always a problem, which is why I'd really appreciate it if you keep wearing the cloak."

"Fine," I said, rolling my eyes as he twisted the end of the braid on itself to tie it. "I'll keep wearing the cloak." I ran my fingers over it, pulling it forward to feel the well-woven braid. I dipped the hard cracker in the tea to soften it and put it in my mouth.

"Knife?" Anza asked, holding up the wax-sealed cheese wheel. He didn't need to elaborate. I passed him Sil's knife and he carefully cut some cheese before passing the blade back to me. We ate together quietly as I watched the light of the fire bounce around inside the eggs, making splattered colors on all the walls.

"You think we're actually going to make it?" I asked as we finished our meal.

"I don't know, but honestly, I wouldn't bet against you."

"Really?"

"You got torn down a Nazzir hole and didn't die. I don't know about you, but I think that's pretty impressive."

"You're just saying that."

"No, really," he said, putting away the food bundles. There was plenty of food left, and it was clear when he put them away on the shelves that we weren't taking them with us. I put the eggs back in the egg bag and tucked them close to me.

"Well, I hope you have enough hope for the both of us, cause this is...a lot."

"I know, I'm sorry. Maybe getting some rest will help?" he asked.

"Yeah, maybe," I said, getting up.

"You're taking the bed, right?" he asked.

"Um, no, you're taking the bed," I said.

"Not if you're going to sleep on the floor," he insisted.

"But there's only one bed, and it's not fair that one of us sleeps on the floor."

"Well, the only other option is to share the bed," Anza said, raising his eyebrows, his voice pitching a little.

"I guess that's what we're doing because I'm not letting you sleep on the floor, and you're clearly not going to let me sleep on the floor either," I said, matching his tone as I put my hands on my hips, and he hesitated, looking me over. Deciding if I was serious. "Come on, it's getting late," I said, moving to the bed.

"Are you sure?" he asked.

"Yeah, neither of us should get a bad night's sleep. Come on," I said, waving him over to the bed. He climbed on one side and I climbed on the other. Back to back, only about an inch between us, I settled down under the thick blankets, the warm fire crackling and the heat of our bodies welling up under the blanket made it easy to rest back into the bed, Anza careful not to touch me as he settled into sleep himself.

The next thing I knew, it was morning, the soft light filtering through into the cabin. As I shifted, Anza's foot rested against my leg, as if he had to ensure I was still there. I sat up, ready to stand, before I heard a pounding sound on the door.

"Anyone in there?"

I jumped up and pulled my thick clothes over the egg bag, and the children inside, hiding them. Anza was right behind me, pulling his coat and cloak on before helping me with mine. The door burst open, and four Maraung rushed in as I grabbed my axe.

"Well, well, well, what do we have here?" Anza stepped forward, getting between them and me, but they rushed us at once. I buried my axe into the shoulder of one of them, Anza cutting the other before we were overpowered and pinned to the ground. "Look at this, boys," one Maraung, who had a long scar down his face, said before flicking my hood back. "We have an Endering."

"Go fuck yourself."

"A feisty one at that," he said as one of the others tied my hands together.

"What should we do with her, Dashra?" It only took them a moment to search us and I went tense as they patted my stomach. Dashra. I needed to remember that name.

"Leave her alone." Anza's voice was like cold death as I

kicked out, catching the handsy Maraung between the legs. His grip loosened, but as I tried to pull away, it was clear it wasn't enough.

"Easy. She looks like she might be carrying," Dashra said.

"Or well off," one of the others said before they forced us to our feet.

"Either way, they'll fetch a good price." Anza shot me a glance, his eyes asking me if I was alright; I nodded. We tried to fight back against them as they dragged us out of the warm cabin and down the cold and icy path ahead, but we had no luck. It wasn't long before they led us into a camp. Roughly a dozen tents were arranged in a semi-circle around a makeshift fire pit. Maraung and Photomyran men and women were scattered about the space, packing, cooking, and counting the money they had probably stolen. Along the left side of the semi-circle and on the opposite side of it, closing the circle, was a series of posts. They dragged the both of us toward the posts opposite the tents. It would be easier to watch us from comfort there. The posts were made of wood and dug into the cracks of the mountain. I tried to shove the Maraung leading me and make a break for it, but all I got for my efforts was a smack to the head.

"Settle down, Endering," Dashra said, tying me to the post before reaching down and untying my shoes.

"What are you doing?"

"It's hard to run away with cold feet," he said, taking my boots. I looked over at Anza, who had also had his shoes taken.

"Our feet are going to get frostbite."

"You really are a bright one, aren't you?" Dashra asked before waving the other Maraung away, leaving Anza and me on the cold stone. A warm rage started building up inside me. The minute I got out of these bonds, I would make them pay. They had made the biggest mistake of their lives.

It wasn't until I felt the soft, familiar feeling of a mind against my own that I snapped out of it, tearing my eyes over to the other posts closer to the tents where several Barbarza were tied up. All of them looked gaunt, but one had flecks of gray running through her fur, and there was a single beaded, feathered earring in her ear. Her eyes were locked on me as she breathed steadily. It took a moment before the conversation Arlo and I had had when we started our trip rushed back to me. With this lithe, age-spattered, gaunt Barbarza's eyes boring into my soul, I knew, without hesitation, with complete certainty, exactly who this was.

"Tamaj."

9

"Don't move your mouth when you speak. Whisper, I'll be able to hear you, please by the grace of the stars, tell me you're Brian's child." Her voice was quick, worried; she shifted slightly on her paws.

"Yeah." I kept my mouth still, letting the air carry the word out as I looked away from her. The people in this camp couldn't know that we were talking.

"Do you know your power?"

"No."

"Damn it, alright, do you have the Echalon eggs?"

"Yeah."

"They didn't find them?"

"No."

"And the Maraung you're with? He's a friend?"

"Yeah, Anza, I'm—"

"Mira, I know; I helped pick your name out."

"You knew my parents?"

"I certainly did." She knew about the eggs, about my parents; she was on edge, worried. She didn't know about Arlo yet. Should I tell her before we hatched a plan? *"Your friend isn't going to do well without shoes."*

"Neither of us will do well with bare feet like this."

"You're not wrong, but he'll be worse off." My feet already ached; I shifted one up off the ground, trying to keep it off the cold rock. As I moved it though, it was clear there was a hole in my sock, and I sighed, trying to maneuver it. It was on top of my foot, but after a few moments that didn't work. I only managed to get the hole over my big toe before I gave up. Struggling with a sock was a waste of energy. *"Alright, I have a plan, but you're going to have to be quick once we start it,"* Tamaj said.

"What is it?"

"I've been whittling down the chains that keep me tied here; they're thin enough where I can probably break free. In about an hour, the camp will get very quiet because there is something bigger and meaner out there that does not like things in its territory."

"You're going to make noise."

"Which will draw it to us, and when they're distracted, I'll come over and cut you both loose," she said, gently snapping her jaws.

"Sounds good to me; think he can last till then?"

"I hope so. It'll be hard to vanish in the daylight, but there's a blizzard moving in; it'll give us cover."

"Warn me before you call whatever it is in?" She snorted, nodding. "Tamaj?" She looked away before looking back at me. "Thank you."

"Don't thank me yet; we're not out of the woods because we have a plan. He's...he's not with you?" I didn't need to ask who she was talking about.

"No, he's not."

"He's gone, isn't he?"

"I'm so sorry." She turned her head from me, her body shaking as she tried to hide her reaction for a moment before breathing in through her nose and out of her mouth, steadying herself.

Silence fell between us as we waited and the hour crept by, each second agonizing. People bustled about, setting our packs down near to where Tamaj was, eating and talking, but slowly, the camp grew quieter and quieter until, finally, the campfire in the fire pit got extinguished. Anza and I shifted our weight from foot to foot, frostbite threatening us both with pin-pricking pain, making it hard to move our feet. One down, one up, trying not to freeze as we stood there.

I tried to think about how to get out of there as the snow started. We had a plan, but what if it didn't work? What if we were still stuck in this camp? What if they killed Tamaj for bringing whatever she was going to bring? It took so long, and I watched Anza getting worse as the camp slowly quieted. With the camp now quieter than the blizzard beginning to rage around us, Tamaj looked back at me.

"Now," she said before throwing her head back and letting a loud, booming howl into the sky. Maraung jumped up, rushing toward her to silence her as she reeled backward against her chains. The chain snapped, but not before the creature she talked about descended from the sky. Silver armor-plated scales covered its entire body, horns protruded from its head, and large beady eyes looked around the camp before it opened its mouth and leveled a section of the tents in a blast of fire and rage.

"You summoned a dragon?" I said, looking to where Tamaj was. She had ducked down, trying to throw off the Maraung near her. At the dragon's first snarl, though, all but one left her alone.

"No, I pissed off a dragon."

"Mira, we have to move!" Anza's voice cut through the screams.

The plan had gone wrong. The Maraung had the tail end of the chain still attached to Tamaj, and no matter how short, that was all he needed. With a yank, she stumbled. A foot found her front leg forcing her to the ground with a cry of pain. I was trapped, and so were the both of them.

The dragon turned its attention toward the remaining tents as Tamaj managed to grab the leg that pinned her down, lifting the Maraung like he was a chew toy, and threw him into the drag-on's path before she turned and headed for us. Its lashing tail

forced her to duck, whizzing over her head as Anza and I struggled at our ropes. They were too tight. We had to get out.

"Oh no…" The dragon turned, facing Anza and me. I planted
both my feet, looking dead into the eyes of the dragon, its maw
open with red-hot coals raging within, ready to burn us alive. I
braced myself, knowing that if I was about to be burned at the
stake, I wouldn't do so with my foot up like a damn flamingo.
The minute that bare toe touched the rock beneath my feet, a
raw, bounding rage boiled through me. The thing that had
settled within me on the Sky Fields, the innate feeling that something was warm and sure. The buzzing and singing sensation
was now far stronger than ever. It needed to get out, out, *out*.
The dragon breathed out, a fiery inferno lashing out toward me.
I turned my head and body, expecting to be engulfed with
flames, but all I felt was warmth. The sharp sound of rocks
sliding into place rumbled around me as flames licked around
the stone that had leaped from the mountain, covering my body
in a curved shield.

"And there's your power; use it!" I didn't have time to process
what had happened. I needed to get loose. I pulled on my
restraints again, and in a single thought, before I could register
what was happening, a spike of rock dashed up the side of the
wooden post I was bound to in a single spike and cut the ropes.
It was second nature, innate. I turned, the hole in my sock
tearing wide, pivoting on my feet to Anza, who, thankfully, the
dragon had not yet turned to target, and in a swift motion,
commanded the rocks at the base of his post to move upward,
cutting his ties as well. He dropped, struggling to regain his feet
as I ran to him.

The dragon shrieked. It had spotted me, and it didn't sound
happy. I turned to face it, finding it readying another blast, and
summoned a stone wall just in time. Energy, light, and song
bounding upward, drawing stone upward, sliding it into place
to buy us time. Fire licked all around us, right and left, and even
above us. I knew where I had last seen Tamaj, but we couldn't

move. The dragon wasn't letting up this time. Anza stepped forward, and each step shook, but I supported him with an arm as he put his forearm against the thin stone slab I had summoned, which was already warm with the flames.

"Shield," he said before pointing toward where we had seen Tamaj as the dragon's fire faded. It could only keep going for so long, and as the flames subsided, I could see her again. She was still trying to avoid being struck by a lashing dragon tail. I didn't need to ask him what he meant. Pulling a section of the small, thin wall over his arm, I commanded the entire section to break from the earth, making it into a small, portable shield. Anza held the shield up as the dragon blasted us again. I pressed my body into his, lending him support as we ran together for Tamaj.

"*Hurry up!*" she said as the dragon moved to follow us, freeing her from being bombarded with the lashing tail. She turned and lunged toward the pile of belongings, grabbing our bags, our weapons dangling from them, right where they had been left, before turning again to meet us. Anza dropped the shield as we got to Tamaj, and I commanded an enormous wall up around us, my head screaming with pain, blood dripping from my nose.

I could hear the dragon desperately trying to find a way around the wall, scratching and blasting it. I helped Anza onto Tamaj's back before taking the packs from her jaws. "Up," Tamaj said, helping me get up onto her back as I slung the packs over my shoulder before she turned and thundered out into the cold. Snow rushed around us as she found her footing in the uncertain terrain.

"Go, go!" I said as she plunged deeper into the blizzard, the sounds of the dragon and the camp vanishing behind us. Anza and I clung to Tamaj's back for dear life as she ran, and after what had to have been only a few minutes, she had to slow down. "We need to keep going."

"*At that pace, I'll collapse before we find shelter,*" Tamaj said. She wasn't wrong; her legs were shaking already, her breath heaving, and her body wasn't exactly healthy. She could only handle short bursts of speed.

"Should we get off?" I asked, Anza tucked against me.

"No, it'll still be faster if I walk, but this blizzard will take its toll. You might want to get your shoes on."

"Right," I said as she stopped. Anza and I slid off, opening our packs and pulling out our shoes. We put them on, Anza slipping me a pair of dry socks. He fumbled, trying to get his own socks and shoes on, and I pushed him back against Tamaj, taking his socks and shoes and carefully helping him get them on.

"You didn't have to."

"I don't want to get caught out here again, and wet socks are going to be a death sentence, so thank you for bringing extra socks."

"Extra socks are important, almost as important as that newfound power of yours," he said, his teeth still chattering as I urged him to get back on Tamaj.

"That was quite some power back there."

"Yeah, I'm really fucking glad it came through when it did," I said, lacing up my boots and getting onto Tamaj's back. The soft, warm feeling of rightness had passed, though, and when I tried to imagine the ground beneath the snow, I was only guessing where it could be. The power was gone. "We need to get out of the weather."

"Yes, but we won't be safe until we get much farther from that camp."

"Safer," Anza and I spoke at the same time.

"What?" Tamaj asked.

"Nothing. Do you know any places where we can take shelter?"

"Yes, but I'm all turned around and I can't see the stars; I don't know where we are," she said as the wind picked up, digging into our clothes, making it hard to think.

"Let's just keep going," I said. How bad had Anza's feet gotten? Mine were still in so much pain. How bad were we to be letting such a malnourished Barbarza carry us through this? Where were we going to go?

"Once we can see the stars, we'll know where to go," Tamaj said, Anza trembling against me as she trudged forward. This plan was shit, but there weren't exactly any other options. We had to keep moving until we found shelter. Slowly, gradually, the cold sank in, wetting and chilling our clothes; even Tamaj shook violently with every step.

The blizzard raged on and we had no idea if we had run headfirst into our frozen demise.

10

"Come on, stay warm," I said, rubbing Anza's shoulders. The cold was biting through my cloak and the rest of my winter gear, chilling me to the bone, and like Tamaj had said, Anza was much worse off, bent over her back, clinging to her fur as she forced her emaciated body through the thick snow.

"We need to get into a cave!" Anza said, the wind whipping his words away so fast I barely made out what he said.

"I can't see anything," Tamaj said, each step shaky and tired as she moved.

"I can't see anything rock-wise," I said, Tamaj fumbling to a stop, her legs shaking as she tried to take another step but couldn't. She stood, the wind whipping against us viciously. I got off her back and trudged to her face, covered in ice and snow. I wiped away the mess on her face, her eyes meeting mine as I did. "We have to keep going."

"I can't keep going without direction. My body will stop on me and you'll freeze to death, too," she said as I wiped the snow from her face. My mittens, which were already drenched through, didn't help much. We were going to freeze to death. Should we have stayed at the camp? Waited to make our escape? Tried a different path? What could we have done differently?

I reached into my pockets, trying to find anything to switch my gloves out, anything that may encourage warmth. I had to at least be able to clean Tamaj's face off with something that wasn't already soaked. I knew in my heart that there wasn't anything in those pockets. Still, my right hand found something hard. I pulled it out, and sitting in my wet mitten was a single, smooth, round, ordinary stone. Tamaj met my eyes.

"Can you move it?" Part of me knew that if I could figure this out, I could do something to save them. I tried, but it didn't budge. The warmth wasn't there.

"No."

"Take your glove off."

"What?"

"We're about to freeze to death, anyway; take your glove off and physically touch it," she said, the wind continuing to batter us as she spoke. I did what she said, carefully removing the glove on my left hand, my fingers aching with the movement. I ignored the lack of color in my fingertips before dropping the rock onto my palm. It bit deep, cold, and harsh from being in my pocket for so long, but the minute it touched my hand, it sang. A bounding vibration rang through my body, warm and natural and right. I reached outward, away from me, knowing that feeling would follow, searching. It followed, the ground beneath the snow revealing itself to me as I looked. It didn't move, but it was moveable, right there in front of me, at the ends of my fingertips. There had to be a shelter somewhere, somewhere out of the wind. It only took a few moments before an opening became clear to me with a tunnel that dove downward.

"This way."

"You're certain?" Tamaj asked. We couldn't afford to keep trailing around without direction.

"I can see under the snow. There's a cave. It drops down-ward." Anza still clung to her back, but he was no longer shaking. We needed to move.

"Does it drop quickly?"

"Yeah," I said, keeping my focus on that cave.

"Geothermal heat. It'll probably be warm in there, and even if it's not, it's out of the wind," she said.

I turned to the cave, leading Tamaj toward its entrance. It was only a few dozen yards away. We would have missed it had it not been for that stone and probably walked off to freeze. I gripped it as tightly as I could in my left hand, my right on Tamaj's shoulder, leading her past an outcropping of stone. As we rounded a corner, there it was, the hidden mouth of a cave.

"Come on," I said, guiding her inside. She stumbled as the snow got less deep, and it was just a few moments before we were standing in the cave's mouth. Safe from the raging wind and blizzard outside. I held my hand up to stop her.

"Anyone in here?" I called. We had pissed off a dragon to destroy a bandit camp, and we needed to avoid those bandits. Silence. Together, we slipped into the cave's darkness, leaving the battering winds of the furious blizzard behind. I held Tamaj's shoulder as we stumbled forward, moving carefully to help her avoid larger obstacles. We slowed to a stop as the cave started to level out, opening into a cavern around us. The sound of water drip-dripping settled my nerves as my skin tingled from the drastic change in temperature. Tamaj quietly settled down on the warm stone ground. A soft glow came from the ceiling, thousands of tiny bugs flittered about on the roof of the cave harmlessly and I could almost hear the water ahead of us.

"It's okay, we're safe," I said, trying not to think about how big the cavern ahead of us was as I touched the wall.

"Safer, Stone-Slinger," Anza said as I went to his side.

"Stone-Slinger, huh? Come on, Beetle-Brain," he cracked a smile as I helped him off of Tamaj's back.

"If you hadn't found this when you did..." Tamaj said but didn't finish her sentence.

"I know, I know. There's water ahead. Do you think it's safe?"

"It's probably from a spring. It may not be safe to drink, considering it's down in this cave, but it may be warm."

"A warm bath sounds good right now," I said before helping Anza sit and trudging over to the water. Reaching out with the hand holding the stone, I reached for the water but had difficulty finding it. Only after a few moments did I realize the water was the same temperature as my body. I splashed it a little, and it rippled outward, impacting the rocks, which vibrated back to me like a symphony.

"Whoa."

"What is it?"

"Oh, nothing. This water is warm," I said, Tamaj coming over to where I stood, lowering her head and sniffing it.

"It does not smell that bad," she said, stepping into the warm water, the snow and ice dripping off her.

"Hey, Anza, want a warm bath?" I asked. He nodded, but was having a hard time getting his gloves off. I moved over to him and carefully pulled them off, revealing dark fingers, too-dark fingers. Quickly, I helped him get his shoes off to find even more heavily damaged feet. This was bad.

"Um, Tamaj?" I asked, and she begrudgingly padded back over, looking over my shoulder.

"They're definitely damaged from the cold, not quite frostbitten, though. He should be able to get into the water, and the color should come back,"

"Should?"

"It's tough to see in this light, and I'm not a healer, but it could have been worse," she said.

I carefully helped Anza out of his wet winter gear and shirt. His muscular but lithe body wasn't easy to ignore, but I forced myself not to let my eyes wander. Leaving his shorts on, I tossed his shirt onto the pants he had been wearing over them and took my winter gear off, stripping down to my underwear. He turned his head away as I removed my clothes, careful to be respectful, before I took his hands and led him into the water.

"Easy," I said as he winced.

"Wanna talk about how you're basically an earthen goddess?" he asked out of the blue as the water lapped at our hips.

"Not really," I said, feeling my face flush as we moved into the water. It was totally because of the heat of the water.

"At least you know what your power is now," Tamaj said as we waded to our shoulders in the warm water.

"Yeah...is it common for Endering to only be able to use their powers in certain circumstances?" I asked, mere inches from Anza, using my arms to guide him, his hands sliding to my elbows so he could rest his forearms against my own. His elbows were in my hands as I led him and I almost missed Tamaj's response.

"Like, if you're touching a stone?" Tamaj asked. Her sarcastic tone caught me off guard, but she kept talking, dropping the sarcasm. *"Yes, all Endering have a downside to their power, a situation where they cannot use it. For example, your grandmother, Silvia, could create fire, but she could not control it."*

"So if the wind shifted after she set a blaze..."

"It would be terrible."

"Sounds like it would be more than terrible," Anza said, and I couldn't help but smile. He rested his head on my shoulder and I leaned mine down to rest on his as we stood together in the warm water. The silence stretched comfortably and the tingling from the lingering cold faded as we stood together. Tamaj stayed a few yards away but clearly was enjoying the warmth. After a few moments, though, she spoke again.

"Mira?"

"Yeah?"

"Was it quick?" I didn't have to ask what she was talking about. Arlo had been her mate, her ally, throughout all of her life. He had her back as she had his; now he was gone. I had to lie to her. No one wanted to hear the gritty details of the death of their partner.

"As quick as it could be," I said, lifting my head to look at her. I swore I could see the tears running down her face. "I'm sorry."

"Did he…talk about me?"

"He sure did."

"Your axe?"

"From him, Anza got someone in his village to make it." She nodded her approval, looking up at the bioluminescent mass on the cave roof.

"How did you…get…stuck up here in the mountains?" I didn't want to say kidnapped. She had clearly been through enough, but I didn't want her story to go unspoken. "You don't have to say anything if you're not ready."

"I'm not ready yet."

"Alright, sorry, I didn't mean to push."

"It's alright, Mira, but I can say that Agrenon…is not in a good place." Her voice in my mind was soft and quiet, as if speaking too hard on the subject might unravel her.

"It wasn't this bad back when you were a kid?" I asked.

"Oh, no. We had our hardships, but there are more bandits now, especially from Korrewen. Add in The Fever and the hardship both bring to the people of Agrenon and before you know it, poverty and crime run rampant."

"Can't my uncle do anything about it?"

"I know your uncle. He means well and tries his hardest, but he's no Saha. People left positions in the military and national medicine sects once he took power. They missed her."

"Have you seen him since he took the throne?"

"No, I haven't seen him for some time; I'm just familiar with his nature. That man could fix any problem if he put his mind to it, it just might take some time."

"So you think he's trying?"

"I would be shocked if he wasn't. I know he's spread too thin," Tamaj said, heading toward where we had left our clothes.

"What were my parents like?" She managed a scoff but settled down on the ground, drip-drying in the warmth.

"Your parents were simultaneously the best and worst Endering to plague the royal family," she laughed.

"How so? Was one of them bad?"

"Oh, no. They were two sides of the very same coin; your mom leaped headfirst into anything, completely unable to keep herself from running straight into danger."

"And my dad was more careful?" I asked.

"Much, but he often also ran head first into danger. I'm talking about dropping off of cliffs onto the backs of dragons, or talking to a Nazzir like it's a sock puppet of danger."

"A sock puppet?" I laughed.

"Oh, yes. It was quite comical. Though it gave your poor grand-mother her fair share of near-heart attacks."

"And Saha?"

"She often defended them from Sil; they were always so 'creative' or 'inventive' or 'independent'. In fact, I remember once, they had destroyed dinner, it was a complete loss, and Sil tried to scold them."

"How far did she get?"

"Not very. Saha told her to pipe down, that food could be replaced, but memories couldn't."

"It...almost sounds like Saha lost a lot before my family showed up."

"She did."

"They're gone, right? My parents?" I asked, and Anza shifted away from me, lifting his head.

"I don't know."

"I hope they're not...they didn't come back for me."

"Mira?"

"Yeah?"

"If they didn't come back for you, you can rest assured that it was because they couldn't, not because they didn't want to."

"They really loved me?" I didn't think four words could make my throat so tight, but they each came out strangled.

"More than you will ever know," Tamaj said steadily, confident.

"Tamaj?"

"Yes?"

"Thank you," I said.

"You're very welcome; now get out before you both turn into wrinkly little fruits."

"Raisins?"

"What's a raisin?"

"Right…" I led Anza toward the edge of the pool, helping him out, and together, we sat beside Tamaj; the air was cooler, but at least we were warm.

"I wish I was bundled up on a warm cot right now," he said.

"Same," I said.

"Oh, what I wouldn't give for a warm bed."

"Tomorrow, we're going to have to find some food," I said, my stomach snarling.

"Food sounds amazing," Tamaj said.

"Maybe the sky will be clearer in the morning? We'll be able to find our way?" Anza suggested.

"If we're lucky," Tamaj said in my head as I stood up. Moving to our clothes, I picked them up, passing Anza his.

"Thanks."

"You should thank me for having holes in my socks; I don't think we would have gotten away from that dragon without them."

"That does not make it alright to keep wearing socks with holes, especially when we can get new ones right out of my bag."

"Socks?" Tamaj asked

"I'm pretty sure he has a magic sock section in his backpack; he materializes a pair every time I ruin one."

"How often do you ruin socks?"

"Very often," Anza said before starting to dress.

I carefully put my clothes back on, leaving my winter gear to dry a little longer. Anza settled in against Tamaj, and I sat near him, leaning against her boney frame as we settled down to rest.

"Mira?"

"Hmm?"

"Thank you for everything."

"You shouldn't be thanking me; I didn't summon a dragon."

"Summon and irritate are two totally different things," Tamaj said. *"Now, settle down before I add a new word to my vocabulary."*

"What word would that be?"

"Murder." I rolled my eyes, knowing this bag of bones wouldn't kill us. I held the egg bag close and settled as close to Anza as possible.

"Night."

"Night."

"Goodnight."

11

The sound of dripping water woke me. My eyes fluttered open, seeing Anza lying beside me, sleeping safely, as comfortably as possible in this deep, dark cave. When I remembered we had fallen asleep against Tamaj, I jumped up, Anza startling awake beside me.

"What, what is it?"

"Where's Tamaj?" I looked around the room but didn't see the Barbarza. We scooped up our stuff quickly before I heard her voice.

"Settle down. I'm watching the snow fall." Anza and I took a breath and shared a glance before starting to more carefully prepare for the day. After we packed our things together, we climbed the steep tunnel back toward the entrance, to find Tamaj looking out at the softly falling snow.

"Any chance at seeing the stars?" I asked, but Tamaj was already shaking her head.

"It's far too cloudy."

"It really is as beautiful as it is deadly," Anza said, pulling on his now-dry winter gear.

"Yeah, it is," I said. "We're going to need to hunt down some food."

"I think I can see a small grove of trees not far from here; there may be animals that live in or near them," Anza said.

"Great, we'll head over there, try to get food for a bit, and head out," I said, pulling on my warm and dry winter gear. "Is there anything we can do to make you warmer?" I asked Tamaj.

"Oh, no, my dear. Us Barbarza are built for the cold. I'm fine."

"You're sure?" I asked.

"Yes, I'm sure."

"Alright," I said, rechecking the eggs, making sure they were close to me before we started heading out toward the grove of trees.

"I don't smell trees," Tamaj said only a few yards into the trip, her nose lifted to the wind.

"Maybe they're not trees," Anza said. I peered across the barren white expanse at the mass Anza pointed to. In the distance, towering silhouettes that looked like trees stood, but they were so far away it was hard to tell what they were.

"Worst we could do is find out what they are and keep moving. We can't stay in that cave forever, they'll just find us again," Tamaj said, trudging toward the masses. She wasn't wrong; if we took too much time in that cave, they would inevitably find us again. The wind was still sharp and cold as we walked, but the soft snow made it easier to see. As we approached the space we had thought was a forest, though, Tamaj slowed to a stop. It wasn't trees. Each pillar stood taller than us, arranged in sets of fours and sixes in boxes. Some walls still stood, but most of the small village rested in ashes.

"There will be no comfort there," Tamaj said quietly before heading away. I kept watching the village, hoping for a fluttering movement or a glimpse of a figure, hoping help would come. Help wasn't coming. It hadn't come for the people who had lived there, and it sure wasn't coming for us. I turned to face forward, trudging through the snow at Tamaj's side as the snow picked up, putting the burned-down village in the distance. Had we been the reason it burned down? Had irritating the dragon

brought an entire village to its knees? Was it burned down before we escaped or afterward? I tried to shove the thoughts out of my mind, trying to focus on the snow, the cold, and kept moving.

"Hey," Anza said, glancing over at me over Tamaj's back from his position at her other shoulder.

"Yeah?"

"That was old damage, at least a week old; it wasn't our fault."

"You're sure?"

"Yeah."

"I still don't like it."

"Me either, but all we can do is keep going," Anza said, reaching over Tamaj's back and offering me his hand. I took it for a moment, holding his gloved hand with my own, trying to push away the shame and worry inside me before letting it go. Tamaj was slowing down, though, having difficulty trudging through the snow. I focused on her, trying to help her keep moving through her panting breaths. I kept my focus on her until my stomach pitched upward and the ground gave out from under me.

"Mira!" A sheet of snow and ice had given way, plummeting downward. I reached out, seeing a flash of brown, Anza heading headfirst toward me. His hand caught mine, but as he tried to pull back, he slipped. Tamaj dug her legs in, grabbing Anza's foot as he lost his footing. In a heartbeat, a single moment, we were dangling over the edge of a sheer cliff, with only a malnourished Barbarza between us and a deadly fall.

"I'm okay." I said.

"Your shoe's slipping," Tamaj said, speaking to Anza.

"We need to do something," Anza said, meeting my eyes, my heart slamming in my chest as I clung to him.

"Give me a second to think," I said.

"We don't have a second," Tamaj said, trying to back up as she started to slip. I pulled my hand that wasn't occupied by Anza's up

and bit the end of a finger of my glove, taking it off before searching my pockets; as my hand found the rock in my pocket, the whole mountain sounded like it was singing, like someone had hit play on a choir recording. The warmth returning to me, I reached out, pulling a slab of the mountain out as Anza's boot slipped. I landed on the slab on my back, Anza landing on top of me.

"Oh, thank the stars," he said before lifting his head to look at me again.

"I've got you."

"Yes, yes you do," he said, his golden brown eyes on mine. I tore my eyes away as I saw Tamaj peek over the edge.

"You alright?" I asked.

"I could ask you the same thing, considering you're the one who fell off a baby cliff," Tamaj said Anza's boot still in her mouth.

"We're good," Anza said. "Baby cliff…" He laughed before carefully feeling how big the slab was to lift himself off of me, rolling over onto his back beside me.

"It's just a baby," I said, smirking up at Tamaj as she rolled her eyes.

"You're alright enough to make jokes. Good, I didn't want to have to scrape up piles of people goo off the bottom of a ravine." I couldn't help but laugh,

"Ah yes, with those opposable thumbs of yours," Anza said softly, chuckling as we sat up.

"What was that?" Tamaj asked.

"Nothing."

"I thought so."

We carefully stood, the rock still in my hand, and I pulled a set of stairs up the cliff's edge. Tamaj had backed up as we climbed. I looked over my shoulder at the extensive cliff we almost plummeted off. Another mountain's jagged cliff stood across the expanse. The warmth still sat in my chest as I tucked my hand back in my pocket, but left as soon as I released the stone.

"Thank goodness for powers," Anza said quietly taking his boot back and putting it on.

"Yeah, thank goodness," I agreed, returning to Tamaj's side before we turned to walk alongside the cliff, farther away from the edge. Anza had moved to walk on the same side as me, keeping himself between me and the cliff as we walked. I kept my hand on Tamaj but could feel how much she was struggling. We needed food.

"Do you think there are any more Holds around here?" I asked Anza.

"Yeah, there were enough to get through the mountains, but the bandits threw us off our course."

"So, there's the potential for finding one?"

"Maybe," Anza said as the snow started falling harder. Tamaj stopped, and Anza and I stopped as well.

"Hey, are you okay?"

"*Shh*," Tamaj said, lifting her head, her ears twitching as she turned. We fell silent before a voice rang through the storm. We stayed still until we heard it again.

"They're over here!" Dashra.

"*Get on.*"

"But—"

"*No buts, I'm faster than you, get on,*" Tamaj said. She wasn't wrong, and I scrambled onto her back, Anza right behind me, before she bolted through the snow. I turned, clinging to her mane, looking past Anza to the two figures approaching us quickly. No, there weren't two. There were two Barbarza, each with a rider. I could pick out Dashra on one of their backs.

"Tamaj, we need to move."

"*I can't move as quickly as I used to,*" she said as they closed in.

"Tamaj," Anza said quietly as she tried to pick up the pace, the thick snow becoming harder to run in, though she was going faster than we would have been able to on foot.

"Turn toward the cliff," I said, slipping my hand back into my pocket.

"What?"

"Do it!" They were upon us, Anza drawing his sword as I drew my axe, Tamaj turning to head toward the cliff's edge.

"Get them!" Dashra snarled as Tamaj ran for the edge of the cliff.

"Tell me you have a plan!" Tamaj said.

"I do!" I said, the Barbarza snapping at her legs. I threw my power at the edge of the mountain, out, and out, and out as far as I could reach. Her stride got wider as realization hit her, throwing herself headlong into running, breaking away from the pair of Barbarza as they skidded to a halt near the edge of the cliff. Tamaj nearly slipped as the terrain went from snow and ice to bare stone, but she kept her footing and charged forth on the path I had created over the cliff's edge, reaching, reaching out toward the other section of ground across the deep chasm.

"Tear it down behind us!" she said as I worked up another piece of the bridge, bringing us closer to the next section of the mountain.

I turned, looking back at the group, trying to use our same path. I grabbed hold of the first section of stone and ripped it out from under their front paws before turning around and focusing on where we were going. My head pounding, the warmth within me burning as it rose up, like a fire was trying to break out of my skin, a warning. As I set the last section in place, the burning sensation and warmth flickered and died. Tamaj quickly got across the bridge I had made just as it began crumbling, and something hot ran down my face as she finally got to solid ground.

"I can't believe we just-Mira, Mira, you're bleeding," Anza said, his delight turning to panic. I lifted my hand to my nose, bright red blood spattering my hand and the rock. He pulled out a cloth and carefully held it to my nose.

"She'll be alright, Anza; she pushed herself too far."

"I feel like I woke up with the worst headache," I said, pinching my nose as my head slammed with every heartbeat.

"*It will pass,*" Tamaj assured me.

"Good," Anza said, getting off Tamaj's back and reaching up to help me. I stumbled when I got down, and my vision blurred momentarily. I used Tamaj's flank to steady myself before I saw Anza take a few steps along the path. "Wait a minute."

"What now?" I said, feeling like if one more thing went wrong, I would dismantle the planet rock by rock.

"That's a Hold sign."

"A Hold, like tea and food and a warm place to sleep?" I asked.

"*On a comfortable bed?*" Tamaj added.

"Yeah, this way, we're almost there."

"*No way, there's no way,*" Tamaj said as my vision stabilized and I led her after Anza.

Limping, cold, and tired, the cabin came into view. The door was snowed in, like the first had been. Together, we dug it out, desperation and hope pushing us forward. Salvation was on the other side of this door. I could feel it. The door gave way, and with a strong push from Anza, there was enough room for us all to slip in.

This cabin was larger than the first, with two beds instead of one, though one was lower to the floor and much larger, built for a Barbarza. I spotted the shelf packed with food like the Hold we had been in before. Anza went to the fireplace, sparking a fire, and I went to the food wraps. I pulled out some dehydrated meat and took it to Tamaj. She carefully climbed into the larger bed to claim it. She ate quickly, ravenously, munching away as Anza and I dug out food for ourselves, sitting on the remaining bed, eating as the fireplace warmed the space. After he was full, Anza found a teapot similar to the one the first one had and went out to get snow. Upon his return, we made tea.

"Feeling better?" I asked Tamaj, and she nodded, reaching back to grab a pillow in her mouth and arranging it before snuggling into the warm bed. I didn't want to think of how long it may have been since she had a warm, comfortable place to sleep.

Anza passed me a cup of tea, and we quietly ate and drank until we couldn't eat or drink anymore.

Carefully, we removed our winter clothes and climbed into bed, ensuring we laid back to back. I expected sleep to come quickly, but it didn't; I couldn't help but feel like an ambush would be waiting for us in the morning. Had I torn away enough of the bridge? Had I done enough to keep us safe? No one had been here for quite some time, that had been clear by the snow at the door, but were we really safe? Slowly, a warm hand gently touched my elbow, and I turned to look at where Anza lay.

"Worried?"

"Yeah, what if they get us in the morning?"

"They won't," he said, rolling over to face me.

"This is gonna sound weird, but...never mind." I wanted to feel safe, warm, comfortable; I wanted to be tucked against him. He was safe.

"I promise it's not weird," Anza said, pulling the blanket back and inviting me closer.

"No funny business, right?"

"Of course not," he said as I inched toward him, tucking myself against him. A single arm of his draped slowly, carefully over my side, almost as if he was ready to snatch it back at the first semblance of an idea that it might not be wanted. I rested my head against our shared pillow and finally relaxed, sleep quickly taking me. He was here, so was I, and we would be okay.

<h1 style="text-align:center">12</h1>

The light filtering into the cabin woke me and I pulled the blankets over my head and heard Anza chuckle.

"No one's here, right?"

"No, we're safe, Stone-Slinger."

"Safer, Beetle-Brain," I grumbled, and he gently pulled the blanket back.

"We are going to have to go back out there."

"Can't we just lie here for a bit longer?" I asked, warm against him.

"Just a little longer." He brushed a few locks from my face.

"Can you two be any louder?" Tamaj grumbled, burying her face under a paw.

"Sorry," we spoke together as she shifted slightly, removing her paw from her face before stretching.

"Well, if we're up, there's no point waiting to get going."

"We're not awake," Anza said, covering our heads with the blanket again.

"Oh, no. If I have to be awake, you two do too." I heard her get off the bed and the blanket was pulled away before I knew it. Anza tried to hold on to it, but there was no match in strength against a Barbarza, even one in as bad of a condition as Tamaj.

"Fine, fine, we're up," I said, rubbing my eyes as we got up.

"Not that we want to be," Anza grumbled.

"Good." We stumbled into our winter gear, eating again before we collected our things and prepared to head out.

"Hey, Tamaj?" I asked as a thought crossed my mind.

"Yes?"

"Have you noticed that there are a lot of bandits up here?" Anza snorted as I asked, and Tamaj chuckled in my mind.

"Yes, Saha once had quite a few battalions of troops stationed up here, they cycled out and were refreshed regularly, both because Korrewen tried their luck any chance they could and because the people of Korrewen knew crossing the border was a good way to make money, so there are lots of bandits from Korrewen. It's been hard for some people to make a living, so they fall to…well, crime."

"Why up here, though?"

"It's easier to hide in the mountains. You can vanish down one tunnel, and no one can find you."

"Sounds great." I rolled my eyes. "Gonna have to talk to my uncle about getting more troops up here."

"We can only do that if we manage to actually make it to the castle," Tamaj said, and Anza sighed.

"Which we can only do if we head out?" he asked.

"Oh, what a fantastic idea." She tossed her head and snorted.

"You could open the door," I said,

"Ah yes, me and my seventeen thumbs." As I put the last of my winter gear on and trudged to the door, I hesitated for the drama before opening it. *"My savior!"* She bowed dramatically before trotting into the snow.

"We should totally have a thumb war one of these days," I said, mostly to taunt Tamaj more.

"What's a thumb war?" Anza asked.

"A thing Endering do to flaunt their opposable authority," Tamaj grumbled from her spot on the other side of the now-open door.

"I can see why Arlo loved her."

"Was he as sarcastic?" Anza asked.

"Oh, you have no idea." I followed Tamaj into the snow, Anza behind me. The snow had subsided, soft flakes drifting around, but the blizzard was gone. Sunlight bounced off everything, nearly blinding us with its glare. After a few moments, my eyes adjusted and Anza took my hand to lead me after Tamaj, dropping my hand after a moment.

"Do you think we'll be able to see the stars tonight?" I asked, resting my hand on the egg bag as we moved; they were still both there and okay.

"I really hope so. We're pretty turned around right now," Tamaj said, trudging on.

"There are a lot of different Holds, but only a few of them have direct paths through the mountains; we were at one our first night here, but—" Anza started.

"People suck."

"Yeah, people suck," Anza said, matching my step, staying together.

"At least the snow is pretty." Tamaj looked out over the rising cliffs and expansive layers of white. She was right; I would call this place beautiful if the circumstances were different. The few rising trees and the sheer cliffs caught in the startling sunlight reminded me of winters at home. The warmth of a fireplace, hot chocolate on a cold winter's night. Tamaj stopped, Anza and I beside her as she tilted her head.

"What is it?" Anza asked.

"Shh…" We fell quiet, standing still, and heard snow shifting. *"Get on."*

"There is no way they found us again," Anza said, drawing his sword.

"Oh, yes there is. If you came face to face with a luxurious future, you'd hike through the night to keep it from getting away, too," she said.

"It might be shifting snow," I said, biting my lip. She was wrong. She had to be wrong, right? A footstep. Anza and I moved at once, rushing to Tamaj as footsteps burst forth. They now knew that we knew they were there. As a Barbarza crashed against Tamaj, a Maraung on his back, we scrambled on. I drew my axe as Anza clashed his sword against the spear the Maraung had, more people moving out of the snow, slipping from behind trees and heading toward us.

I swung, crushing my axe against the Maraung's head as Tamaj scrambled away from the Barbarza, nearly knocking him clean off his mount, who stayed hot on our heels regardless of his injured rider.

"Tamaj!" I said, pointing toward an expanse that looked like the snow wasn't as deep. Tamaj turned toward it, a wall of stone behind it as far as the eye could see, wrapped in a layer of ice, and there on the other side of the expanse was a cave. A series of cave entrances we could get lost in.

"No, no, that's a lake!" Anza said, clinging tighter to Tamaj.

"No, it's a frozen lake," Tamaj said as she gained speed, leaping out over what must have been ice. I expected it to crack, expected water to rush around us. Expected to be soaked to the bone. The ice groaned beneath us, threatening to pitch us into the cold water beneath it, and cracking started. Still, Tamaj kept going, running headlong for the cliffs.

"Don't you dare stop!" Anza said, turning. I looked back at what he was looking at, the crack in the ice jutting outward toward us at a stilted but furious pace. Tamaj didn't let up, even though those chasing us had stopped at the edge. Tamaj spun at the last minute, turning us around so we could easily slide into the cave while facing our enemies. Anza and I each wordlessly lifted a hand and flipped them off as we vanished into the darkness. Skidding to a stop, Anza and I quickly got off, the ground still slick underfoot.

"Do you think they'll follow us?" I asked.

"It should be difficult to do if they can at all," Tamaj said. *"Either way, we can't go out the way we came in; that ice will give way, even if they aren't waiting for us."*

"Right. Do you think there's a way out?" Anza asked. We fell quiet. Why hadn't we thought of that? Were we trapped in a cave with a dead end? I tried not to let the idea sink in, my heart slamming in my chest from the chase.

"Only one way to find out," I said, and slowly, we started forward, heading deeper and deeper into the tunnel. The only sounds were the soft drippings of water and our footfalls. I could feel the tunnel getting thinner, smaller, and more compact. My heart fluttered in my chest and my throat got tighter and tighter. It wasn't until I heard Tamaj's fur against both sides of the tunnel that I realized we truly were trapped. It hurt to breathe; there wasn't enough air, and there wasn't a way out. I slid my hands against the singing stone and focused my attention upward. We needed more space.

"Mira, what are you doing?"

"It's too close, it's too close."

"Mira, don't. If you push or pull the wrong thing, it'll collapse." I tried to stop, feeling the warmth burn within me like it had when I built the bridge.

"Mira," Anza said, his hand finding mine in the dark.

"It's too close; I can't see, I can't breathe, we're trapped."

"You need to calm down." Tense and scared, the fractures from my power began to creep all around us, every wall threatening to fall inward.

"Easier said than done."

"Hey, hey, what are you scared of? Where is this coming from?" I didn't want to tell him the truth. I didn't want to tell him all the things bubbling at the back of my mind, all the things I had tried to push back to focus on today's problems, because they would be tomorrow's problems. "Come on, tell me."

"I've been trying too hard not to think about what we've been through, worrying about how bad this will get before we get to the castle. We haven't talked about my place; princess, heir. Are you kidding? I can't see anything and it's small in here and I feel like we're stumbling through this trip."

"That's why they call it a trip."

"Tamaj, this isn't really the time," Anza said.

"I just…I feel trapped."

"Are you trapped or surrounded?" I turned back to where I knew Tamaj was hearing the cracks growing larger around us.

"What the fuck is the difference?" I couldn't help the hot tears running down my face, the tension in my chest, the lump in my throat.

"The focus you have, your perspective, will determine our outcome at this moment. Are you trapped by this mountain, or are you surrounded by it?" It hurt to breathe, the cracks growing as I clung tighter to the stone. All I had to do was drop it, but I was holding the walls up as much as I was tearing them apart.

"Breathe with me, come on, in and out," Anza said, taking a deep breath. I tried to calm my breathing, matching his, and as I did, slowly, the panic subsided and my headache faded. The singing of the stones became soft and gentle and the range of my power crept outward.

After a few minutes, I could feel my power expanding. Up the sheer cliffs and winding trails of the mountain. There were stone squares that barely graced the surfaces of the mountain, each with a fireplace within the Holds, craggy peaks, and shifting stones rising and up.

"Mira?" Anza said softly. He had stopped guiding my breath, but I kept breathing calmly, focusing on the world around me. There were deep ravines and sheer cliff faces, boundless and breakable. We could die in a thousand places and there were dozens of routes that would lead us to safety. I had been so afraid of this tunnel beneath the ground, so afraid of all the things we knew we would face. I was terrified of a ballroom or trying to be polite and royal. I was terrified of being everything an Endering shouldn't be. At that moment, though, with the mountain singing to me, I realized I had nothing to fear. It knew me, every inch of my being, and I knew it, every winding path, every broken piece, every safe route forward. I was the mountain, and the mountain was me. So long as I didn't focus on any particular thing, I could feel the whole fucking mountain. I turned away from Anza, bringing my focus to the situation at hand, and carefully put the stones back how they had been.

"Tamaj is right; we're not trapped, we're surrounded." We were surrounded by stone, abundance, potential, and vibrance. Surrounded by opportunity. Turning to the cave wall that was closest to the air, thin or thinner than the rest of the cave. I took another breath, keeping myself as calm as possible, imagining a tunnel in the depths of these walls. Carefully, I reached out and pushed; the stone moved an inch backward as I stepped carefully forward, leaving a gentle ridge in the floor so we could all keep our footing. I kept a mental note of the mountain above us, shifting positions and moving properly to keep the tunnel from caving in on us.

"Is she…?"

"She is." They didn't speak anymore as they followed me down. I didn't have to look back to know Anza walked beside Tamaj, close enough to have a hand on her shoulder. I could feel their feet touching the stone. They led one another behind me, and after several minutes of concentration and focus, we were bathed in light as I let the long pillar I had carved out of the mountain drop into the valley below.

"Holy shit."

"You can stop freaking out about it at any point."

"You carved us out of a mountain."

"Without killing us or collapsing the mountain," Tamaj added.

"Yeah, yeah," I said, but I couldn't help but smile as I pulled steps out from the side of the mountain, leading us down to a more forested area. Craggy stone sections rose between thin sections of trees as we pressed forward.

"Don't pretend you don't like how that felt," Tamaj teased. *"Admit it, it was cool."*

"Fine, fine, it was really fucking cool," I said, looking back. I could still see the hole we had left.

"And it likely put much more distance between us and that horrible man."

"He's not the only bandit out here," Tamaj said.

"Or the only threat," Anza said.

"Why, in this or any other world, would we be able to catch a break?" I said, garnering a sharp chuckle from them both.

"Think of the castle, it'll make it worth it."

"I've never been so…what exactly is 'worth it'?" I asked, and Tamaj turned to look back at me for a moment.

"I'm so sorry I keep forgetting this is your maiden journey." She turned to face forward, continuing, *"Think expansive and cozy, hot baths, warm meals, comfortable beds, and all the space in the world to stretch. Oh, and the library. I'd kill to be in that library again."*

"I don't know if you'd *actually* kill to be in a library," I said.

"Oh, you haven't seen that library. I'd find a way," she said, coyly.

"Oh, yeah…you're so intimidating," I said, rolling my eyes as we trailed behind her. A wall of brown fur tore from around a tree, slamming into Tamaj. Barbarza's teeth locked in on her as she whirled to bite him back. Anza and I rushed forward, but not before two more Barbarza, with riders, got between us.

"Tamaj!"

"Run." Her voice was firm and clear in our heads. They had divided us. We were outmatched. Anza and I stepped backward as I met the eyes of Dashra.

"No way."

"There you are, pretty thing." I didn't think. I reached for my axe, the Barbarza lunging. In one smooth motion, I unsheathed it, taking off the egg bag as we turned to run.

"Anza!" I threw the bag. He barely caught it as they tore off after us. They wanted me. They didn't care about the eggs and didn't know they existed. They didn't want Anza. Or Tamaj. They wanted me. I broke away, rushing into the small forest close to our path, leaping through and dodging trees. I looked to my left, hearing movement and seeing Anza running for his life, sword drawn, blood dripping down his back. The Barbarza was rearing back, faster than him, ready to grab him with a mouth full of teeth. In a flash, my hand found the stone, and a spike shot out, angling back behind Anza, right into and through both the Barbarza and the rider. With their momentum, they didn't have any opportunity to stop.

I dodged around another tree. Hearing a second Barbarza fall in line with the one chasing me. I looked back, seeing the Barbarza that had attacked Tamaj. Blood spattered down its maw and chest. *Tamaj.* I sent another spike out, slamming into that Barbarza's chest. He coughed blood, his legs still trying to push forward for a moment before the light left his eyes. Dashra was still on my heels as my feet found moss and I readied myself for the next strike. As I turned to lash out, I saw him; he had leaped from the Barbarza, a thin, glass vial in his hand. No. Not a vial. A syringe. I lashed out as he stabbed me in the neck, dropping my axe as he hit the plunger.

"Gotcha" White-hot fire leaped through my veins. I clung tighter to the rock, but the warmth that came with my power fluttered out like a candle flame snuffed out by the wind. His knee found my sternum. I tried to get up, only for his foot to crack into my side. Pain erupted through me, my breath gone as I tried to scramble away.

"It has taken me so long to catch you, little Endering."

"Fuck you," I hissed, my legs and arms already heavy. They didn't want to move, and every time I tried, there was a delay. My body was already shutting down.

"Hmm, a little spitfire. We'll take care of that."

The last thing I saw was his boot crashing down on my face.

13

"If you don't leave her alone, she will kill you."

"I have fought for days for this payday and—"

"And you're going to have to keep fighting for it; this stuff only works for so long." I opened my eyes, vision blurry, head pounding. I tested my arms and legs. I was bound, and what was that taste? A gag, a fabric gag in my mouth? My head burned and my legs screamed with pain as I looked up at the man and woman standing over me.

"And you have enough of it to get us back to Korrewen, right?"

"Of course, and we have the people to take turns carrying her. We still need to be careful. If she's on her way to Agrenon, she's likely that Endering Kings best chance at an heir,"

"So we don't only have an Endering, but one in line for the throne."

"Exactly."

"This is going to be easy." My body was still trembling with pain, my mind trying to fathom what was going on, but I couldn't think straight, my throat thick with a thirst I hadn't noticed at first. Even my eyes itched, dry and scratchy, the cold biting up from the ground I lay on.

"No, it isn't. She's too spirited. We have to break her before we get her to Korrewen."

"I'll break her before we even leave this cave."

"Well then, we better get to it. You're better at this than I am." I tried to move my head as they moved out of my line of sight, but I couldn't. It was only a moment before I was on my back, my hands twisted under me from behind, pain lashing out as I was shoved back against my own hands. Pain erupted in my hip, and my already blurry vision fragmented as the man slammed a heavy club against me. He was trying to physically break me. To keep me from physically being able to leave.

"If you're not careful, you'll kill her." He struck again, tears slipping from my eyes. I could barely blink as the strangled sound made it out of my throat.

"She killed at least four of my men."

"And they will have died in vain if you kill her!"

"I won't kill her, but I'm going to get my revenge for the lives she took."

"Fine, just keep her alive," the woman said before leaving. I was going to keep my life, but at what cost? What would be the cost of getting to live another day? Anza had the eggs, Tamaj… was Tamaj alive or dead? Anza was likely out there with the burden I was supposed to bear. Out in the cold, alone. I was here, trapped, bound, in more pain than I had been since I came to Agrenon. My hip seared with pain, unstable as Dashra pulled out a knife. Kneeling over me, he dug it into my shoulder. I tried to lash out at him, to stop him, but I could only scream around the gag. My already dry, raw throat cracked at the sound.

"That's right, scream; no one's going to hear you out here, and even if they did, they wouldn't care." He pressed the blade deeper into my shoulder. "Don't worry, I'm not going to cut open your veins or arteries, not like that little Barbarza you were traveling with." My heart dropped into my stomach. Tamaj's attacker had come back covered in blood. Even Anza had been bleeding the last time I saw him. My stomach twisted, threatening to vomit, but there was nothing in there to come up. How long had I been out? He pulled out the blade, and another scream escaped me. I could scream. I could scream. I pressed my tongue against the gag, pushing it out of my mouth.

"P-please, don't," I managed. I could talk, but how long would that last? I had clearly lost time, but how much of it? When was the last time they had dosed me with that stuff in the syringe? His hand found my throat, cutting off my air as his blade bit down shallowly into my side, drawing down my ribcage. I tried to scream, but nothing came out. His hand clamped firmly on my windpipe.

"Keep begging." He held me until my vision tunneled before releasing me. I gagged, gasping for air as his knife bit into my chest. His movements were blurry at first, but the slashes that bloomed across my chest were real. Each cut burned, some deeper than others, as he slashed open my shoulders and my arms, coming close to my neck but moving downward every time he got too close. I tried to move my arms again and found I could as he moved to get a new, larger blade. I turned onto my stomach with a hard push, trying to crawl away. My right leg wasn't working, too weak from him bashing it moments before as I tried to struggle forward across the dirt.

"Oh, look at you. So pathetic," he started before his hand wrapped around my ankle and pulled me back to him. "Come here." I cried out, each movement jarring and painful as I tried to summon my power to find that the warmth wasn't there. Pain erupted from my foot, bounding up my leg as I screamed. My throat tasted of blood as he stabbed clean through my foot.

"Stop!" I tried to choke out.

"You're not going anywhere," he growled at me, pinning me down by my neck as his blade found another foothold on the outside of my thighs, slashing my legs open as he held me down. The pain lashed through every bit of my body as he worked, moving quickly. I desperately searched the wall I was facing, hoping to see something that would help me, but there was nothing, nothing but raw, unbridled fear and pain. They were going to sell me to Korrewen; they were going to keep me alive, barely, long enough to get me there.

I wasn't going to have my powers at all, my only companion for the trip would be fear and pain. What was going to happen when I got there? When they sold me away to a different kingdom? What was going to become of me wrapped up there in that nation? Sil had told me about them, about how they treated their Endering. It was only a few moments before he moved back to the club he had. My vision started to spin as he began slamming the weapon into me again, pain erupting with every bone he struck. Every single bone in my body was screaming from the jarring pain.

There was no point in screaming. My throat was too raw to make noise, and my vision was too unstable to make much sense of what was going on, but it was beginning to stabilize through the fog of the drug.

Tamaj was probably dead, Anza had probably taken off in order to get the eggs to the castle, and I was going to be sold away to a rival kingdom and used for who knew what. I had to make sure I never made it to Korrewen. I had to make sure that the moment I got ahold of my senses, if they made a single mistake, I ended my life. I couldn't live the life Sil had described in Korrewen, pinned down and used for only one thing. I had to get free. Or I had to die trying. If I could move one little pebble, I could force it through his brain and kill him. I could buy myself time. I could do something besides lie here, bleeding heavily, head spinning, and pain in every inch of my form.

"That's enough."

"I'm not done yet."

"You are for now. I have to dose her again, or do you want me to let her kill you?"

"She doesn't even get a say in if she takes another breath; she's not killing me."

"She will if she shakes this off." The man stepped away, the woman coming closer. I tried to writhe away from her as she pulled the syringe close to me. "Shh, it's alright, little Endering," she said, as the pricking sensation of the syringe bit down into my neck. "Sleep."

I tried to fight the flooding agony, but the pain was too much, driving my mind deeper and deeper as I thought of my friends. Of Tamaj, who had been so tired and scared when we met her. How she had the confidence to piss off a dragon as a distraction. How she had helped me unintentionally manifest a power I couldn't access when I needed it most. I barely knew her, but Arlo had loved her, had cherished her, and I understood why: she had been willing to give everything to those she believed in. Now she was dead because of it.

As my vision started to fade, tears silently sliding from my eyes, I thought of Anza. Those bright, gilded brown eyes. The snowball fights and the warm smiles, and how he always moved with care and grace. How he had untangled my hair and helped me all this way. How he seemed to know what I was thinking as I thought it, how he reached to comfort me every time I wasn't sure of myself. We had gone separate ways. He was safe with the eggs. Safer. He would keep the kids, *my* kids, safer than I could. That was all that mattered. He was safer, so were they, and I had to find a way out of this mess.

Even if that meant I died alone in these mountains.

14

<hr>

"This will wake her up." Pain. Unbridled, unrelenting pain. My eyes snapped open, the strangled scream rising in my raw throat. Everything ached, but my biggest concern was a wooden spike being driven into my side.

"Why do you even want her awake? She's less dangerous asleep."

"She can't do shit without touching her precious rocks, especially when we've got your miracle juice running through her veins," Dashra said as I finally focused on him, my head pounding and every inch of me aching.

I noted my knees and ankles were weak as I dangled by my wrists, dried blood dripping from every inch of me. I tested my toes and fingers. I could move, dangling now from the roof of a cavern. Was it the same cave? Carefully, I grabbed the rope holding me up before driving my knee into his chest. Knocking him clear back onto his ass. Even that movement sent pain through my body. I tried to move my legs again but couldn't. The woman sat in the corner at a small makeshift table.

"You little—"

"Serves you right. No one enjoys getting woken up." I tried

106

to move my mouth, but the gag was back in place, bound against my tongue with a scrap of cloth tied across my mouth this time.

"She shouldn't be kicking or scraping at someone with her life in their hands," Dashra said, stalking over to the table to snatch up a sword and pivoting it to place it beneath my neck.

"You really shouldn't do that."

"Why not?"

"Endering don't forget faces, especially the ones of those who have wronged them. She hates you. If she ever got away, she may…want to make good on how badly you've beaten her." The other Maraung didn't look up from what they were doing, moving pieces to what looked like a game. I looked back to Dashra, meeting those dark eyes and glaring into their depths. "There's also the chance she knows she's worthless dead; convenient that there's a sword at her throat." I shifted my weight and Dashra snatched the sword away.

"Now she knows for sure. She's going to be trying to kill herself or grab rocks the whole way to Korrewen," Dashra said, turning on the Maraung at the table. He had already guessed my plan. She looked up, her eyes steady, calm, controlled.

"No one ever said this would be easy, only that it'd be worth it. Remember the riches we're heading toward, with literally every step."

"It better be better than my wildest dreams for this pain in the ass."

"It will be. Now, go relieve Gremush before you wake everyone else up," she said, gesturing behind me. Dashra stalked off down what I assumed was a tunnel to the right. I didn't want to look behind me at 'everyone else.' How many people were there? How many people were willing to take my life, give me away to a kingdom I had only heard horror stories about, to get rich?

"It won't be as hard as he thinks it'll be," the remaining Maraung said, reaching into a nearby bag and pulling out a cloth-covered satchel. Laying the satchel out, she unraveled it, revealing dozens of syringes packed full of the amber-colored liquid. "You won't even have your powers."

I wanted to tell her to go fuck herself, rip her head off and hurl it into the sea, but my vision was still blurry from the last syringe she had used on me, and my legs hurt so badly. They probably weren't broken, but they were weak. *I* was weak. I still couldn't move them. I tried to move my fingers and hands again and roll my shoulders, but I couldn't.

"One of the many pros of this lovely little drug is that you become dead weight, so much easier to move you around when you can't fight," she said, but I had figured that out already.

At least Anza had the eggs. At least he could get them to the castle safely. I didn't matter compared to them, and these Maraung hadn't known about the eggs, so they had what they wanted as far as they knew.

"Hmm..." She glanced to the cave entrance, tilting her head slightly as a sound, like metal against stone, rang out. She leaped to her feet, reaching for something on the table. She wasn't fast enough, and my vision was blurry, I could only vaguely make out the form that rushed in, but there was no mistaking what I saw as he drove a sword through her middle. She shrieked, and in an instant, there was movement behind me.

"I'm coming. Hold on!" My heart leaped, eyes watering again, relief washing through me at first, followed quickly by fear as I recognized the voice.

Anza.

He pulled the sword from the woman's middle, turning to the enemies approaching from behind me. I had to blink hard to clear my vision, but I wanted to see this. Two Maraung lunged for Anza, barely awake long enough to grab swords. Anza dodged, grabbing the sword-wielding hand of one as he ran the second through with his sword, leaving it still inside him before punching the first in the gut, taking his sword from him in less than a second and stabbing the attacker clean through. Every moment was cold, calculated, and ready. Blood spattered against him as he turned to the third with his stolen sword, quickly decapitating him with a single swing. Two more stood between him and me, Anza's golden-brown eyes glittering in the low light of the cave.

"Hmm, seems you two have made a critical error. She"—he stopped to point the sword he brandished at me— "is *mine.*" They tried to rush him, but he grabbed the sword-wielding arm of one to twist it, bringing the Maraung to his knees and stabbing the still-approaching attacker in the stomach. He dropped his sword as his breath left him, but Anza didn't wait for that. He tore the sword out of him and, with a single movement, killed the last attacker with a swift slash to the throat.

Anza stepped back before retrieving his sword from the woman, who was now bleeding out on the stone floor. Her breathing was still ragged as he made his way over to the space where the rope that held me up must have been tied, carefully stepping over their bodies. I watched as the woman took her last breath, watching it leave her. It was only a second before I fell from the ceiling, landing against his chest as he rushed to catch me, his arms solid and safe around me. He had only been here for a few moments, and in those few moments, he had eradicated everyone. Carefully, he took off my gag.

"Anza? Anza..." My voice sounded thick, wrong; I couldn't talk for long.

"I'm here."

"Dashra, he's..." I said, looking toward the door.

"Dead. It's okay, you're safe now."

"Safer," I said.

"Can you stand?"

"I don't know," I rasped, as he carefully tried to set me down, but pain ran up my body, my legs refusing to function. "No-nope," I said, burying my head into his shoulder.

"I've got you; it's alright," he assured me, carefully setting me down long enough to cut the rope from my hands before he picked me up again. I looked up at him. "Come on, let's get out of here," he said as he stood fully, heading toward the cavern's exit, stopping long enough to scoop up the syringes.

"What are you gonna do with those?" I asked.

"I'm gonna get rid of them so no one else can hurt you like this," he said, and I couldn't help but worry. Was he hurt? Had I seen all of that correctly? Was my idea of what happened skewed? The tunnel to the outside was quiet, the raging storm the only sound.

"I'm sorry."

"For what?" he asked, keeping me close.

"For...for..." I lost the train of thought, desperately trying to find it again.

"Shh. I've got you." He brushed my hair out of my eyes as we stepped into the blizzard.

"T-Tamaj?" I said, trying to think through the waves of pain from my legs and head.

"We split up to find you. We've got a spot to meet up though. She's probably already there; I gave her the easy area." She was alive. How the hell was she alive?

"The eggs?"

"Safe with her."

"Safer."

"She's faster and smarter than us, she'll keep them safe. There's a light inside her when she talks of them. She cares for them greatly."

"Alright...am I...I feel like I'm gonna pass out." I fought through every word.

"I know, everything hurts."

"Is...pain something you can...?" I didn't finish the sentence, but I didn't need to.

"No, but the stress and...desperation that comes with pain, the willingness for it to end, at such an intensity, it's unique to pain, and *that* I can feel."

"Sorry."

"You've got nothing to be sorry about." I fell quiet, trying to focus on staying awake, trying to count my heartbeats as we moved forward before a peaceful mind met mine.

"Oh my stars, Anza, are you alright?" Seeing us both splattered with so much blood, I hadn't thought of what Tamaj might think.

"It's not mine," Anza promised.

"T-Tamaj," I managed, her blurry shape coming into view as she touched my hand with her face.

"Oh, sweet one."

"We need rest," Anza said, shifting me slightly in his arms.

"There's a Hold over here. Hurry," Tamaj said, leading Anza toward a Hold hidden in a cliff face. I couldn't see the door for a moment, but when it came into view, I knew inside would be a warm little sanctuary, a bubble of comfort in the blizzard-like expanse. Someone was saying something.

"Mira? Mira, can you hear me?"

"Hmm?" It took all my focus to listen to Anza, hear him, and turn my face to see him.

"I'm going to open the door, alright? I'm going to have to set you down."

"'kay."

"This is bad, Tamaj."

"I know, but we have to take it a step at a time." It was easier to hear Tamaj; her voice was already soft and smooth in my head.

I didn't remember Anza setting me down in the snow, but I was suddenly there. The cold sank into my legs momentarily as Anza opened the door. The chill soothed the sliced and irritated skin, comforting me as I tried not to think about all the wounds that asshole had inflicted. He returned to me, still covered in blood, with something more in his gilded eyes. Carefully, he slid his arms under me and lifted me up again. A sparking warmth, similar but different to the feeling of my powers, sounded in my chest. The drug was really messing with me. I couldn't think straight.

"Alright, alright," he said, stepping into the cabin built into the wall. Before I knew it, he set me in a soft, comfortable bed.

"Anza?"

"What is it, Stone-Slinger?" he asked, his voice tight, eyes wet.

"Th-thank you, Beetle-Brain." He closed his eyes, tears slipping out as he carefully covered me up.

"I know you're out of it right now," he started as he opened his eyes, crouching down next to me, looking into my eyes as he wiped my face with a warm wet washcloth. Where did he get that from? I was losing chunks of time. I had to be. "But you never have to thank me for anything I do for you. I...I will rip the world apart to get back to you, Mira. If anything ever stands between us, if anything ever hurts you, I don't care how big or powerful it is, I will end it. I will come for you every time; never forget that."

The sparking rang in my chest again before stilling, but my tongue was thick in my mouth. After I made a few soft noises, he rested his head against mine.

"Rest. Please rest. I'm right here." I tried to relax back into the mattress, but every inch of my body was on fire. Agony itching through my body, burning across my skin. I was on fire and I could do nothing about it as I lost control of more and more of my body. When was the last time they had given me a dose of that crap?

I stared at the ceiling for what must have been hours, limp, unable to move an inch. Was this what it was like for other Endering? Being stopped in this way? What happened to them when they couldn't move? I didn't want to think about it. How much time was I losing right now? Were they going to be alright?

I tried to remember Anza when he wasn't covered in blood, but I couldn't stop myself from pulling up that image of him, drenched in the blood of our enemies, eyes on me. At some point, Anza joined me in bed, clean of blood, but he didn't touch me. I wanted him to hold me, but he had no way of knowing that. Would the pain be worse if he held me? I tried to pull up a feeling of longing, trying to give him consent without being able to speak, but it wasn't enough. I lost track of time, my vision getting more and more blurry before I slipped back into darkness, my head pounding, my body screaming, unable to move an inch.

15

The feeling of a single finger brushing up and down my jawline woke me, but I didn't open my eyes.

"Do you think she's going to be alright?"

"I don't know, Anza. All we can do is wait for her to wake up."

"If she's not…I don't know…I don't think I can—"

"Let's not jump to conclusions."

"Right," Anza said, and I shifted my body, trying to feel out my legs and arms. They were there. I could move, but everything was still stiff. "Mira?"

"I'm here," I said, opening my eyes to find his concerned face above me, furrowed eyebrows framing his gilded gaze.

"How are you feeling?"

"Like a Barbarza hit me at full speed."

"See, she has jokes. She's fine," Tamaj said as I got my elbows underneath me. *"You are alright?"*

"Yeah, I'm good, I think. What was that syringe shit?"

"Echalon Heart." I felt cold all of a sudden, my stomach threatening to throw up what little it had. Still, Tamaj continued, *"The drug that is derived from the hearts of Echalon can stop an Endering's power, paired with the numbing and paralyzing effects, it's…an effective way to control an Endering."*

"I was losing time. Like, a lot."

"One of many side effects," Tamaj said. *"But you're alright now?"*

"Stiff, but yeah, I think so."

Anza sighed with relief, the dark circles under his eyes clear as I studied his face.

"You didn't sleep at all, did you?"

"A little."

"Don't lie," Tamaj said.

"Okay, I didn't, but I couldn't; I tried," he said, fighting a yawn.

"Neither of us did."

"Why? It wasn't like I was gonna die, right?" Silence. "Guys?"

"We didn't know…how much they gave you."

"Or if you'd wake up."

"Oh…" I let it sink in. Had I been on the brink of death again? If I was, this time they couldn't have done anything to save me. All they could do was sit, wait, and see if I woke up. "Can we…like, never do that again?" Anza rested his head on my shoulder for a second, sighing as tension left his shoulders. I didn't need his empathy thing to realize the level of relief he must be feeling.

"I'm going to get you some water, alright?"

"Water sounds amazing right now." I waited until he stepped out, going to get freshly fallen snow.

"You've…you've seen that before, haven't you Tamaj?"

"Yes…once or twice," she said.

"How bad was it, really?"

"It wasn't good, Mira, but you're up, you're alive, and we can figure out anything else. You are going to feel, um…a little withdrawal later; it shouldn't be bad, just some irritation," she said, trying to be soft about it.

"Fantastic," I said, stretching out my legs and arms and trying to sit up. My legs trembled in pain. The injuries from

Dashra were all wrapped and bandaged, taken care of. Anza came back in.

"Whoa, take it easy."

"I'm not made of glass," I said, trying not to roll my eyes at him.

"I know, but near-death experiences aren't exactly fun."

"Anza's right; you must get up slowly. Your muscles are probably fragile and tired."

"Great…is anyone, and I mean anyone, able to give me any good news?"

"Well," Tamaj started. *"I hoped not being dead was good news."*

"Don't get me wrong, it is."

"Alright, the only good news is that we're almost out of these damn mountains."

"Thank fuck," I said as Anza passed me a cup filled with the barely melted snow. I sipped at the water and took a bite of the snow as it tried to assault my face, letting my body heat warm it in my mouth before I swallowed.

"Slowly," Tamaj said.

"Fine." They shared a glance. "What?"

"Nothing," Anza said, brushing my hair from my face. The weird feeling, like warm sparking again, but it faded as soon as he withdrew. I attributed the feeling to the drugs.

"We should rest a few hours and get started now that those assholes aren't right on our tail anymore," Tamaj said as I sipped the snow water.

"How long do you think it'll be before we're out of the mountains?"

"Not long, by the end of the day, so long as things go well."

"That sounds amazing," I said as Anza settled in next to me, gently touching my side. I lifted my arm, giving him room to rest his arm over my side as I lay down. It took more effort than I cared to admit, setting the cup on the stand beside the bed. "A little actual rest before we go?" I asked.

"I will collapse if we don't." Tamaj laughed, settling back into her bed as Anza pulled the blanket over us.

I pulled him closer, and he rested his arm over my side, pressing his lips against my neck for a moment before resting his forehead on my back. It wasn't long before they fell asleep. I tried not to be annoyed. We didn't have all day to sleep, but they got me away from the bandits and stayed up all night to make sure I lived.

I lay there in silence for a few hours, walking through how things had happened in that cave, the spraying blood, how Anza had moved. Had I imagined it? If my perception of time wasn't reliable, was there a chance I had hallucinated? Before I knew it, Anza roused again, hours gone as he rubbed his eyes.

"So, you're still alright, right?" Anza asked.

"Yeah, I'm good. Good luck waking Tamaj, though."

"Tamaj is already awake," she said, lifting her head. *"Ready?"*

"As ready as we can be," Anza said as I nodded. He helped me get up, giving me fresh socks and lacing my shoes. I finished the warming water and stretched my limbs, trying to push the irritation buzzing inside my head away. We should have moved by now, but they needed rest. Was this the withdrawal talking? I pushed the thought to the back of my brain as Anza led the way out of the cabin and into the wooded, snowy expanse.

"Which way?"

Tamaj nodded toward a narrow path leading into a thick forest, the trees still green, like pine trees rising around the entrance.

"Are we guessing?"

"Kind of," she said. *"We know the direction, but without the stars, it's impossible to get a proper heading."* I took a breath to calm myself, reminding myself that hadn't changed. We had been doing this for days. Anza's hand found mine.

"Easy," he said as we started toward the path, Tamaj leading the way.

"It's frustrating."

"We'll feel better when we're out of the mountains. Here, do you want these back?" he asked, pointing at the egg bag.

"Yeah, that might make a difference…hey, I didn't get to thank you for last night," I said, watching as he unfastened the bag and passed it to me. I put the bag on, fastening it tightly to me.

"Don't worry about it."

"I'm not, you guys had the eggs. You didn't need me. I appreciate you coming back and what you said when we got to the Hold."

"You remember that?" he asked, dropping my hand. I looked at his face, finding it had changed color.

"Yeah, I remember that," I said, resting one hand on the egg bag and the other on my axe, trying to meet his eyes.

"And?" he asked, finally looking at me.

He had been ready to give up everything. When I met him, killing people had clearly not been his nature. He couldn't kill his sister when she had been taken by The Fever. The bandits in the woods lived. He even left Sanji and Jinera to find their own fates. Ending a life wasn't easy for him, but last night it had been as easy as breathing. He helped me because he could, like he had the day he first met me.

"Feeling's mutual." A smile touched his lips as we fell quiet, keeping close to Tamaj as the trees grew more plentiful, rocks and stones springing up on occasion. The smells of the trees and the ground made me feel better. I looked back at Anza, seeing he, too, had relaxed a little, looking off into the woods as he lagged behind closer to Tamaj's haunches.

I took in the moment—there had been so few moments of peace on this trip. The sound of birdsong and the smell of the forest made last night feel like it was a few weeks ago and not a few hours. Even Tamaj seemed more relaxed, lowering her head to sniff here or there as she walked. I rested my hand on her shoulder, keeping myself steady as we moved. The patches of sunlight filtering through the branches almost made the forest feel magical.

"How are you feeling?" Tamaj asked.

"Alright."

"Not as irritable?"

"Yeah, sorry about that."

"No need to apologize," she said as I reached into my pocket, feeling the small stone there. The warmth of my power was weaker than usual, but it was at least there. I let the rock go and breathed deeply, taking a moment to revel in the peace as the day progressed. We kept walking, but as the sun descended toward the horizon, the cold started to creep in and we needed to start searching for a place to rest.

"Do you think there are any more Holds up ahead?" I asked.

Tamaj shook her head as darkness descended upon us.

"We should start a fire, settle in for the—" Anza was cut off by the softest, quietest sound of a child's laughter. We all froze.

"Get on. Now," Tamaj ordered.

Anza and I didn't hesitate to scramble onto her back as she lunged forward, picking up speed. Before I could blink, there were Hazzal at both of our sides, their mottled brown forms only showing The Fever in their too-white eyes. I drew my axe as Anza drew his sword. He defended Tamaj's left, and I took the right. A Hazzal lunged for her leg and I leaned down to slam my axe into its head, twisting its body while my axe was still stuck in its skull to trip another. I saw two bodies collapse from Tamaj's other side, feeling Anza moving beside me. I focused on my side, trying to keep the pack from her legs. She rounded a corner, and my head burned with a scream so loud a headache sprouted at the back of my skull.

Tamaj skidded, and I turned my attention from the pack, seeing the cliffside she was trying to avoid before we launched over it, plunging down toward the ground below.

I scrambled, kicking off of Tamaj as we fell, and lunged toward the cliff, reaching my hand out, desperate to touch the massive stone wall. It took longer than I hoped to graze the edge of the stone with my fingers. I pulled the warmth forth, slamming a slope into the air beneath us, hoping we could slide to safety. We had to hit the slope first, though.

As I crashed down, I tried to roll, but my leg crumpled beneath me. Pain shot up my body as I tumbled downward, my head smacking off of a stone. I tried to control my slide better before turning to look at Tamaj and Anza as they slid. Tamaj was limp, a twisted mess of fur and bones, and Anza clutched his arm, blood running from his mouth.

We slid to a stop at the bottom of the slope I had made and I tried to scramble over to them, pulling my broken leg behind me, pain ripping through my body with every movement I made. I didn't get more than a few feet before I was too exhausted to keep going. I lay on my back, trying not to listen to the noises coming from Anza as the clouds parted for the first time in days. Stars glittered above us, cold and bright against a darkening sky, as laughter trailed down the cliff face. They were coming for us. I planted my hand against the ground, ready to defend us if I could, but the pain made it hard to find the warmth within me.

"Anza?"

"Alive!"

"Tamaj?" Silence. "Tamaj!" I watched her form, unmoving in the brush for a moment, until the laughter grew closer. I tried to sit up, another wave of pain almost putting me out as the Hazzal stalked closer, patiently moving toward us now. One lunged, heading right for me. I tried to pull up a stone spike to stop it, but it didn't work. There was movement behind me. A woman who was at least twenty years older than me, with umber-brown skin and tightly woven braids streaked with thin strands of gray, came into view.

"Hold your breath!" she said, as she slammed into the Hazzal. The moment she touched it, a shock went through the creature's body, its atoms ripping apart at the seams as it collapsed into black ash and smoke. She turned toward the rest of the pack, gray eyes wide and bright.

I held my breath, terrified by the delight in her eyes. It wasn't the fact that she had no problem standing between us and a pack of infected Hazzal that scared me. It wasn't her too-familiar eyes or her smile as she approached them. It wasn't even how her body moved, poised and skilled, dangerous and elegant. What chilled me to the bone was that she had sent that Hazzal to its death with a single touch of her fingertips. *She was an Endering.*

16

"Come on, puppies, let's play!" Her smile made my stomach churn as she turned to face the other two Hazzal heading for us. One leaped for her, and she grabbed it by the top jaw, not at all concerned about the teeth as she twisted it around, flinging him into another beast. The first disintegrated as it was thrown, and the other Hazzal also started to break down once the first hit it. It was only a moment, but we were out of immediate danger for the span of a single, fleeting breath. She turned her attention to us.

"Tamaj," she said, her accent thick. It wasn't a Maraung accent; no, it came from somewhere else, but I couldn't quite place it, and honestly, I didn't want to.

"Don't you dare hurt her!" I said. She had sent those Hazzal to the beyond, to their deaths, with the touch of her hand and she was moving toward Tamaj.

"Hush, child."

"I'm not going to let you kill her!" Trying to pull myself toward Tamaj while keeping my eyes on the woman, tunnel vision took over my eyesight for a moment.

"Oh, sweet young one, you're not going to stop me from doing much of anything," she said, walking past me and resting her hand on Tamaj's shoulder. A shockwave ran across her body, similar to the shockwave the Hazzal had experienced, but she didn't break apart into little atomic bits and pieces. It was only a moment before Tamaj lifted her head, turning to look at the woman.

"Don't tease the girl, Emai." Something wasn't right. Was that *banter?*

"It is good to see you too, old friend,"

"Emphasis on old? Low blow."

Emai smiled but turned to Anza as Tamaj stumbled to her feet.

"Tamaj…" he said, distrust clear in his tight voice.

"Relax, she's a friend."

"And if I'm not, I'd at least give you a chance to hit me once; fair is fair." Emai rested her hand on Anza's shoulder. The shock also ran through him, and I watched as his wounds slowly stitched together, catching a glimpse of a familiar mark, a banishment mark, at the back of her neck. She turned to me.

"Don't move, little one, stay still," Emai said. I did, trying not to think of how she may have gotten that mark and stayed in this realm, keeping my eyes locked on her. As I forced myself to remain still, she rested her hand on my shoulder. "Your spine and leg are badly damaged." Tamaj had been alright, Anza was okay; there was more to Emai's power than death and destruction.

"Okay, okay." A tingling ran through me, almost like an electric shock but softer, more subtle, and the pain slowly subsided until it was gone. I sat up cautiously, expecting to be in pain, but felt none. Even the wounds from the night caused by Dashra and those other bandits no longer writhed with pain. I got to my feet, helping Anza up as Emai stepped back. Anza rubbed his ears hard and shook his head as Emai said something in another language to Tamaj, who sighed, almost disapprovingly, but nodded.

"Let's get you three inside and get some food into you. When was the last time you ate?" She pointed at Tamaj, who rolled her eyes.

"It's been a very long journey."

"I bet," Emai said, her eyes meeting mine for a moment. A tingle rolled up my spine and the hairs on my arms rose. Something wasn't right about those eyes, slate gray, they bored into my being every time she even glanced at me. Between the bandits, thieves, and the infected, it wasn't wise to blatantly trust anyone, even if they seemed like a friend at first.

"What do they call you?" I asked.

"Call me?"

"Sil's called the Wildfire. You don't have a special super-secret code name?"

She smirked, her smile reaching her eyes as she nudged me toward what looked like the silhouette of a cabin in the distance.

"My name's a little...intimidating."

"They call her The Reaper." Anza and I moved closer to each other without a word as we walked toward the cabin. Tamaj was one step ahead of us, but I was still tense with Emai's hand on my back. Tamaj didn't seem worried, but a sinking feeling settled in my chest.

"Fitting," I said as we stepped onto the porch. She could quickly turn each of us to dust. Even the trees petered out as we approached the home, leaving nothing but the cabin standing in a small clearing. An Endering outside of the castle and its rules; I wasn't sure if we should admire her or tremble beneath her gaze, but she stepped forward regardless, past us, and led the way into the cabin.

"You have a downside, right?" I asked as we stepped into the warm cabin.

It was roomy and cozy looking. Thick blankets draped over a couch, and a small counter jutted out to part the space between the living room and kitchen. It almost looked like a natural home, with its hallway stretching back to what must have been bedrooms. The walls were littered with art from different cultures, depictions of life in Maraung villages, and African artwork, which filled the space with color, joy, and calm. A single twisting branch rose from a mount on the floor, settled by a window as if something usually perched there. Emai had put me on edge with her power, but her home was comfortable, like…a home. Safe. Safer.

"That's very forward. I don't even know your power. Why do you ask? Scared I'll turn you to dust?" she asked, moving toward the kitchen.

"Honestly, a little. I mean, with a name like The Reaper… makes me queasy."

"I second that," Anza said, resting a hand on one of the thick blankets.

"Feel free," Emai said, nodding to him. He quickly took one from the couch and bundled himself up in it, still cold from outside. He reached an arm out to me, inviting me in, but I lifted my hand slightly to turn him down. I wasn't as cold as he was and I didn't want to get too comfortable here. "Well?" she asked, turning her attention to me.

"Tamaj?" I asked, glancing over to the Barbarza, who seemed comfortable in the house.

"For star's sake, Mira, if she was going to kill us, she would have already. Relax," Tamaj said, walking toward the couch and stretching before lying beside it.

"It's true," Emai said, leaning over the kitchen counter to watch me, propped up on her elbows, chin in her hands. I took a breath to steady myself. I hadn't thought Sanji and Jinera would have tried anything either, but they had stolen the egg bag from me. But Tamaj hadn't been around for that.

"I can manipulate the earth," I said, looking back at Emai, watching the sparkle in those sharp, unsettling eyes.

"Downside?"

"I'm pretty sure I've gotta be touching stone to do anything," I said.

"How delightful," she said, her smile getting even bigger

before she looked to the counter again. "I can heal people or I can kill them, but to kill, they must be within range of the dust I release. It's like a cloud. If you breathe it in, you die. It's easier to kill them when I can touch them. To heal, I must be able to touch them, and they must still be alive," she said. "Once a heart stops and all activity is gone in a brain, I can't save them." It almost sounded like she had experienced trying to save the dead before.

"So opponents with bows and arrows at a distance…"

"Is a weakness for me, yes," she said, looking back at me. Tamaj cleared her throat. "What?" Emai asked.

"Stop staring, you're creeping everyone out, and I'm hungry."

"I did not miss you one bit," Emai said, her voice dancing across the room as she flashed a sly smile in Tamaj's direction before she turned into the kitchen.

"Believe me, the feeling is mutual," Tamaj responded, smirking, her tail wagging as I moved to her side and sat on the couch. My body ached the minute I sat down, and though the couch was crudely made, it was the softest thing in the world for a moment.

"How are you doing?" I asked Anza. His response was to wiggle closer to me and rest his head on my shoulder as an earthy herb-like smell filtered in from the kitchen. He offered me the blanket again, and I settled into it with him.

"Good, I guess?"

"She's terrifying, but I'm warm. Food is on the way, and she kinda saved us back there; what would we do if she wasn't here?" The small valley was surrounded by mountains, well off the beaten path. There was no chance for a good person to find and save us. We would have died.

"I guess she's not so bad."

"You think she's going to eat your toes in your sleep or something?" Anza joked. Then he lowered his voice to add, "Maybe she will."

"No, I remember Sanji, Jinera, and all the other bandits we've encountered. I seem to bring trouble everywhere I go."

"You think I don't? Why do you think I live in a cabin in a valley in the mountains?" Emai said.

I hadn't heard her approach, but she set a large bowl of food in my lap, passing one to Anza, who sat up, pulling his head from my shoulder. Tamaj sat up, eating directly from a larger dish Emai had prepared for her as Emai found a spot on the arm of the couch, eating from her own dish. I looked down at the bowl; it had a small round ball of dough and a thick stew-like dish next to it. I leaned in to smell it. Filled with spices and flavor, I knew immediately that this was a dish she must be good at making.

"You take a piece of the dough with your hand, give it a toss, flatten it, and pinch the food with it, and then…" She demonstrated, picking a piece, tossing it softly before catching it, flattening it and folding it around a section of the thick meal before popping it into her mouth.

"Do all Endering bring trouble where they go?" I asked, picking a piece of the dough off the ball she had given me. Emai nodded as I did.

"It comes with having abilities. Every Endering will bring trouble. The good thing is that we get good at dealing with trouble," she said.

"Or you die," Tamaj noted.

"Death? Me? Hah, I've won so far. Who's saying I'm not immortal?" Emai laughed, and I leaned into Anza as he ate quickly.

"Think this is poisoned?" I asked. He swallowed hard before shrugging.

"Probably not."

I nodded, feeling Emai's stare boring back into me.

"Do you have The Two?" she asked.

"The what now?" I asked, mirroring her movements to shove a scoop of food into my mouth. The flavor burst against my tongue, delicious and starchy and warm. It tasted like home. "What is this?"

"That is Fufu, and I'm talking about the Echalon." A piece of food lodged in my throat and I coughed, almost choking on the meal. I moved the egg bag behind me. Anza moved to pat me on the back as I coughed to clear my throat.

"You okay?" Tamaj asked, and I nodded, looking at Emai.

"I, um, I don't know what you're talking about."

Tamaj snorted and Emai smirked.

"Mira, Emai is an Endering of Agrenon. She's safe to be near, and she was there when your dad was given the mission."

"You were?" I asked as Emai got up.

"I was just in the same room when Saha asked him to do it. I'm going to take all that as a yes, though." Emai said as she gestured to me in general before she moved back to the kitchen, returning with a wooden cup of water and offering it to me. I took it and drank until the cup was empty before speaking.

"Yeah, I have them."

"Good. I was worried they may not return in time to hatch here, but that's enough questioning for one night. You all look like you could do with some rest," Emai said, and Tamaj nodded.

"Especially me. You try carrying these two freeloaders over those mountains!" she said, wagging her tail, light in her eyes.

"Freeloaders? I don't see you thanking me for us not dropping to our deaths, and don't get me started on that dragon," I said.

"Dragon? Never mind, I don't want to know, alright? Let's get to sleep," Emai said, shaking her head.

"Are you alright?" Anza asked as we got up, and I nodded.

"Yeah, I think so," I said as we walked behind Emai.

"I'm sleeping on the couch!" Tamaj called, and Emai looked back to nod before moving down the small hallway.

"Hey, Emai?"

"Hmm?"

"Why aren't you at the castle?" I asked as we stopped before the two rooms.

"The Endering of Agrenon can do what they please, though other kingdoms are more..." She hesitated. "Possessive. And I don't really care for your uncle," she said, shrugging as she gestured to a room. I nodded quickly and entered the doorway as she gestured for Anza to take the other room. Once she left, he stepped toward me.

"Are you sure you're okay?" My throat grew tight, and after he spoke, I couldn't stop my eyes from filling up with tears. "I don't know. Seeing another Endering, especially one so powerful, is just..."

"Overwhelming."

I nodded, and he held out his arms. I stepped into his hug and sighed, shaking as the tears fell.

"I feel like maybe she could do this better. Like I'm not good enough."

"Listen to me for a second?" I nodded. "You have kept them alive so far; you have trekked over plateaus riddled with agitated Nazzir, stumbled through mountains, lost your friend, and not only changed my life but saved it once or twice."

"But that doesn't feel good enough," I said, my throat getting tighter and tighter.

"Mira, if you are anything in this world, you're good enough. I swear by the stars, you're good enough."

"How do you know?" I asked, looking up into those golden-brown eyes as he sighed.

"Because you're giving it your best. Sure, it's not perfect; yes, we got a little banged up along the way so far—"

"A lot banged up," I interrupted.

"Fine, a lot banged up, but you got us away from a dragon for stars' sake, and those damn bandits. You're good enough; you're so much more than good enough." I rested my head on his collarbone and tried to get the tears under control as he rubbed my back.

"Safe, Beetle-Brain?" I asked.

"Safer, Stone-Slinger."

"Like, probably the most safer?" I asked.

"There is literally an Endering in the other room with death touch; either we're the safest people on the planet, or we're about to die, and I don't think it's the latter." I couldn't help but laugh.

"We're going to be okay?" I asked.

"We're going to get to that castle. I swear we will."

"We almost died again."

"Yeah, we really have to stop doing that." I smirked, and we laughed together as I looked back up at him.

"We should get some sleep."

He nodded.

"Good night."

"Night," I said, stepping back toward my room.

"Mira?"

"Hmm?"

"We've got this," he said. I nodded and stepped into the room.

The only thing in there was a small bed, which I settled into, bringing the egg bag around to the front of my body, and pulled my legs up to my chest over the bag. Wrapping my arms around it, I held them close and took a breath as the dark of sleep pulled me under.

17

The bed was comfortable, but there was something wrong with sleeping alone. I was still tired when the daylight broke through the small window in the room. I didn't get up until I heard a bang from the living room. I jumped up, pushing the egg bag behind me and grabbing my axe. I headed out the door to my room, ready to fight a death-wielding Endering, only to find Emai holding her foot.

"I am so very sorry."

"No, no, it's my fault, not used to people being here." I lowered my axe as Tamaj looked to me.

"Everything alright?" I asked.

"Someone's on edge," Emai said, putting her foot down as she jerked her head toward me.

"Everything is fine. Emai...kind of forgot I was sleeping on the couch."

"The couch and the floor are very different places," Emai retorted, heading toward the kitchen and getting herself a drink.

"Who broke what?" I turned, seeing Anza standing at the entrance to the hallway, rubbing sleep from his eyes.

"I blew up the house with my thumbs," Tamaj said, Emai almost choking on the drink as she laughed.

"I'd like to see you and all of Agrenon's army try to take my house."

"They wouldn't even think to dare."

Anza approached as the two bantered, gently taking the axe from me.

"Didn't get much sleep?"

"Is it obvious?"

"Not really, but…me either."

"Guess I'm used to sleeping propped up against lady thumbs over there."

"Yeah, me too. I'm gonna put this back in your room."

"You really don't think she's a threat?" I asked, and we looked over to the two. Emai was now trying to grapple with Tamaj, who was laughing at her as she scrambled onto the Barbarza's back.

"I think we're good." I let him take the axe.

"I'm gonna spin you!"

"Not in here! You're not outside!" Emai declared. Tamaj padded toward the door. "There's food in the kitchen," Emai called over to us, looking at me before unlatching the door.

Tamaj burst from the cabin and I padded to the door to watch as she started spinning like a dog chasing its tail, Emai holding on for dear life. Laughter rose. Real laughter. Not Hazzal laughter, fringed with death. Anza stepped to my side, passing me another bowl of aromatic deliciousness, fufu and all. Eating with Anza and watching those two goofballs, my nerves finally settled.

Emai could be trusted, not because I knew her, but because Tamaj did. Emai fell off and Tamaj pivoted, slamming her front legs into the dirt like a dog begging to play. Emai got to her feet and stared her down before running for a tree, Tamaj hot on her heels, her delighted screams of laughter caught on the breeze.

"It's nice to see her happy," Anza said.

"Yeah…"

"What are you thinking about?"

"That maybe we could stay here. I know we can't, but it feels like…" I said, unsure if I should say what this place reminded me of. The cabin rising up in this grove was so similar to the cabin I lived in with Sil. It had a different layout and design and further additions to it, but after convincing yourself The Reaper wasn't coming for you, it felt safe.

"It feels like home."

"Yeah,"

"Maybe one day we could stay here."

"Hey, Mira, get out here!" Tamaj called. *"Help me catch this slippery little Endering!"*

I finished the last of my meal, Anza laughing as I fumbled down the stairs, leaving my bowl on the steps as I headed toward them. Emai stole a coy glance at me as I ran for her. She doubled back, heading for Tamaj, but I hooked the rock out of my pocket, slamming a v-shaped wall between her and Tamaj.

"Get her, Mira!" Anza said as Emai whirled again, but I was at her only exit.

"Hi."

"You're really good at that."

"Yes, yes I am." She looked up, and it hit me what she was about to do a moment too late. Hands up, she grabbed the top of my *V* shape, flipping herself up and on top of it. She stood before I could even make a move.

"You need finesse."

"Finesse?" I asked.

"Yeah, fine—" She got cut off as Tamaj leaped for her, grabbing her arm and yanking her down. I dropped the stone in time to see Tamaj pin her down. Emai, looking up at the Barbarza, smug.

"Got you."

"I let you win."

"You don't want to admit I won," Tamaj said, getting up.

"As I was saying," Emai said. "Finesse." She got up.

"And how could I do that?"

"Hmm, here's an idea," she said, circling me. Anza started down the stairs, and I held my hand up to him, tension in every movement.

"She's trying to teach me something, I think." Emai's soft chuckle danced in my ears for a moment.

"He really thinks he could take me?"

"No, but for her, I would try," Anza said, locking eyes with her before backing down and moving to Tamaj, who sat.

"Hmmm, I like that one," Emai said, returning her attention to me.

"You know anything about this?" Anza asked Tamaj.

"When it comes to Emai, she's either brilliant or about to trip over her own feet; you never know what she's up to."

"Here." I turned to Emai, who had come back, and in her hand was my axe. She set it down, stepping in front of it. "Get your axe."

"How is this supposed to help me?"

"Just do it."

"Alright," I rushed forward, trying to dodge around her to get to my axe. Still, she sidestepped quicker than I expected, her foot catching my own, tumbling me to the ground as she danced away from my grabbing hands to kick my axe farther from me. I glared up at her, pushing my hair out of my face.

"Come on, you can do better than that," Emai taunted.

"How is this helping with my powers?"

"Well, considering you're not using your powers, it's not," she retorted, grating on my nerves.

"I don't want to hit you."

"Hmm, a shame," she said, standing over my axe, watching me expectantly. I planted my hand on the ground, feeling the warmth, and picked up the slab of earth my axe lay on. She sidestepped away as I tried to pull it toward me, simply picking my axe up off the slab I had made as she moved.

"Ugh."

"What? Did you expect this to be that easy?" she asked.

"Not expecting it to be impossible."

"It's not impossible. You're thinking big; think tiny, think finesse."

"You can say finesse a billion times and I still won't get what you're trying to say." Emai smiled.

"Watch."

And I watched, sitting up as she casually bent over. With what must have been an astronomical amount of control, she touched a single blade of grass. I watched as the familiar shock-wave rattled through it, and that single blade disintegrated, the surrounding blades remaining unharmed. "You must learn to be graceful with your powers. Grace and finesse lead to precision, which can save you in difficult situations," she instructed. As she was speaking, I grabbed a stone, weaseling it into the small hole Anza had left for decoration, securing it firmly around the end of the handle. As she stopped talking, I drew the rock to me and my axe skittered across the ground and into my hand. She didn't try to stop it.

"Like that?" I asked.

Her smile widened

"Took you long enough! That's the snowflake on the tip of the iceberg, though. Keep practicing."

"I will," I said, spinning the axe. Tamaj padded forward to put her head on Emai's.

"I missed you, Death-Dancer."

"I missed you too, Sunstorm," Emai said. "Know what I wanna do?"

"Hmm?"

"I wanna try him," she said, pointing to Anza.

"Excuse me?" Anza said as Tamaj lifted her head from Emai's, a defiant understanding in her eyes.

"Here we go."

"Are you worthy of accompanying an Endering?" Emai asked, starting to move closer to him. He crossed his arms and something about her made him move.

"Hey," I said, tightening my grip on my axe.

"It's fine," Anza said, dropping his crossed arms as they started to circle each other. "She's testing me, but there's no malice there."

"An Empathic Maraung," Emai said, eyes flicking to Tamaj, who simply padded to my side as Emai's eyes slipped back.

"Calm your nerves."

"It almost sounds like she's—"

"She's messing with him, and it looks like he's well aware." Tamaj wasn't wrong. They circled each other, that crooked smirk on Anza's face.

"Why?" I asked

"Because it's Emai, and she can."

I kept a firm grip on my axe when Emai lunged, moving to throw a punch right in Anza's face. Still, with a smooth motion, Anza palmed her forearm, moving her arm out of the way as he moved behind her, twisting her back to him and pinning her at her arms against him.

"Oh, quick," Emai said as Anza released her.

"And he has saved me more times than I can count," I said as they stepped apart.

"Yeah?" Emai asked. "From?"

"Yeah," I looked at those eyes, deep gray, unsettling; she wanted to know he was good enough. "Nazzir, bandits, being clumsy as fuck on those mountains, a dragon, there was even a point where I couldn't use my powers, we had been split up, I had been taken, and he came for me, even when he didn't have to."

"What do you mean you couldn't use your powers?" Emai said, the playfulness dropping out of her face. Her eyes were suddenly fringed with pain, a pain I couldn't place. I carefully moved my shirt away from my shoulder to show her the injection mark. Healing, but there. "No, no!" I watched as her face twisted, almost crumbling, and felt her hand find my shoulder as Tamaj got up.

"It's alright, it's alright," Tamaj said as I stepped back.

"You have experience with this, too…"

Emai nodded, her thumb running over the wound. A slight shock ran over it, healing it, but tears had sprung to her eyes.

"I'm okay; Anza got me out."

She nodded, quickly wiping away her brimming tears before looking at Anza.

"You're worthy."

"I'd hope so," Anza said as she nodded.

"Come, today we feast and rest," Emai said, leading us collectively toward the cabin.

"Did Emai seem a little…intense there?" Anza asked.

"Yeah, a little," I said.

"She cares deeply for people quickly," Tamaj said.

"Hmm…" Anza watched Emai, his brow furrowed, as if he was trying to figure something out. I tried to let it go as the day stretched on.

Emai fed us lunch and dinner and I lounged around the living room with Anza and Tamaj the rest of the day. Anza found a book of stories, handwritten in Maraung, and settled in, reading them to me, stories of bravery and adventure from the great country of Ghana back on Earth. Emai smiled in the kitchen as she listened to him, occasionally correcting his pronunciation of different names and places. The sunlight skittered across the floor as the day rose and fell. Night was dancing at the edge of the windows when I started to doze off.

Emai came to my side, gently removing something from around her neck and placing it over mine before she moved to lift me up.

"Oh, sorry, I can—"

"Oh no, you're alright," she said, backing off. "Thought you were asleep."

"I was almost there. I'm gonna get to bed," I said, looking to Tamaj, who had fallen asleep to Anza's storytelling. I nudged Anza, and he groaned but sat up. Together, we haphazardly made our way back to our respective rooms. I closed the door, curling up in the bed and pulling the egg bag close to me. My head had barely touched the pillow before I slipped into sleep.

"So, she left?" I opened my eyes to Anza's voice and sat up, feeling the egg bag shift as I moved.

"Who left?" I asked, and he poked his head in the doorway.

"Emai. She left a note and a bag for each of us at the door," he explained as I pulled myself up out of bed, fastening the egg bag tighter to me and patting them to make sure they were there before following him down the hallway to the living-room where, sure enough, there were three bags packed. I reached up, almost instinctively, to the new weight around my neck. Light, but it hadn't been there before. I remembered her placing something over my head and around my neck the night before just before we went to sleep.

A single pendant of stone hung from a thick piece of cordage. The stone had a strange symbol carved into it. I left it where it hung around my neck, looking up as Anza started going through a pack.

"Does Emai disappear a lot?" I asked, turning to look to Tamaj.

"*Unfortunately.*"

"I didn't even get to ask her if she wanted to come," I said.

"*I have a feeling there's a reason she left.*"

"Anything in the note she left?"

"No, it was simple," Anza said. "I've got something to tend to, supplies by the door, Em."

"Shit," I said.

"At least she left us supplies," Anza said, pulling out each item one by one. Rope, a map, dried meals wrapped in thick papers, and a change of clothes. I went to the bag with my name on it, going through it as the smell of what must have been breakfast made my stomach growl. I had everything Anza had, at the bottom of the pack though, a few pretty and light stones sat glittering in the dim light along with a writing pad and charcoal. I picked up the rocks, one by one, feeling the different rumblings each held.

"I'm gonna have to name my rocks," I said, hearing Anza and Tamaj both chuckle as I set them down, picking up the notepad. I flipped it open, expecting it to be blank, but it wasn't. Each page had a carefully crafted symbol on it. "Hey, what's this?" I asked, holding one up.

"No clue," Anza said.

"That's a sigil," Tamaj said. *"Magic. I don't know what they do, though. Emai is very good at crafting sigils. Why don't we eat, get changed, and get ready to go? If we leave soon, we can reach an Echalon city by nightfall."*

"Echalon city? That sounds so fucking cool."

"Then hurry!" I quickly packed my stuff back up and went to dress with the fresh clothes. Dark pants and a shirt with an equally dark zip up jacket. I carefully ran my fingers over the inside of the neck of the jacket. The thin white embroidered *E* glaring back at me before I pulled it on, slipping back out to the others. Anza did a double take, Tamaj moving to nudge his mouth closed as it opened.

"What?"

"Nothing." He looked away a little too quickly, and I shook my head and headed for breakfast, giving his shoulder a light punch as I walked by. He had changed his own clothes as well, donning a dappled gray and black button shirt. His buttons were bone and carefully carved, spilling down the far side of his shirt and equally dark pants, as well as a similar jacket to mine.

"You don't look half bad yourself," I said.

He pursed his lips before following me toward the kitchen. We ate quickly before we headed for the door. I checked again to make sure I had everything—Sil's knife, Arlo's axe, the egg bag, my pack—before I stepped off of the porch, looking back at the now-closed-up cabin. For a moment, I longed to stay. To stay in the warm and cozy cabin, to eat delicious food and spar with The Reaper. But she was gone, and the castle called me.

I took in the cabin with that last long look and turned my back to it, knowing in my bones that I would be back one day.

18

"Holy shit," I said as we walked up to the broken and burned doors of the small city surrounded by young trees. The remnants of fenced-in fields surrounded it, but up close, the doors alone were striking. Towering stone walls stood beside them, one door hanging on a single hinge, the other crumpled and half burned.

"*It was a bad day,*" Tamaj said.

"You say that like you were here," Anza said as we slipped past the remnants of the doors.

"*I was,*" Tamaj said. "*This is—was—the city of Teramor.*"

"You lived here." It wasn't a question, but Tamaj nodded to me, anyway.

"*Once upon a time, a long time ago, I grew up here; it's where they're from,*" Tamaj said, nodding to the egg bag. The kids were home. We had gotten them home. Now we had to get them safe. Safer.

I turned my attention to the city itself. There was ample space left open for activities; some of it, a rounded area, clearly a gathering area, was set with cobblestones. Grass had overgrown the rest of the open space before eventually giving way to buildings. Each was similar, except for a larger building off to the left.

There were houses to the right of it, but Tamaj led us to the large building.

"What building is that?" I asked.

"At the front, it's a library; the side and back serve as a school," she said, her voice soft in my mind. Anza took my hand and shook his head as I was about to ask her if we should go in. I noticed her drooping tail and tentative gait before nodding to Anza. Who knew how long it had been since she had set foot in this city. How much pain being here and remembering must bring.

I tried to imagine the lanterns on the white stone buildings alive with light. The window shutters intact, and children playing in the street. Instead, plant life had overgrown everything it could, old burn marks bolting up and down different buildings, and debris from a variety of weapons littered the streets.

It didn't sink in until I saw the fragmented body, dazzling in the remaining sunlight. They were partially buried, as if the ground was trying to take them back, and the state of the remains made it impossible to tell their gender or identity. Only a shoulder and their head were visible, the dirt and grass growing out of their chest as Tamaj passed without looking at them, their cold eyes sunken in, unfocused.

I squeezed Anza's hand, and we kept going, picking our way past dozens more bodies scattered throughout the streets. We were at the library faster than I thought we would be, the sun threatening us with darkness as we slipped up the elegant stairs and past the statues of towering books that stood as pillars at the front then through the broken doorway of the library. Running my hands over the stone as we walked in, a tingling radiated down my fingertips, the energy warm. That's when Tamaj stopped.

"Hey, are you okay?" I asked.

"Something's wrong," she said as I looked at the library. The stacks were tall, the ceiling-high shelves had several ladders

haphazardly leaned against them, books lining the vast majority of the dark expanse, tucked into some kind of order.

"Why do you think something's wrong?" I asked as we started forward again. Keeping close to Tamaj, my hand still in Anza's.

"They ransacked the library when they came, and it's—"

"Neat, too neat; someone's been here," Anza said.

"Think they're still here?" I asked.

"Maybe," Tamaj said as the last fragments of sunlight that dashed through the windows in the elegant and expansive library vanished.

"We're planning on staying the night here?" Anza asked.

"It was traditionally the safest place in the city; heavy walls, thoroughly fortified."

"It might not be the safest place now," I said, turning to look at the doorway we had walked through, only to find that it was gone. Nothing but a vertical stone wall in its place. I reached for the rock in my pocket.

"You're not seeing what I'm seeing, right?" Anza said, dropping my hand to draw his sword. I drew my axe.

"What the fuck is going on in here?" No sooner had I asked than a spattering of light flashed against the wall, bounding quickly along the shelves, soft and dappled, like it was filtered through shattered glass. It was simultaneously everywhere and nowhere all at once, like a bouncing prism. I pulled out the stone from my pocket. "Tamaj..."

"I'm thinking."

"Think faster," I said before the laughter started. Echoing. Haunting. My heart slammed, the noise almost sounded like a child's laughter, but it sounded less like a Hazzal and more like a child laughing in a large room.

"It may be the ghosts of the past," Anza said quietly. "Why would the door vanish if it wasn't?"

"I don't know," I said.

"There has to be a logical explanation," Tamaj said. I turned to

her, hoping she had something positive to say, only to see, poised on the top of a bookshelf a few rows down, a gray silhouette. The light caught in her body reflected where her tiny white dress didn't cover her. Her wild hair and large eyes made her look otherworldly, like a moonbeam incarnate.

"Guys..." At the single word, she bolted, Anza and Tamaj looking to where she had stood with enough time to catch the movement.

"I told you it was a ghost."

"I fucking hate ghosts," I said, feeling Anza's back meet mine. He would cover me, and I would cover him. Tamaj stood with us at her tail, able to pivot quickly from one side to another if she needed to.

"Something isn't right."

"No shit," I said. "We need to get out of the library and out of the city."

"It's too dark to go out there, the Hazzal will find us before we get to the next town." Anza was right. We were stuck here. Facing this ghost for the night.

I could hear it moving as we breathed, back to back, skittering closer instead of farther away, testing our boundaries. Light spiraled everywhere until I heard it at my right-hand side. I lashed out, feeling my hand connect with a pillar. No, not a pillar, paper on a pillar. I caught the tiny flash of a smile in the darkness as a symbol flashed, and instantly, there was noise. Screaming, bells, and crashing noises came from every inch of the room as Anza and I held our ears, dropping my axe. It didn't get any quieter. Tamaj was still looking about, unfazed by the noise. I reached for Sil's knife, knowing it was easier to wield in close quarters, only to find it was gone. I turned to Anza, seeing his pack was open too when it had been closed moments ago.

"It's not a ghost. Ghosts don't need knives!"

"What is it?" Anza cried.

"Dead as far as I care," I said, hearing it scrambling. I threw my stone out, carving it into a point, trying to pin it to the wall. I missed before hearing the being to my right, I lashed out, my hand meeting the paper before a bright and blinding light flashed in my eyes.

"Mira, you have to stop going for it," Anza said.

"It's preparing sigils, and you're unintentionally activating them," Tamaj said. I could hear the tension in her voice, almost as if I could hear her brain working to figure out what this was.

"How the hell am I supposed to hit it?"

"You aren't," Tamaj said.

"What?"

"I think I know what it is."

"Well, it would be nice if you could tell us?"

"Do you trust me?"

"Of course we do," Anza said.

"Mira?"

"Yes."

"Take out an egg."

"What?" I asked, seeing the creature caught in the moonlight for a moment. It was moving toward us, fast, Sil's knife drawn and fire in its eyes.

"Do it!" I quickly unzipped the bag and pulled out the amber egg as fast as possible, holding it up. Brilliant orange-brown flashes of color spattered the walls as the moon caught its image. I could see the tiny creature had stopped inches from me. Knife to my throat. Eyes on the egg. Realization hit me like a freight train as it slowly tore its eyes from the egg back to me.

"She's an Echalon…"

"Echalon can't do magic," Anza said.

"Endering can." The small girl's voice was so quiet that if the dust had sentience, it could have snatched it from her.

"Mira, do not move."

"Not planning on it."

"Wise girl," the Echalon said before looking at the egg. "Is this the only one?"

"No, there's another in the pack." She moved slowly,

reaching to the pack and gently opening it enough to see the other egg before meeting my eyes again.

"Why do you have them?" The knife was still at my throat. Could I reach the stone before she killed me? I heard Anza shift and the Echalon girl shifted closer, the knife touching my throat. "Try it, and she dies."

"I have them because I'm finishing a mission. To bring them to the castle, to help save the species," I said. "But I can't do that if you kill me." Her eyes, a deep gray like the rest of her, stared into my own for a handful of seconds, and in that time, I forgot how to breathe.

She slowly lowered the knife and backed up to a nearby bookshelf, hiding halfway behind it. The noise and light spells she had made were fading now, as if they had only been temporary. I didn't take my eyes off her as Anza got to me.

"You alright?"

"Yeah, the door?" I heard him turn to check for it.

"It's there now."

"You're pretty well versed in magic, aren't you?" I asked the girl.

"Why?"

"What?"

"Why are you asking me that question?"

"Why aren't you answering it?" If she could play mind games, so could I.

"*Mira drop it,*" Tamaj said.

"You better be careful with names," the little Echalon said. "The wrong creature hears your name, your whole life is theirs."

"I'm not worried," I said.

"Then you're an easier target than you look."

"Are you going to kill us or let us stay the night?"

"Shelter is what you seek? We can...arrange for a single night."

"No more invisible doors or lights or noises?" I asked, and

she shook her little head before turning and vanishing into the darkness. I put the egg away, trying to calm myself down.

"Tamaj? How could an Echalon live out here?"

"I don't know. She wouldn't have been able to unless she had help, especially in the early months."

"Wait, did you say months?"

"Echalon grow very fast. That one can't be more than a few months old."

"A few months old, and she's laying traps?"

"Not just any traps, a variety of traps," Tamaj said as a snapping rang out.

"Why would she need a variety of traps?"

"To be prepared," Tamaj said. *"You never know who's coming for you when your heart is the most precious thing on the planet."*

"Still makes me fucking sick every time I hear that," I said.

"At least The Two aren't alone," Anza said, a hand on my shoulder.

"Yeah, but I doubt she'd want to leave, and if she did, I doubt that she'd trust us enough to actually get her to the castle."

"Right," Anza said. "Tamaj?" I hadn't noticed her look out into the rows of library books, but as I looked in the same direction, I saw the girl tucked into the darkness, listening as she played with Sil's knife.

"We should probably not be talking about all this," I said, turning to Anza, who peered into the darkness but nodded upon seeing the small girl.

Carefully, we moved toward a corner of the library, the light moving with us; she was watching us. Tamaj tucked into the corner, Anza and I leaning against her, weapons still drawn. The girl was fast, intelligent, and steady. She could, at any moment, decide we weren't worth the effort and lash out at us.

"Get some sleep. I'll take the first watch," I said to Anza.

"You just had a knife to your throat. You should rest."

"I wouldn't be able to. Too much adrenaline. Sleep. We'll switch when I calm down."

He pursed his lips but sighed and nodded.

"Don't forget to wake me," he said.

"I won't."

Tamaj was still looking out into the library. I said nothing to her as Anza slowly fell asleep against her. Eventually, Tamaj fell asleep as well. It was only an hour into my watch when I saw a motion creeping slowly toward us. The Echalon slipped into the light of one of the windows.

"Hi," I said, trying to keep quiet. She didn't talk, just slid a paper and Sil's knife to me. I carefully took it, looking at the paper. It was Anza's map. "Is this what you took from him?"

"No, I magically materialized one out of thin air." Sarcasm dripped from her, but I thought it best not to return it.

"Right."

"You were talking about a castle, about getting them safe," she said, nodding to the egg bag.

"Yeah, we were. What's it to you?"

"This place is…getting more and more dangerous. King Olaf isn't doing all he can to keep bandits out of Agrenon, meaning more show up here looking to get lucky."

"Meaning you have to make more traps and hide more often."

"It's not new, but it is getting harder daily."

"So, what are you going to do about it?"

"Follow you to the castle, whether you like it or not."

"Really now?"

"Yes."

"What if I told you that we wouldn't hate having you with us?" She inched closer, looking me over as if assessing my body language before inching closer again. She was still on edge, and I couldn't blame her. All she had known was scrambling to survive. Even though she had a knife to my throat not long before, I knew this kid didn't deserve this.

"Which castle are you going to?"

"Agrenon's."

"Not Korrewen's?"

"No, not Korrewen's."

"Because I know the way to Korrewen. I've seen it on maps. It's very different from the path to Agrenon's castle; you couldn't trick me."

"I'm not planning on tricking you," I said. "And even if I was, I don't think it'd work."

She looked me over for a few seconds before she quietly crawled toward me. I didn't move, flinch, or try to get away as she pulled herself up into my lap, slowly leaning her head against my shoulder. Eyes ever moving to ensure every movement was alright. As she settled in, I slowly moved my hands to wrap underneath her bottom, supporting her against me like one might support a sleepy child.

"What's your name?"

"Names are dangerous." Her voice was still and soft against my cheek. As if a single word spoken wrong could crush it.

"I don't even know sigil magic, hun. I can't control you with your name."

"Whisper," she said. It was fitting.

"It's nice to meet you, Whisper."

"Try to hurt me in my sleep and I'll gut you."

"I wouldn't have it any other way."

19

A single tap on my shoulder woke me. I looked up, meeting Anza's eyes as he looked between me and the little Echalon still tucked against my shoulder.

"How?" he asked, his voice barely a breath in the early morning light.

"I'm just awesome."

"She just came right up to you?"

"Kind of. She threatened to kill me if I hurt her before she passed out."

"That seems pretty standard for her," Tamaj's voice was soft in my mind as she turned, looking at us. *"I wonder how hard life is, knowing anyone you meet might want to kill you."*

"It sucks," Whisper said, nuzzling closer to me.

"Will you be accompanying us, little one?"

"I'm not little. I've gotta get my stuff first," Whisper said, yawning and burying her head in my shoulder.

"This is Tamaj and Anza and—"

"Wait, Tamaj? Like, the third house down on the right, Tamaj?" Whisper asked, sitting up and turning to look at the Barbarza. Tamaj took a steady breath but nodded.

"That's me."

"You're really old now."

Tamaj closed her eyes for a moment, taking another breath before she opened them again.

"That I am."

"My name's Whisper."

"It suits you," Anza said as I reached to move Whisper's hair out of her face. She let me before she stumbled to her feet, the sunlight dazzling across her skin, throwing spirals of light across the library.

"I'm gonna go get my stuff," she said before walking off, rubbing the sleep out of her eyes.

"I don't know what you said to her, but I am delighted she's coming," Tamaj said.

"Yeah, she's gonna need everything we can give to her."

"Everything," Tamaj said, looking after her. For a moment, I almost swore I could see the tears at the edge of her eyes before she blinked, and they were gone. We got up, preparing our things to go. I could see the remnants of the sigils at the door and pillars from the night before. I heard the soft tap-tapping of stone on stone as Whisper found her way back to us, a small pack on one shoulder, now covered in a dark cloak and ratty little shoes to cover her feet.

"We're gonna have to do something about that," Anza said, and I nodded.

"How close is the nearest town?"

"A ways off," Tamaj said as Whisper approached me, reaching for my hand. I took hers, feeling the warmth of her little fingers wrap around mine.

We led the way out of the city. Tamaj hung back as we passed the fragmented bodies of Echalon embedded in the ground. Still, Whisper didn't seem disturbed by them. I looked back at Tamaj, who trailed even behind Anza, and upon meeting his gaze, he gave me a worried look. It wasn't until we were out of the city that Tamaj matched our stride again. Light filtered through the trees and Whisper slowly held out her other hand, grabbing at a low-hanging tuft of Tamaj's mane. We walked quietly before her hand slipped from mine. She nearly stumbled, trying to keep up with Tamaj.

"Would you like a ride, little one?"

"Could I?"

"You could," Tamaj said.

Anza and I stopped, Tamaj slowing to a stop as Whisper reached her little hands up higher. Tamaj lowered her body, using a paw to help Whisper onto her back. Tamaj trotted forward, her gait changing as if leaving sadness behind her as Whisper's laughter rose. It had been a long time since a child's laughter meant nothing else. I took a breath as Tamaj spun and Whisper's shrieks of delight eased the tension in the air as Anza stepped to my side.

"You know, there will be three of them, right?"

"Shit, you're not wrong."

"Think we're ready?"

"No," I laughed. "But I can't wait to meet them." I held the egg bag closer.

"Stop, stop!" Whisper asked Tamaj, stepping to a dizzy stop.

"You guys okay?" It was a redundant question. Their laughter made it clear there was no danger.

"Yeah, I have a question for you, Mira."

"Shoot."

"Your powers are moving the rocks, right?"

"Yeah."

"Do you gotta touch the rocks to make them move?"

"This is more than one question, but yes," I said.

"Why, why do you not make the rocks like…bracelets or something?" she asked, and suddenly, the burning embarrassment left me completely and utterly convinced I was too short sighted for this trip. Heat rushed to my face as the embarrassment rose. I wouldn't have to worry about grabbing at a fucking rock if it was already touching me.

"Because I didn't think of it," I said, fishing out the stone we had gotten before the mountains, the warmth flowing through me as my fingers graced its steady, rumbling body. I moved it carefully, flattening it out, shaping it around my wrist and willing it to be solid. In a moment, I had a well-fitting bracelet resting around my hand, warmth still pouring through me.

"Hey, Tamaj?" I asked.

"Yeah?"

"Do Echalon always make you feel dense? Like damn." They broke out in laughter, Anza leaning over to pat my back.

"Yes," her voice said, a giggle still dancing within it as it made its way to my mind. I shook my head, getting my bag out and digging for the interesting rocks Emai had left us, moving past the sigil pack.

"Oooh, what's that?" Whisper said, as she looked back at us.

"Oh, sigils, but I don't know what they do or how to activate them," I said, passing the pad to her. "Maybe you can make them out?"

"Oh yes, yes," she said happily, taking the notepad.

"Why do you know about magic again?" Anza asked.

"You don't ask an Echalon why they know things, Anza," Tamaj said as Whisper held back a giggle.

"Cause I can."

"Echalon hyper-focus on a variety of different things. Sometimes — well, most times — they learn much faster than any of us could dream of, and there were several books on magic in that library back there," Tamaj explained.

"Which is the same as 'cause I can'," Whisper said, looking over the different sigils.

"How did you get them to activate again last night?"

"Oh, I didn't. You did. Touch activates them, but you gotta touch the ink, and usually, you have to have intention in mind. Not always, though. Once I figure out what these are designed for, I can help you use them. They look pretty advanced, though."

"Awesome. I'm gonna smack Sil for not teaching me about them."

"Sil…wasn't super magic driven," Tamaj said.

"Honestly, the longer I'm here, the more Sil seems super Sil driven," I said.

"Eh, she'd fight for those she loves, but she's stubborn in her beliefs."

"You can say that again," I said before turning my attention to the rocks I had dug out of the bag. There were three, and, carefully, I crafted them like the stone before them, wrapping them around my wrists to solidify them there. Two on each wrist. The warmth within me hummed, steadying into a vibrant feeling of rightness. Anza shuddered beside me as I breathed out, feeling confident in my power for the first time.

"You good?"

"Yeah, I can still feel your feelings. That power, the sureness-it's…" He trailed off, looking for a word. "Amazing?"

"It certainly is," I said. "Don't take this the wrong way, but you can't turn that off, can you?"

"Eh, not really. You can differentiate between what is and isn't yours, and everyone has a different range, and you can choose to ignore some, but you still know, it's hard to explain," he said.

"That must suck sometimes."

"Yeah…but there are times, like right now, that I wouldn't give it up for the world." I tried to ignore the heat on my face as he smiled. "Come on, they're getting too far ahead of us," he said, leading me after Tamaj and Whisper. Tamaj bounced about with Whisper protesting playfully on her back. I picked up the speed of walking after him, getting to Tamaj's right side a moment after he got to her left, Whisper sitting atop Tamaj between us. I buried my fingers in Tamaj's mane, her thin frame beneath my fingertips.

"What's this?" Before I could stop Whisper, she had the necklace Emai gave me in her hand. Tamaj glanced back at me, her eyes narrowing on me before she looked back to the path ahead of us, daring me to say something negative to Whisper about being grabby.

"Not sure. Someone left it for me."

"The sigil almost looks like a strength sigil, but it's...wrong, different," she said, dropping the necklace. I watched as she pulled her bag to the front of her body.

"What do you think it means?"

"Not sure, but I'm gonna find out," Whisper said, pulling out a book and a piece of charcoal. I tried not to pay attention to what she was doing, hoping she could figure it out.

Turning my attention to the surrounding forest, I took in the way the light filtered through the towering trees, fallen logs alive with mushrooms and moss, birdsong in the air, and the sound of other creatures in the forest. It was almost comforting. A call of a bird of prey sounded in the world's chatter. At that moment, the world didn't seem so bad. Even the crisp air wasn't too cold or warm. For a moment, a singular moment, I tried to savor where we were, savor the little giggles from Whisper as Tamaj bounced happily down the trail. Savor the small talk that came up as Anza asked Whisper questions about magic.

The day was slow, simple, and sweet; no one threatened our existence. It wasn't the world that was broken. No, the world was happy to keep turning around. It was the people who were having a hard time. The people of Agrenon were broken. Facing a plague, a bandit invasion, and a king who wasn't being as effective as the queen who had stood before him, though, as Tamaj had said, he was likely spread too thin.

How quickly had Korrewen's forces taken advantage of my untrained uncle? How quickly did he get thrown into the hot water of this world's stage? How thin were he and his resources spread? Could I help fix this? Agrenon was on the brink of collapse; even I could see that. Between the plague, the unsure attitude toward him as king, and the bandits from Korrewen, we would have to work together to make this work. If we even got to the castle, could I fix this? I wasn't sure, but one thing was inevitable as we walked through the serene forest. Trying was the only option. Not trying to solve all these too-big issues was the same as lying down to die.

"What was that?" Whisper asked, tilting her head to look into the forest.

"What was what?" I said, Anza letting Tamaj get a few steps ahead to see around her with a better view into the forest. When I saw movement, a person moving between the thicker trees, eyes locked on us.

"Bandits," Whisper said, keeping her voice low.

"*Up,*" Tamaj said.

"If we all get on your back, you won't be able to go far," Anza said as I took off the egg bag, handing it up to Whisper.

"Hang on to these for me?"

"You're not gonna end up like my mom, right?"

I wanted to ask her who that was, but it wasn't the time.

"We're gonna be fine," I said.

"*At least get ready to jump on, should we need to,*" Tamaj said. I shook my wrists, verifying the bracelets were still there. There was movement to our left, louder. Tamaj didn't stop, but she started picking up the pace. Anza and I moved to keep up, hearing more movement in the forest all around us. There had to be a dozen people or more, quick, blurry flashes of brown darting between the trees.

"They have Barbarza!" I said. Anza and I grabbed Tamaj's mane, shoving our legs in tandem into the ground and vaulting ourselves up onto her back righting ourselves and clinging to each other as Tamaj ran, Anza sitting behind Whisper, and me behind him.

I turned, seeing a Barbarza already on our heels, jaws open, ready to snap shut on Tamaj's leg. I slammed a short wall up, tripping them head over tail. They had been so close that they almost hit us as they fell.

"Powered!" A Maraung said from the back of a Barbarza, the

group scattering, many picking up the pace to get ahead of Tamaj.

"Toadstools!" Whisper said.

"Mira, we need to break left!" Tamaj said. I didn't question it. Slamming a wall up to the left of us, I stopped the few mounted bandits in their tracks, giving Tamaj space. She broke left.

"No, no, that's a—" Anza stopped mid-sentence as Tamaj bolted over a line of toadstools. "Fae ring," he finished as we kept going, the bandits halting at the toadstool line. A line which they didn't seem to think they should cross.

"We have an Endering. So long as we don't say each other's names, we should be able to get through this, in theory," Whisper said.

"Theory and actuality are very different things, Whi—" Whisper slapped her hand against Anza's mouth.

"No names," Tamaj slowed, panting hard, her legs trembling. Anza and I quickly dismounted.

"You good?" I asked Tamaj, and she nodded.

"We need to be careful," she said simply, looking around. I couldn't hear the birdsong. There were no more noises from the forest and a thick, eerie fog had begun settling between the trees; even the light was duller.

"Careful? There are things out there that can—"

"Shut up," Tamaj said, growling lowly as she glared at Anza. More movement in the forest.

"Everyone chill out. What is out there?"

"Names are dangerous," Whisper said sternly. "There is nothing out there."

"But—" Anza was immediately cut off.

"There is nothing out there," Tamaj said. I took Anza's hand and met his eyes, taking a slow, deep breath. He held my hand tightly, breathing with me.

"I've got you, I've got you."

"She lived in the city of Teramor for years," Whisper said, gesturing to Tamaj.

"Which means I know what it takes to get through this," Tamaj said, finally recovering from the long sprint before padding forward. *"Walk quickly, don't run, stay close,"* she said firmly.

"Okay," Anza said.

"Alright, let's go," I said, walking with him, hand in hand, as we followed Tamaj. She walked briskly, and we kept close. Anza kept glancing around before turning back to look forward, eyes wide.

"Breathe," I said, squeezing his hand tighter.

"There were stories of toadstools like a line in the sand, of certain life and death. Stories of what lay beyond."

A scream ripped through the fog. Terror rose inside me as Anza and I quickly tried to get to Tamaj's side. As I reached to rest my hand on the top of her back leg, my legs were torn out from under me. I hit the ground, hard, trying to lash stones out at whatever was pulling me, driving itself into my leg. Looking back at it, I could see nothing. None of my stones hit. They all fumbled into the forest. Anza rushed after me, scrambling for my hand.

"Mira!" darkness descended.

20

The darkness didn't last for long before I was suddenly in a dark, sandy hole. A tight, claustrophobic, dark, sandy hole with the sounds of a Nazzir shrieking above me. Reaching up, the image of Anza reaching for me held firmly in my mind, I reached for him as far as I could, trying to pull myself up, but I wasn't moving. I wanted to reach for him, for him to save me like he had a dozen times before. The shifting sand moved, threatening to crash in on me.

"Wait!" In a heartbeat, the scene changed. My heart was pounding as a Barbarza bandit bore down on me. I twisted behind a large tree and it changed again, my hands buried wrist deep into Arlo's stomach, trying to stop the bleeding. Nothing made sense. Time was minced. My stomach twisted and lurched as I moved. Suddenly the feeling of rushing before I hit the ground, feeling broken. I recognized the memory of falling before meeting Emai. The scenery changed again, and I was on my hands and knees, on the forest floor, fog rolling around as a single sound of footsteps circled me. I tried to move, but I couldn't.

"Mira..." The voice sounded like a hundred whispers at

once. "An Endering. Interesting how someone so readily prepared could be so…underwhelming."

"Fuck you." I had a voice. I could speak.

"Hmm, maybe later. There's still quite a lot of your mind to play with, thanks to your friend." I tried to look up at it but couldn't. It didn't want to be seen. I tried to move, pushing forward. Every muscle screamed, but I crawled an inch forward. "Interesting. You shouldn't be able to move."

"Why not?"

"I have your name." I was no longer there, but the voice stayed. "We'll take care of that."

Agony. Raw, unbridled agony as I was thrown into the memory of the bandit camp on the mountain where we had met Tamaj. The dragon was the only thing there. I tried to move as it turned its attention to me, but I was tied to the post again. Fire. Every inch of me was on fire. The flames licked at every inch of me, tearing across my flesh. The scream tore out of me before I was suddenly on the forest floor again. The footsteps sounded around me. I tried to reach for the warmth within me, but it was cold. I had no power here. Slowly, a touch drew itself across my shoulders.

"What do you want?"

"Hmmm, want? Interesting inquiry. Desire doesn't matter when you're eternal. Still, the expansion of being is essential… what better way than to puppeteer an Endering?"

"You can't make me your puppet."

"Oh, little one, it seems you've misunderstood what you're capable of. Let me assure you, beating me is not within your skill set."

"You're being rude." The voice wasn't mine but rang with an ethereal familiarity. Resounding, familiar, warm, accusatory. The being behind me, touching my shoulder, stopped. In a rush, I could suddenly see the edge of the toadstools. Tamaj had Anza pinned on the other side. He desperately tried to draw his sword on her as she struggled to keep him pinned to the ground. He was not above harming her to get into the toadstool ring he had not wanted to enter only moments ago. Whisper must have given her the egg bag. It swung from her neck and Whisper stood a few feet within the toadstool circle.

"My apologies, little one. How am I being rude?"

"You have guests and don't even care to introduce yourself?"

"I will give you my name if you give me yours."

"N- no." With a breath of wind, I found my voice gone. I could do nothing but watch as Whisper smiled.

"That's not how my culture works. See, if you weren't rude, you would know that, and considering we are in your home, you should know the cultural significance of those you invite in."

"But I did not invite you in, little Echalon."

"Didn't you? You're an eternal fae, from the old times, even you know an open door is an invitation to peek your head in, and if you don't, you're clearly not doing enough research on the past, present, and future." Silence. "You have been rude to me and my friends."

"My apologies, young Echalon. How could I ever make it up to you?"

"Give me my friend back."

"Your friend?"

"Yes, Mira."

"I'm sorry, young one. I can't do that. Her name was given; she's mine." I do not know how I did it, but I found my voice.

"Mira's not my name."

"What?" That thousand-voice chorus was suddenly on the brink of irritation.

"It's not my full first na—" I was suddenly home, at the cabin, Sil before me.

"Go on, put your name on the paper," she said. I wanted to. It was Sil; she had taught me so much, even when I hadn't paid attention. She was my parental figure; she had raised me. She had helped me when my hair got tangled and made my favorite meal on my birthday. She had taught me how to live out here in this world, and for all her shortcomings, I still wanted, needed, to make her proud. I started to write my name, but after I got the A down, the dread crept in. "Go on."

"Don't."

"Do it."

"I'm right here, just reach out!" I looked up to where Sil had been a moment before and found Whisper, hand outstretched toward me. I tried to reach for her, tried to move, and at first, I found I couldn't. I pushed, my muscles aching, pain ripping down every nerve. Every inch of my body was in pain again suddenly.

"Your name," I pushed hard. "Your name!" I pushed harder, my hand now an inch from Whisper's. *"Your name!"* My hand touched hers, and in an instant, we were no longer in the cabin. Now we were both in a fog-filled clearing, no longer near the border of the toadstools, my hand in Whisper's.

"Mira?" she asked as I met her eyes. I tried to move. My body didn't scream. I slowly got to my feet. "Run."

"But T said not to."

"Run!" I didn't ask again. We took off together, hand in hand. Raw anger thundered around us as the fog turned dark, cascading down and around us like a never-ending blanket.

"Where are the others?"

"Doesn't matter. It's a circle, if we run straight, we'll get to the exit!" she said, keeping her hand locked in mine as the smoke took different forms. A disemboweled Arlo snapping at us, I lashed out, my fist connecting with nothing, the fog transforming from Arlo's form back to fog again. Jinera and Sanji leaped from behind a tree, a Nazzir sweeping toward us. Whisper didn't jump, plowing through the visions of the three like they weren't there.

"You can't see this?"

"What we see is going to be different. Nothing is real. Assume I'm the only thing that's real!" she said. Could she be real? Was she the real Whisper? Or was this some other sick trick? I did not know, but I clung to her hand like she was the only tether in the world.

The fog was closing in, collapsing around us, transforming into islands from the sky fields, bandits in mid-attack. Still, I pressed past them, through them, clinging to her hand as we ran together. I barely saw the sight of toadstools as we crossed them. As quickly as the darkness had descended, like walking through a dirty sliding glass door, it was over. Whisper slowed to a stop, quickly pulling me down to my knees.

"We're okay, we're okay, you're okay. I've got you," she said, sounding far away, like she was yelling down a cavern. It hurt to breathe, hurt to move, fire still tingled on my skin, my hands were still slick with blood and sand, smoke still burned my eyes, the sins of my past crashing in on me from every angle.

"Anza! Tamaj!"

The ground radiated the movement of the others as they moved toward us, but trying to will my body to move was hard. I had killed so many. Arlo. Arlo's death was my fault, Rania's too. Did Sanji and Jinera die? What about the bandits? I knew that most of them were trying to survive and that seeing me made them hopeful of a life without pain, hunger, and fear.

They were doing what they had to in order to survive. Whisper took my face in her hands, they were cold on my cheeks. Cold.

"Anza? Is she feeling anything?" Tamaj asked, panic in her voice. Panic.

"No, nothing, it's like she's empty."

The cold on my cheeks was grounding me. I blinked and reached up, resting my hands on Whisper's where they sat on my cheeks before meeting her eyes.

"Cold."

"Good, good, Mira, good. Focus on that. The air is cold too. Deep breath," Whisper said. We took a deep breath together. I could feel the cold, crisp air rush through my nose into my lungs, and I breathed out slowly. I took another breath, cleared my head, and closed my eyes. I heard movement but still couldn't react, feeling the warmth of something on my shoulders. I looked up at Anza, now resting a blanket around my shoulders. I willed my body to move, but it was too heavy, as if it wasn't my own.

"Anza?" I asked, feeling Whisper pull my hands down from my face.

"Hey, hey," he said, his face twisted in worry as he moved to my side. "You're alright. Whisper got you out. You're okay."

"Out."

"Right, out," he said as I turned, looking back at the toadstools. Panic struck me like a lightning bolt and Anza grabbed me, holding me tight as I scrambled backward, my whole body shaking.

"I've got you. You're alright," he said before I buried my head in his shoulder, trying to think about what I saw. Arlo disemboweled. Jinera and Sanji. The Nazzir. The dozens of bandits. The dragon.

"I saw-I saw things. I saw…" My throat was raw, choking the noise out as I clung to him.

"I'm sorry."

"He lit me on fire. He lit me on fire!"

"I'm so sorry."

"He was going to use me! He called me his puppet. I couldn't move or do anything!" Tamaj curled around us, Whisper hugging me tightly from the side.

"You're not in there anymore. You're safe. You're safe," Tamaj said, Anza gently pressing small kisses on my shoulder.

"I couldn't beat him; it wasn't in my skill set," I said, feeling the hot tears pouring into Anza's shirt.

"No, it wasn't, but it was in mine. They have to play by their own rules. We're okay. You're okay," Whisper said.

"Can we please get the hell away from this place?" I asked, lifting my head off Anza's shoulder. He brushed away my tears and nodded. I tried to get up, but my muscles ached. Tamaj supported me on one side, Anza on another. It was only a moment before he carefully picked me up. I rested my head on his shoulder, seeing the pain in his eyes as he turned his back to the toadstools, leading Tamaj and Whisper farther into the forest. The sun dipped down toward the horizon. Every flickering shadow and unexpected movement made me cling tighter to him, burying my head deeply into his shoulder. Every muscle ached, my skin still felt crispy, though I didn't have any actual burns. We got as far as we dared before Tamaj stopped, the sounds of the night rising up around us.

"We'll tuck in here," she said, settling in and gesturing for Anza to set me beside her. He did and built a fire, Whisper padding toward a patch of grass nearby, scaring a small group of fireflies. I watched her, not paying attention to Anza until I heard his voice quietly brush through the cooling night.

"Here." I looked up, reaching for the tea Anza passed me. Settled on the ground near a campfire, I turned my attention back to Whisper, who was still chasing bugs at night. Their little bug forms occasionally light up little fireflies in the dark. I could feel Tamaj's breathing, the steady pulsing of my heartbeat in my ears as Anza sat beside me, the cold night air around us. I was safe. Safer.

"Thanks."

"Feeling any better?" he asked as I sipped the tea.

"Yeah, I think I am," I said.

"I'm sorry. I know I messed up back there. I almost lost—"

"You don't have to say anything."

"What?"

"You don't have to apologize for anything. We all messed up back there."

"All of us?"

"Yeah, Whisper and Tamaj knew what dangers we were heading into, you said my name, and I didn't listen to you when you tried to warn me; we all messed up."

"*We* didn't get lit on fire."

"It was only in my head."

"An ancient fae lit you on fire within your own mind *with* your own mind. It doesn't matter *how*, it still happened, and if it wasn't for Whisper..."

"I don't want to think about it."

"Alright," he said as I sipped at my tea. "At least she's having a good time," he said, gesturing toward Whisper. I was thankful for the change in the subject. We sat in silence, watching her. The only light revealing where she was in the darkness was the light of the fireflies and the weak moonlight filtering through the trees. She giggled as she caught one, letting it go and chasing it, dancing around the spiraling light.

"I know she's lucky we found her...but I'm thinking maybe we're the lucky ones," I said, still wondering how a child so precious had saved me.

"Yeah, I think we are," he agreed.

I opened the blanket, pulled it over his legs, and inched closer to him, listening to the soft noises of the night, a cry of a bird of prey hunting above. I saw the flutter of wings as it landed in a nearby tree and leaned back against Tamaj, watching it for a moment before looking back to Whisper, who was stepping carefully toward me. Her feet avoided the twigs on the ground, finding moss creeping, almost as if she didn't even have to think about where she was walking.

"Look," she said, showing me a handful of fireflies.

"They're beautiful," I said, opening the blanket to let her in. She settled in my lap, Anza looking up to stare at the stars. The sounds of the night stretched on. The little lights in her hands were warm and bright, flashing at random intervals. It was about an hour before I realized Anza had slipped into sleep.

"Whisper?"

"Yeah?"

"Thank you."

"For what?" She seemed genuinely confused, eyes still focused on the fireflies in her hands.

"The...fae?" I asked, and she shook her head.

"You don't have to thank me for that."

"You didn't have to do that, though."

"I was taught many bad things before I was left alone, one thing was if someone needed help, *truly* needed help, you should help them."

"And if they're trying to trick you?"

"Oh, that's easy, then you just disembowel them." I couldn't help but smile.

"Right." I wanted to feel put off by her statement, but I wasn't. This feral little disco ball was someone I owed my life to. Someone I'd give my life to in a heartbeat, just as I would for The Two. She was my responsibility, and the castle still seemed so far away.

"There's something you want to talk about," she said.

"I...I feel like I'm losing hope, like we're not getting any closer."

"I haven't been with you for very long, but we're gaining ground. Maybe you're having a hard time because you've been walking much longer, but every step technically gets you closer to the castle. There are just a lot of steps to get there."

"I hope so," I said, resting my chin on her head. "I guess it's hard to see the light sometimes."

Whisper didn't look up at me as she spoke again, letting the fireflies run from one finger to another. "It's hard to wrap my head around sometimes, how the light can come from so many places—the moon, the stars, even fireflies—but the brightest light I've ever seen is hope. It's hope that will lead you through the dark."

"I don't know if I have much hope anymore," I admitted.

"That's alright, I have enough hope for the both of us."

21

We started out when light crept across the sky. Still tired, I tried to push what had happened the day before behind me. We had a castle to get to. The quiet morning left us hungry, cold, and wet as the rain started, thundering violently downward, making every step difficult. After a few hours, my feet ached like I was walking on swollen pincushions.

Movement a few yards away in the trees made Anza and I look up. There was a Barbarza, walking with a woman and child on its back, a man guiding them. The man looked at us, a sword in one hand, and with his free hand, made a motion, bumping his fist against his chest before turning to reveal an open and empty palm to us. Anza nodded, repeating the motion, and the group continued on.

"What was that about?" I asked, keeping close to Tamaj, trying not to lean on her as she walked.

"It's a gesture of intent. By showing the bare hand, he clarified that though he's armed, he would prefer not to fight."

"And by showing him the same, we agree?"

"Exactly," Anza said. "Repeating it makes it clear that everyone involved has the potential to be dangerous but hopes they won't have to be."

"Do people ever use that to get someone's guard down and attack them?" I asked.

"Yes, which is why you still keep your weapon close," Tamaj said, Whisper snoozing comfortably, even in the thundering rain, on her back. I kept my hand on my axe, ready to draw it, but the group continued, the woman occasionally looking back at us before the paths drew apart.

It wasn't long before the village rose in the distance. I pulled the hood of my cloak up and kept close to Tamaj, fixing Whisper's cloak to ensure she wouldn't be seen.

"Should we avoid it?" I asked.

"We're getting closer to the castle, the villages and towns get more frequent. Soon, it'll be impossible to avoid people," Tamaj said.

"And if we keep walking in this weather, I'm gonna cut my feet off," Anza said.

"You and me both," I said, watching as the edge of the village came into view. I expected bustling merchants, running children, and a bright, vibrant village. Instead, we met streets lined sparsely with people, closed-up houses, and closed-up shops. The few people out and about looked like they had traveled there. They stood still, laden with their packs in their groups at the few open merchants.

"Something isn't right."

"Hey, look an Endering!" I turned to the voice, seeing a Maraung man striding toward me already. I kept close to Whisper ready to do whatever was necessary to protect her and The Two.

"Oi bawbag!" The voice came from the right. I didn't look at it, though, my eyes locked on the man who had stopped in his tracks. "Last fella that fucked with an Endering through here shite his britches." That accent. I couldn't place that accent. It wasn't Maraung, it was one I hadn't ever heard before.

I didn't look at the speaker until the Maraung man did, catching a glance of the light green Photomyran woman on the porch of a nearby building. She stood about my height, with a thick braid down the back of her head, russet brown flowers tucked throughout. She had soft features built around sharp brown eyes. She wore her petals and leaves arranged in a skirt, blouse, and a shawl in a way that was hard to track how they flowed. The way her eyes pierced through me made my throat feel suddenly very dry. She was built like she could be a problem. I pushed the thought away, noting the building behind her was clearly a tavern inn, bustling with people inside, drinking and arranging their things.

"And what are you going to do about it?"

"Do you really wanna know, you daft jobbie?" she said, looking out at him from beneath her eyebrows. A hand shifted behind her, as if reaching for something affixed on her back. I didn't give her a chance. Bolting forward, I twisted one of my bracelets into a sharp point, holding the end tight as I held it beneath his chin before he could move. He looked back at me, putting both hands up slowly. A crude stone dagger resting at his throat.

"I promise you don't want to know," I said as he met my eyes. He nodded slowly and backed up. Turning quickly, he returned to his group as the woman looked at me before beckoning me to her with a hand.

"You alright?" Anza asked, resting a hand on my shoulder as we approached her.

"Yeah."

"Who the hell is that?"

"And what's a bawbag?" Anza asked, his voice hushed.

"No clue, come on." We quieted as we got to the bottom of the stairs. "Thanks for that. We're all tired of the attention."

"Well, you'd better get used to it, lookin' like that," she said, eyeing me up and down. I tried not to take it personally. "People don't know how to leave people be these days."

"Yeah, well, thanks anyway. Is this an inn?"

"It is. You lookin' for a place to stay?"

"Yeah, we have the coin somewhere. Who would we talk to?"

"Me, but I won't take your coin."

"Inns don't come for free," Tamaj said, snorting.

"No, they don't," the woman said.

"What's the catch?" Anza asked, rubbing his face with a hand.

"A Barbarza comes in the night, rattled with The Fever. I've been trying to take care of him, but he's a sleekit beastie."

"I'm not even gonna pretend to know what you said. You want help with it in exchange for a room?"

"Aye," she said, waving us in. Carefully, we followed her in. Anza kept himself between the prying eyes of the tavern and the hooded sleeping Whisper on Tamaj's back.

"Another round?"

"Yer drunk enough!" the woman called back, waving us to the front of the tavern. "Yer fair done in, so I'll give you the rooms now. So long as ye actually help me tonight."

"We will," I said.

She snorted, looking us over.

"Good, go get some rest." She passed me a key. "Up the stairs, second door on the left."

"Thank you."

She nodded her response before going back to tending the bustling tavern. We stayed close to one another, holding tight to Tamaj's mane as we made our way through the crowd to the stairs at the left of the bar. I slipped up first, Tamaj next, Anza behind, watching out behind us. I got to the door, unlocked it, and opened it to a small room with a large bed, a smaller bed, and a low-to-the-ground nest-looking bed. I closed and locked the door behind us.

"What was up with her?" Anza asked.

"Something was off, for sure," Tamaj agreed.

"She was so...protective and defensive at the same time, it made no sense," Anza said as he helped Whisper off of Tamaj. She instinctively clung to him, letting him carry her to the smaller bed.

"I don't care so long as we have a warm, dry place to rest," I said, kicking off my wet shoes before tearing off my socks. Tamaj and Anza grumbled in agreement as Tamaj went to the low bed, and Anza sat on the other side of the remaining one, kicking off his shoes. I wanted to sit and think about the strange woman again, but I was too damn tired to launch a full-scale investigation because of a weird girl. I tucked into bed near Anza, looking over at the already-asleep Tamaj before letting sleep take me.

"Oi, time to get up!" Groaning sounded throughout the room as the Photomyran woman's voice rang through the door. Her insistent pounding didn't stop, obnoxious and firm.

"Coming!" I called.

"Hurry it up!" I heard her footsteps retreat and sighed as Anza stared at the ceiling.

"You good?"

"I hate that woman." I couldn't help but crack a smile as Tamaj stretched, Whisper groggily reaching for me.

"Where are we?"

"Warm, but we have to fight an infected Barbarza to stay."

"Alright," she said groggily, rubbing her eyes. I made sure her cloak was firmly fastened around her as we got our shit together and made our way downstairs. The tavern was empty, which was weird. I imagined taverns would be busy at night, but this one was eerily void of people. It made my skin crawl.

"They went home. Can't walk in the dark without it coming for you."

"Gotcha," I said. "Where do we start?"

"By eatin'. Can't help kill a Barbarza this big on an empty stomach," she said, setting three plates on the bar before bringing around a large bowl for Tamaj. I didn't realize how hungry I was until she started bringing out the food. Anza kept looking her over, like he couldn't quite place something, sticking close to me.

"I'm too tired to eat," Whisper said quietly to me.

"Eat," I said, settling her down. The woman did a double take, catching Whisper's face under her cloak.

"We don't have a problem, right?" Anza said, sizing her up.

"No, course not."

"Good," he said as we tucked into the meal, Anza and Whisper meticulously picking it apart. Tamaj didn't question it, eating ravenously.

"For fuck's sake, it's not poison. I can't go 'round poisoning people I need help from."

"Right," Anza said. "We didn't catch your name…"

"Doesn't matter, you'll be gone soon, anyway."

"Right. Where did you say you were from again?" I asked.

"I didn't."

"You're…just so warm and inviting for someone who needs our help," I said, feeling Anza nudge my side. I didn't look at him.

"When you're faced with people who would try to kill you on the daily, nice isn't an option," she said firmly. "You ready yet?" We let the conversation die and finished our meal before Anza and I readied our weapons. I passed Sil's knife to Whisper. She swished it around quickly before sticking to our side.

"You sure you want the wee one out there?"

"No, but we can't leave her in here," I said. She looked us over, but nodded and drew a quite lengthy blade out from under her skirt.

"I don't even want to know where you were hiding that," I said.

She threw her head back as she laughed before shaking her head.

"I like this one."

I wasn't sure who she was talking to, but she led the way to the door. Tamaj met my eyes, and we exchanged a look of uncertainty before following her out into the night. Silence danced across the whole town. There was no birdsong, no noise in the forest, not even the remnants of people in the streets. They were clean and empty. I held Whisper toward Tamaj, who hesitated long enough for the little Echalon to get on her back.

"Low and slow," the woman said.

I scanned the streets, not seeing any movement, as I twisted the axe in my hand, getting ready to use it. Ears sharp, eyes up, Tamaj creeping carefully outward, Whisper checking behind us as the five of us started inching through the streets. I could hear the steady breathing of the others, the soft pat-patting of Tamaj's feet on the cobbled streets, and the wind softly playing with the trees. We passed building after building, but nothing came out. The silence was starting to worry me.

What had this weird Photomyran called this Barbarza? A 'sleekit bastard'? It almost felt like we were the ones being hunted. The tension in the air was still thick and harsh as we crept through the low lit streets until we passed a large stone building and a large creature moved in the darkness like lightning, roaring out of the alley.

I tried to pull up a piece of stone to impale it, but it was upon me, the others fanning out to flank it from the sides. I remember teeth reaching for my head, a paw crashing onto my shoulder as I tried to bring my axe back up. I was dead. I was dead. A soft hand slid onto my other shoulder, and I was gone.

22

"Move, lass, move!" I did not know how, but I was now at the infected Barbarza's side, flanking him, my stomach tossing. Disoriented and shaken as the Photomyran woman impaled it through its ribs, into its lungs. I shook my head and lashed out, trying to aim one of my bracelets toward the back of its head, but I couldn't focus. My stomach was reeling, my footing was wrong, as if I didn't belong standing here on these cobbled streets. I missed, whizzing past toward Whisper and Tamaj. Still, I grabbed it back, changing its direction midair and wrapping it around the massive snapping jaws of the Barbarza.

"Fuck yeah!" Anza said, diving right toward the Barbarza's throat. Tamaj flanked it, heading toward me as Whisper leaped off her back onto the other Barbarza's back. It tried to turn to bite her, but with a bound maw, it couldn't grab her. Tamaj's teeth sunk into the Barbarza's hind leg, holding it in place as I reached out, pulling up a spike of stone into the Barbarza's abdomen. Whisper poised on his back, moving up toward his jaws, almost losing her footing, and reached for its closed jaw, pulling back its head by its nose, giving Anza a clear shot at its throat.

It never had a chance. Sliding steel met bone as Anza cut deep, blood pouring from the Barbarza's throat spilling quickly onto the ground, splashing black on Anza as our Photomyran friend bolted to Anza's side, pulling him away. I reached for Whisper, pulling her free of the Barbarza as he slipped down, Tamaj letting go simultaneously.

"Water, now!" the Photomyran said, pulling Anza back toward the tavern. I held Whisper close as Tamaj urged her to follow her with a nudge. She quickly pushed Anza behind the bar, rushing to get water so he could wash. It was only a moment before she returned, tossing a cloth at him and setting down two large pails.

"Why the panic?" I asked as Anza wetted the cloth.

"Blood in an open wound will turn you, and you don't exactly look like you've been riding on sunshine and rainbows to get here," she said as Anza cleared off his bare skin.

"I'm gonna change," he said, wiping the last of the blood off.

"Alright, be careful," I said, watching him return to the room.

"Well, we took care of your problem," Tamaj said as Whisper kicked her feet out. I put her down, and she moved to Tamaj's side.

"You certainly did. You can rest today and another night, but I need the room back after," she said.

"Sounds fair to me. I still didn't catch your name."

"I didn't offer it."

"Well, what should I call you then?" I asked, looking her over. Tamaj snorted, clearly done tolerating such an ill-tempered woman.

"We're going to get some more sleep."

"While we have comfy beds," Whisper said.

"Alright, I'll see you when I head up," I said, watching them leave before returning to the woman. I hadn't realized she had moved, but she was an inch from me.

"How did you—" Her hand clamped on my mouth, but those sharp eyes weren't filled with a threat. No, not quite. She wanted quiet. I nodded, and she slid her hand from my mouth. Grabbing my hand and beginning to draw a hap hazardous oval.

"How did you—" She drew her finger through the oval, like a blade slashing through a spell, and the Photomyran woman was gone. Standing before me, her finger still in my hand, was an Endering. Her hair was thick and bounded straight down her back, the same russet brown as those flowers had been. The clothes I had seen her petals arranged in were just that, clothes. Her features were the same: soft with sharp eyes, but she was exceptionally pale.

"They called me Flit."

"You-your an Endering!" She pulled her hand back, the disguise sliding back in place.

"And if you tell anyone, I'll rip your spine out before you know what's coming."

"That's how you moved so fast?"

"I'm not fast. I jump through space, teleport."

"Downside?"

"I'm not telling you that."

"I won't tell anyone."

"Damn straight you won't. Shouldn't have even shown you, but I can't take that back now. I don't want to be part of a kingdom, never did, and I have a promise to keep, so when you leave here, forget about me."

"Why did you show me?"

"You're an Endering. I had to move you in that fight if you were going to live. You would have put it together eventually, especially with an Echalon at your side, it's not like they didn't see it."

"You're not wrong there," I said. "Do you think Anza will be alright?"

"Yea, we worked fast. It takes a while to set in and I didn't see any wounds on him. Gotta be careful."

"Right."

"And you are going to need this," she said, slapping a piece of paper down on the table. With a piece of charcoal, she began to draw, carefully inscribing an intricate sigil on the paper before passing it toward me.

"What's this?"

"The sigil I used to hide," she said. "You'll need it the closer you get to the castle; that *is* where you're going?"

"Yes…thank you, this is—"

"The price of forgetting I exist."

"Right, you don't exist."

"Good. Now get before I change my mind," she said, jerking her head toward the stairs. I got up, leaving her there, and headed toward the room. I took a breath before I opened the door. Whisper was buried in the sigil book at Tamaj's side and Anza, clean now, was cleaning his sword.

"Hey, got something else for you to look at," I said, moving toward Whisper and holding up the paper as they looked up.

"Oh, wow!" Whisper said, jumping up and running to me. I passed her the sheet. "This one is intricate! What does it do?"

"Hides a person. The person downstairs said a drunk Endering left it here ages ago." Anza looked me over, raising an eyebrow. I didn't look at him.

"This is gonna be so good."

"I'm happy you like it," I said, moving to Anza's side. "You okay? That blood didn't get into anything, right?"

"No, I'm alright, it was thicker than—" He stopped himself.

"Regular blood?"

"Yeah…I just realized how often we're covered in blood."

"You mean how often *you're* covered in blood?" He shivered as I sat beside him.

"You don't have to keep killing if it bothers you."

"I know I don't, but if it comes down to killing them or saving you, I don't need to think." I tried to push away the heat that rose as he spoke and turned back to Tamaj and Whisper.

"Are we really close? Because it feels like forever away still." *Change the subject, change the subject, and maybe the sparking in my chest will go away.*

"We're closer than we were in the mountains. We'll be at the Shale Tree in a few days."

"We're gonna get to see the Shale Tree?" Whisper said, looking up from the notepad to Tamaj.

"We sure are, little one,"

"Can I carve my name?"

"I don't see why not," I said, shrugging as Tamaj nodded.

"It might be a little scary, though. There are quite a few Echalon there," Anza said.

"The tree calls them home, right?" Whisper asked.

"That's right," Anza said. "But they won't all be in the ground like in Teramor."

"Wait, what?" I asked.

"Some of the Echalon, The Fallen, are walking around. Well, most are, but they're not…there," Tamaj said.

"But I'll be able to see my people," Whisper said.

"They're not people anymore, Moonbeam," Anza said gently.

"They are to me; they matter to me," Whisper said, returning her eyes to the sigil.

"Well, we can't get to them if we don't sleep," Tamaj said as Anza opened his mouth to argue. He let the words die in his throat before forcing a small, sad smile. I could tell we were walking toward a slice of pain from the worry written all over his face. He sheathed his sword, and I took his hand.

"Right," he said, as we settled carefully into the beds we had slept in the night before, his hand still woven in mine. I listened to his breathing, hearing Whisper's and Tamaj's slow as they fell asleep.

"Worried?" I whispered.

"I'm the one who's supposed to read emotions."

I rested my head on his shoulder on the pillow, looking at the room's ceiling.

"That's not an answer."

"I…hope she's ready. The stories I've heard don't make The Fallen sound easy to stomach."

"If anyone can handle it, it's Whisper."

"Yeah…" He didn't sound convinced.

"You care about her."

"She's a kid. It's easy to forget because of how smart she is, but she's—"

"Still a kid."

"And she's been through enough as it is. She puts up a good show, but she's so…" He stopped, searching for the word he needed.

"Fragile."

"Yeah." He was right. I had almost forgotten that she was a child; she wouldn't even be a toddler in human years, but there she was wielding a knife, understanding and implementing strategy, ducking and hiding, making traps, and perfecting sigils. Because she had to. Even before us. She had to. "She doesn't even have decent shoes."

"The shops seemed pretty bare, too."

"They did. I guess there's no point worrying about it now, but…" He trailed off. "The minute we get to the next town, we can get her a pair."

"Yeah," I said, feeling the warmth of the room and the surrounding blanket. "Try to get some rest?" I asked.

"You too."

I stared at the ceiling, mulling over Flit, the way she moved, and how she may have gotten here. Gradually, my mind moved to Whisper, a child, mere months old, fearlessly pulling back the head of an infected Barbarza, fully knowing she was helping us kill them.

23

When I opened my eyes in the morning, I was lying close to Anza, his arm draped over my side, my forehead against his chest. Panic set in as that sparking sounded in my chest and I scrambled back, hitting the floor as it sputtered out. Then I remembered where I was.

"Whoa, are you alright?" Anza asked, sitting up and wiping the sleep from his eyes.

"Yeah, yeah, forgot where I was for a sec," I said, feeling the heat on my face.

"I don't want it to be morning," I heard Whisper grumble.

"*Why?*" Tamaj's voice said, though she still lay in her bed, eyes closed.

"Cause it means we have to leave," Whisper said, and I sighed, knowing she was right as Anza got up, reaching a hand out to me, too, offering to help me up. I took his hand and let him pull me up.

"We can't stay forever," I said, wandering over to Whisper's bed. She pulled her blanket over her head.

"Nooo," she said. I smirked, pulling the blanket off of her and picking the sleepy Echalon up, letting her heavy form rest against mine, her head on my shoulder like a toddler that had stayed up too late. She wrapped her arms over my shoulders as I supported her on my arm, seeing Anza start gathering our things as Tamaj stirred, stretching.

"Make sure we don't leave anything," Tamaj warned. I searched Whisper's bed with my free hand, finding the little pad of sigils and the sigil Flit had given us. Anza reached for them and I passed them over, the little Echalon still asleep on my shoulder.

"She's exhausted."

"Echalon are great at plowing through problems...until they burn themselves out," Tamaj said.

"Her being sleepy could also be because she hasn't been safe, like ever," I said.

"And she is safer now," Anza said. "We've got everything." He maneuvered around me and Whisper to ensure I had my axe and Sil's knife. He slung my bag over his shoulder.

"Let's get outta here before our lovely Photomyran decides we owe her," Tamaj said, snorting, her hair raising slightly.

"Easy, we need to make it to the edge of town," I said as Anza led the way to the door, opening it to let us out. I followed him down the stairs into the tavern area and spotted Flit, a handful of people in the bar.

"Oi, come here." I padded toward her, keeping Whisper close. I could feel Anza's eyes on me, watching to make sure I didn't need him.

"What?" I asked.

"A last gift," she said, passing a small pair of shoes across the counter. "For the little one."

"How did you—"

"Don't ask questions; take them and go," she said.

I carefully took the shoes with my free hand.

"Thank you."

"No, thank you," she said before nodding toward the door. I didn't answer her, but returned to Anza and Tamaj's side as we headed toward the door.

"What do we call such an Endering as you?" a different

Maraung asked. I didn't look back at them as I answered, remembering the feeling of the mountain singing to me.

"The Mountain."

"The Mountain of Agrenon," I heard Flit say.

Whispers ensued as we finally slipped out the door. I held Whisper close, Anza at one side, Tamaj at the other, as we headed toward a castle I hoped existed. The chattering of birds sounded as we got to the edge of town, Tamaj nodding to a section where the trees broke away.

"We should skirt through there, stick to the edge of the forest in case we need to duck out of sight."

"Sounds good to me," I said, urging Whisper to get on Tamaj's back. Tamaj hesitated long enough for the little one to settle against her mane. I swapped out Whisper's shoes and Anza passed me a fresh pair of socks as I worked. Once her little feet were secure, we kept going, tucking her things into my bag in case she wanted them. She stirred, groggy, as she lifted her head.

"Where's that pad?" Not where are we, not what happened, but the pad of sigils. I couldn't help but smile; she knew what she wanted. Anza took the pad out, passing it to her. She groggily looked over the sigils, studying them.

"Do you think we can use that to hide you two?" Anza asked.

"We should be able to. It'd be cool to not be targeted everywhere we go," I said.

"Once I get the hang of this sigil, we can put it on something, like a bracelet or a patch, and I could use it whenever," Whisper said.

"But only Endering can do magic, right?"

"Yeah, but magic is all about intent, at least from what I've read, which, admittedly, is limited. Theoretically, you could create something with the intent of someone else using it. That person could theoretically activate that spell," she said without looking up from the pages of sigils.

The same way she had made the spells that I unknowingly triggered when we met.

"Wait, wait. So, if I knew about sigils when I came in…"

"This journey probably wouldn't have been so difficult," Anza finished as I turned to Tamaj.

"Sil never liked magic. She was very good at lighting people on fire, though," Tamaj said, shaking her head.

"I'm gonna give that woman a piece of my mind the next time I see her."

"I will pay you anything you want to see that. Name it," Anza said.

"Your firstborn child," I grumbled.

"Done."

More giggles erupted between Tamaj and Whisper at our little pact, but I ignored them. The trees thinning out, revealing only the rolling hills beyond. We stuck to the sides of the forest for some time before Tamaj turned, leading us out into the rolling hills. I stuck close to her, the sight of birds above us, and thick, bounding, luscious green grass below. Wildflowers sprang up around the fields; even Anza shivered as the wind whipped my hair around.

"You alright?" I asked, looking over Tamaj's back at him.

"Yeah, I don't like being without cover."

"If we need it, I'll make it."

"Good, good." He didn't seem convinced.

"We'll be able to see people coming too," Tamaj said.

"As well as they'll be able to see us," Whisper chimed in.

"Not helping," I said, but tried to get Anza's mind on something else. "Hey, didn't you trick us with sigils, Whisper?"

"Yeah, how did they get activated without Mira's intent?"

"Anyone can set intent silly, but only Endering can do and activate magic, so I could prepare sigils and get them ready in case I faced an Endering, but I couldn't activate them," she said.

"We're lucky we found you when we did, Moonbeam."

"If we didn't, I'd never know about magic," I said.

"I know, I'm amazing," she said, flipping her hair before turning back to her pad of sigils. I rolled my eyes, looking at Anza, who was shaking his head as he watched her. "Wanna know how else I'm amazing?"

"How?" Anza asked.

Whisper tucked the sigil pad into her bag and scrambled off Tamaj's back, hitting the ground and running off ahead, her little voice shouting back to Anza.

"I'm faster than you!"

"Oh, we'll see about that!" he shouted, running from Tamaj's side after her. I checked around us, looking for a threat, expecting some sort of catastrophic moment. There was nothing but rolling hills before us and the forest standing behind us.

"We're alright," Tamaj said. I picked up the pace to walk shoulder to shoulder with her.

"I'm just…"

"Nervous."

"Right. Can I ask you kind of weird question?"

"Mira, we have fought dragons, crossed the mountains the hard way, taunted fae creatures, and toyed with an Endering of death; I expect weird questions at this point. What is it?" I couldn't help but laugh.

"Alright, you have a point," I started, watching as Anza scooped up Whisper, spinning with her in his arms.

"Faster, faster!" she demanded, and he obliged.

"There's this feeling I get sometimes here," I said, lifting my hand to pat my chest. "Almost like a sparkler, but softer."

"I don't know what a sparkler is, Mira."

"Right, sorry, it's like…tiny fire sparks."

"Oh…hmm…when do you usually feel them?" I shrugged at her question.

"I don't think there's any like, given time or anything. It's…I want to make sure it's not something dangerous."

"If it is what I think it is, you'll be fine."

"Well, what do you think it is?" I asked.

"Ah, you see, that's the beauty of this thing…if I tell you, you'll know."

"That's the fucking point!" I said, the laugh still in my throat.

"Believe me, 'Stone-Slinger', you'll know what it is when it's time," Tamaj said. *"Now come on, before those two get too far away from us,"* she said, trotting faster away from me.

"Tamaj! Come on!"

"No!" She laughed as I ran after her, watching her dance out of my grasp. The sun bore down on the vast open fields, the cloudless skies making for a pleasantly warm start, even as we chased each other across the fields, Tamaj letting me catch her eventually as we caught up with Whisper and Anza.

"Mira, can you help me up?" Whisper asked, Anza patting his own shoulder. I helped Whisper onto Anza's shoulders and watched as she gently patted his head.

"Look how tall you are!" he declared as we kept going, Tamaj at my right, Anza at my left with Whisper on his shoulders, the day stretching toward night.

"We should keep moving," Tamaj said as the full moon illuminated the field, our little moonbeam lighting up with its glow.

"How much farther to the next town?"

"We should get there by morning," Tamaj said.

"We're really becoming nocturnal," I grumbled.

"We'll sleep in a bed at night eventually," Anza said, wiping his eyes.

"I can't wa—"

"Mira, stop!" Whisper was too late. A single sigil, larger than Tamaj, flashed up at us from where it had been carved into the hard ground and, before we could react, an eruption exploded from below. I was blasted sideways, reaching out to catch myself and landing hard. Fire and dirt, stone and pain. I couldn't see them. The eruption rocked my body as I tried to find my bearings. My head burst with pain as my vision settled, seeing the limp, fire-laced body of Tamaj. Her fur was ablaze, body sprawled as she lay on her side.

"Tamaj..." It hurt to talk, a thick grid of smoke fighting into my lungs, the sigil's marker still spilling the thick smoke. I fought my way to my knees as Anza came into view, barely on his hands and knees, patting Tamaj out as I crawled a few feet toward them, Whisper at his side.

"We're gonna run out of air if we don't move!" she said before a familiar sound sang out in the air, an arrow burying itself into Anza's back.

"Anza!" His body slumped against Tamaj.

"We need cover!" Whisper's voice cut through the smoke, and I tried to push past the pain, slamming up a wall along the outskirts of the sigil. I crawled the last few feet to them, feeling with one hand for Tamaj's chest. I could see Anza's chest moving. The rise and fall of Tamaj's chest was subtle, but there.

"Anza," I said, pulling him closer, taking out the arrow and turning him over. I got his head into my lap, brushing the soot and dirt from his face with a thumb.

"Mira?" His eyes were filled with shock and pain. "What happened?"

"An asshole or two blew us up."

"We need to move," Whisper said again as I fought for air.

"We don't know where they are," I said as I grabbed the arrow tighter before the rumbling from the head of the arrow sang out. The idea hit me like a wave crashing on the shore, a warm feeling in my chest. The necklace Emai had given me grew hotter as I focused my power outward, beyond me. It bounded outward quickly, focusing, focusing my power, focusing on all I was and all I would be.

Slowly, arrows came into my view; the small bunches of arrowheads hunkered up off the ground were unmistakable. I dropped the stone wall, folding it outward to disrupt the sigil, the smoke sputtering out as the six bundles of arrows shifted. Where there were arrows, there were people. Another arrow sang out, but in this heightened state, I could both see and feel it coming toward me.

I reached up as quickly as it had been loosed, stopping it between my pointer and middle fingers. Twisting my body, I held it in place, feeling the tension of the speed it had buzz down my fingers and across my palm like a light, a song in my hand, and flung the arrow back the way it had come. A strangled noise sang out in the night.

"Stay together!" I roared, hearing Anza try to draw his blade. Arrows sang out from the remaining five people. As quickly as they loosed their arrows, I pulled up thin stone shields, keeping them in the air so I could move them more effectively. The group positioned around us wasn't thinking straight. They had caught the wrong Endering.

I diverted two arrows, making them follow through to untrue marks in the people firing from behind me. My stone shields crashed in the way of other arrows stopping them before I set the stone shields spinning lazily around me. Three down, three to go. A bundle of arrows moved, getting up, starting to retreat before it fell again, slumping to the ground. Something else was out there, but it did not bear a stone weapon. I couldn't pinpoint it on these rolling hills. More arrows. I twisted my body, blocking the arrows with a shield from hitting Tamaj and Anza before sending the shields toward the two remaining bandits, sharpening them into pointed spear ends as they flew. It had only been a moment when the bandits crumpled under my power. The only sound that remained was the noise of a bird of prey, like a falcon, in the night.

I listened quietly for whatever had taken out that fourth bandit, waiting to face whatever it had been. Just because it killed them didn't mean it was friendly. The seconds ticked on until Whisper spoke.

"Mira, they're…they're in terrible shape." I turned back toward her.

"There's someone out there. Watch my back."

"Okay…this one," Whisper said, pulling out the sigil pad. "I figured it out yesterday. It's for healing. Try it?"

"Yeah, yeah, watch my back," I said again, and she nodded, leaving me with the pad to step a few feet behind me, watching for movement as I tucked in beside Anza.

"Are they gone?" he coughed out, eyes focusing, still slightly glazed from the blast.

"Dead," I said. "Something else is out there, though. I don't know if it's a friend or foe."

"What?"

"It helped me pick off one of the bandits, but we can't think about that now. I'm gonna try this," I said, before drawing the looping sigil Whisper had shown me with a finger on Anza's chest.

"Careful," Anza said. "Don't wanna accidentally make the wrong one."

"Intent, remember?" He barely managed a nod.

In this close-up place, with my anger fading, I could see how badly he had been burned, his flesh pitted and wounds filthy. I pressed my hand against the sigil formed of dirt and worry, closing my eyes and pressing my intent into it. Imagining his wounds healing over, focusing on their healing without pain or infection, focusing on healing all over, even wounds I couldn't see. After those brief moments, Anza's hand found my face and opened my eyes. Looking down at where his wounds had been, I found only whole and healthy flesh and a sudden feeling of tiredness washed through me.

"I'm alright."

"I thought I was gonna—"

"Well, you weren't. I'm alright," he interrupted. "Now, Tamaj." I nodded as he sat up, helping me find a spot on Tamaj where I could draw. Her shaky breaths could stop any moment and I had a feeling, call it intuition or a hunch, that this spell wouldn't work if she died. I pressed my hand firmly against the sigil, breathing intent into the spell as it worked, like I had with Anza, feeling Tamaj's breathing get stronger. I didn't stop until she lifted her head.

"What happened?"

"Take it easy," I started. "We were ambushed."

"Everything's sore."

"Better than dead," Anza said as she stood up.

"Whisper, are you alright?" I asked, turning to look at the little Echalon behind me, who seemed entranced by watching my back. "See something?"

"I did, but it left," she said.

"Are you okay?" I repeated.

"Oh, sorry, yeah, I'm okay," she said, returning to my side.

"What'd it look like?"

"A person. I could only make out the silhouette, though."

"Dang, so you couldn't tell the species or anything?" Anza asked, and Whisper shook her head.

"What matters is it's gone," I said, watching Tamaj to ensure she could balance.

"Thank the stars," Anza said.

Whisper glared at him, but said nothing as I picked her up.

"Let's get to that town before whoever that was decides we're easy targets."

24

Daybreak hit the moment our feet touched the cobbled stone, the busy town before us absent the pain and strife from the night before. Tamaj was still limping, Anza leaning on her heavily as they stumbled forward, Whisper on my hip. I was too tired to hide us, and it wasn't more than a handful of seconds before eyes turned to us and whispers lit up the streets.

A hand reached for Whisper and I didn't have to think to summon the cobblestone beneath us into a spike, rising upward, scratching the hand of the woman who had dared reach for my daughter.

It hit me in that moment how quickly I had come to love our little Moonbeam, but I didn't have time to dwell on it as I turned my focus back on the woman who had tried to touch her. She pulled her hand back, and I glared at her, her weathered face startled at my power. I tried to imagine what she saw, a battered, flame-singed Endering with tangled, half-matted dirty hair smeared in blood, the smell of smoke clinging to my very being; I could use this to my advantage.

"The next person who tries to touch any of us will get one of these directly up their ass!" I said, my voice rattling every rooftop and doorstep I could see. She stepped back quickly, and I put the cobbled stone back where it had lain, returning it to its natural shape.

Carefully, I led them forward, finding the nearest tavern inn, music spilling into the street and the walls practically bursting in their effort to contain the people, and headed toward it. Anza and Tamaj kept close, Whisper quietly clinging to me as we stepped into the tavern, her head tucked up under mine. A lull in the conversation lasted less than a second before hushed whispers filled the space. Some people ignored us, others kept their eyes on me. I was ready, still adrenaline-filled, to kill anyone who even put a toe out of line. I approached the bar and the tavern keeper approached me from the other side.

"What can I do for The Mountain?"

"My reputation precedes me."

"It does, fair but fierce. My question stands."

"A room for me and my companions, how much?"

"For you and your companions? Considering you took care of that pack of bandits that trapped the fields, nothing," he said, fetching a key and passing it over. "First on the left." He jerked his head toward a set of stairs. Part of me knew this was too easy, and part of me was too tired to care. I took the key and led them to the room; no one dared to get in my way. No one spoke until I closed the door behind us.

"Thanks, Mira," Whisper said. "For back there."

"You've got nothing to thank me for," I said, setting her in the bed farthest from the door. She settled down quickly in the blankets, yawning as she did.

"You weren't hurt, right?"

"Naw, I'm pretty good at getting blown up," Whisper said.

"Thank the stars one of us is," Tamaj said, tucking into a bed of her own, moving slowly, aching with every step. Anza even sat heavily on a bed, rubbing his face with his hands.

"Do you and Anza believe the stars are your ancestors?" Whisper asked.

"*I do,*" Tamaj said.

"Yeah, why?" Anza said as I sat on the other side of the bed, kicking off my shoes and pulling the egg bag close.

"I've always wondered what it'd be like to believe my ancestors are looking down on us from the stars."

"You don't?" Anza asked.

"No, but I believe in you, Tamaj, and Mira, and that's more than enough."

"*You've just met us, little one,*" Tamaj noted.

"Yeah, but most people would have tried to kill me by now," Whisper said as Anza and I crawled into bed.

"*Maybe you'll have a change of heart tomorrow,*" Tamaj said.

"What's tomorrow?" Whisper asked.

"*Tomorrow, the hills flatten out and we can double our speed. Tomorrow, we get to the Shale Tree.*"

"Really, really?" Whisper perked up.

"*Really, really,*" Tamaj said, though she was already half asleep.

"Are you alright, Stone-Slinger?" Anza asked as we settled beside each other in bed.

"Yeah, how are your wounds?"

"Sore, but I think I'll live."

"Good, losing you would suck."

"In the words of Whisper, 'I know, I'm amazing'." I couldn't help but laugh as he tucked himself under a blanket. I grabbed my pillow, hitting him gently with it before settling in myself.

"Go to sleep."

"Working on it," he said.

Whisper muttered something in a language I didn't understand. Anza shifted under the blanket and Tamaj's chuckle was the last thing I remember before slipping into a troubled sleep. I woke up a few times throughout the day, but it wasn't until later that I woke up to an empty bed. I got up, feeling for Anza.

"Anza?" Silence. I scrambled over to Whisper's bed, finding

it also empty, the soft snores of Tamaj stopping enough to lift her head.

"They went downstairs, the music," she said. I had heard the music but not registered it as important in my panic. Carefully, barefoot, I slid downstairs and stopped in the entryway to the lower floor of the tavern, frozen by the scene before me. The place was almost empty, but in the middle of the tavern, Whisper laughed, hood down, as Anza twirled her to the music.

"Again, again!" She laughed and Anza picked her up and spun her again. Their laughter quelled my nerves. Leaning against the doorway to the stairs, watching them, I took in the moment. An actual moment of peace, joy, and light in the darkness and pain we had been handed. The low light of the tavern caught and twirled as Anza spun her.

"I'm gonna toss you!" Anza warned.

"Oh, no!" Whisper laughed as Anza gently tossed her in the air and caught her. Whisper wasn't light, but Anza didn't seem to have much difficulty moving her.

"Again!" Whisper said as Anza caught her. He tossed her again and put her down, and together they did a simple little dance, the girl stepping on his toes as they moved.

"If we don't get back to bed soon, Mira is gonna wake up and get worried about us," Anza warned.

"Please, one more spin?" Whisper asked, and Anza rolled his eyes but scooped her back up, spinning her again. I turned, savoring the shrieking laugh that sounded up the stairs as I climbed. I heard the familiar thumping of two pairs of feet on the stairs as I got to the room. I got back into bed and rolled into the position I had been in, feeling the sparking in my chest again as I pretended I was asleep. Quietly, Anza snuck in with Whisper, tucking her into a bed.

"Thanks, I never got to play like that before."

"Anytime. I'm sure there' are plenty of things to do at the castle," Anza said over the sound of gently moving blankets as Whisper settled in.

"I hope so, or I'm going to be so bored."

"Oh, I think there will be. Are you less scared now?"

"Yeah, things have been a little stinky lately."

"More than a little stinky. Try to get some more sleep?"

"I will," Whisper said.

"Night."

"Night."

Anza settled back into bed, stretching as he settled into the blankets.

Whisper was a kid, wrapped in a world that wanted nothing more than to kill her. Small and frail and stuck in survival mode. I heard Whisper gently snoring. She had needed this and Anza had known that. He had felt her distress and reacted, helping her become more relaxed. Relaxed enough to quell her fears and get some rest. I finally succumbed to sleep after hearing Anza's breathing slow.

The morning came too fast, my aching body still tired, smoke lingering on my clothes as I sat up, rubbing my eyes.

"Morning, sleepy," Anza said quietly.

"Morning. Anyone else awake?" I asked.

"*No,*" Tamaj grumbled.

"Define awake," Whisper sounded.

"Oh, it sounds like they're definitely still asleep," Anza said.

"Oh, yeah. For sure," I said as we got to our feet together. I grabbed my shoes as Whisper sighed, starting to get up. Tamaj stretched, and slowly, we started to gather our things.

"Where'd I get these shoes?" Whisper said as she pulled her shoes on, wiping the sleep from her eyes.

"We got them at the last tavern. That lady we fought with gave them to us. I have your other ones."

"I can't believe I didn't notice."

"You've been a sleepy little moonbeam," I said as she pulled her bag to her and her cloak over her head.

"Sleepy, moon," she yawned, trudging over to me, hugging me, and resting her head on my hip.

"Alright, let's get out of here," Tamaj said gently.

"Oh, you want to leave? Like, go through the door?" Anza said, a slight smirk playing across his face.

"Don't make me turn you into breakfast," Tamaj said, deadpan, as she waited for him to open the door. He smirked wider before moving to open up the door. Once he did, we all carefully padded downstairs. The tavern keeper waved us over as we got there and I walked to him, Tamaj, and Anza, keeping a distance, ready to pounce if I needed them.

"There are quite a lot of people between here and the castle, so keep that in mind when it comes to your little one," he said quietly. His eyes were kind. This was a well meant warning. A warning to stay hidden.

"Thank you," I said. "We'll be careful." He nodded in understanding but didn't say goodbye as we headed toward the front door and the edge of town.

Whisper reached for Tamaj and I couldn't help but smile before Tamaj hesitated. I leaned closer as Tamaj let her get onto her back. Anza took up one side of Tamaj, and I took up the other, hell-bent on ensuring that Whisper was flanked from as many sides as possible. Even though her hood was up, we were in broad daylight. People could see us.

But the townsfolk parted quickly when we approached, likely remembering my display from the day before, and before long, the cobbled stone gave way to a clear, well-worn path leading us farther into the rolling plains. We trudged for hours, the plains stretching out in every direction, leaping and bounding before us. In every endless fucking direction. At first, it was beautiful, the rolling grass and Whisper fumbling about to pick wildflowers. However, after about an hour, I was irritated with the endless wind whipping my already tangle-ready hair. Anza made us stop for a moment so he could untangle my hair and braid it again.

After walking for a few miles, I stepped over a small hill to look down the steeper hill to where a massive tree towered toward the sky, its reach far more significant than any I had ever seen. Its branches stretched out, bounding upward. Though I know it couldn't have, the way my neck craned to find the top made me feel like it was kissing the clouds with its size. Stones, broken pieces of limbs, and fragments of gemstones shot up from all around it, catching the light and sending it out into the shadows of the surrounding clouds. Small groups of stones seemed to be beneath it, moving, shifting among the tangle of visible roots that pierced the ground.

"Fuck yeah, there it is!" Whisper declared, the wind weaving through the massive branches as she ran toward the tree.

"That's the Shale Tree?"

"*It is, indeed,*" Tamaj said as she trotted after Whisper. Anza stepped to my side.

"I don't-I can't-I..." he said, trying to get his brain to process such a magnificent sight.

"Me too," I managed, and we laughed, looking at one another. I shoved the thoughts that tried to grab my attention to the back of my head, trying to ignore that sparking feeling.

"Come on, before Whisper falls off a root or something," he said as I nodded, leading the way toward the tree. The closer I got, the stronger my power sang back to me. The warmth of the sun and the rushing wind had become so much, and here we were now about to be under the shade of a tree that was said to give life. The fabled birthplace of all Echalon. The only genuinely holy thing Whisper's amazing little brain had ever dared to grasp.

Whisper didn't get too far ahead as we took in the glint of light, the towering stones, and twisting roots. We were still a few hundred yards from the trunk when I recognized the moving rocks. They weren't rocks at all. I slowed as we walked into the darkness of the tree's shade. Whisper and Tamaj didn't slow down, but Anza hung back, waiting for me. The shapes were not rocks. They were people. Small groups of Echalon shuffled lazily about, their bodies barely moving. Their eyes were dead, chests all broken open. Some didn't have arms, and a few were missing legs. Every few feet, an Echalon poked up from out of the ground. The Fallen.

"Are they safe?" I asked Anza.

"They seem to think so," he said, nodding toward Whisper and Tamaj. "I think Tamaj would know, at least."

"Right, she would have warned us."

"Right," I said, feeling the air filled with an unsparked tension. The light still bounded through them, spattering splashes of light in dozens of hues on the ground.

"I've never seen them walk before," Whisper said.

"Most people buried bodies in mass graves when they ransacked the towns and cities. Those that weren't buried were called back by the tree."

"It feels like…I've come home," Whisper said quietly as she padded through the different shapes of dead Echalon.

"They're quite the welcoming party," I said quietly, following them.

Once we got past the initial barrage of dead Echalon, I could finally slide my hands against the stones that had fallen off the tree. An unbridled feeling washed over me as I touched the stone like no one was beside me. An overwhelming and pain-filled feeling of loneliness. Tears slipped down my cheeks as I realized what I was feeling. I looked at the stone, hundreds and hundreds of marks in neat rows across the surface, shuddering under my touch. I snatched my hand back.

"Whisper, Tamaj?"

"Yeah?"

"You guys are sure we're safe?"

"They are empty, Mira," Tamaj said.

"Right," I said, watching Whisper reach out to pick up a small, simple gray stone.

"I'm gonna add my name," she announced, padding toward a stone that had a little space.

"Should she?" Anza asked.

"Every Echalon used to make at least one trip to this tree, and they would add their name to a stone."

"It's like a living tome of all the Echalon that have come before me," Whisper said, bracing herself against a stone as she started carving her name in a language I couldn't read. It didn't take long for her to finish, but after she stopped, she brushed tears from her eyes.

"There's something wrong," Anza said as Whisper dropped the stone. Pressing both of her hands against the stone, her eyes unfocusing as the tears flowed.

"Whisper?" Tamaj asked as she stepped toward the little Echalon.

"It's...alive...it feels..."

"The Fallen?"

"The tree." Groaning met my ears as the tree shifted. At first, I thought it was moving because of the wind, but now I could see the branches move against the wind. It was moving on its own, rooted in one spot.

"Um...guys?" Anza said. I turned to him then followed his gaze. They were looking at us. The Fallen had each turned to look at us, stopping in their tracks.

"Whisper, we need to go," I said, their dead eyes strikingly clear. I thought they would be empty, but they weren't. Hundreds of eyes looked at us, filled with longing and lonely pain. We needed to leave.

"But the tree."

"Now, Whisper," I said as she stood up. The moment her hands left the stone, the Fallen started moving again toward us. The tension in the air shifted, and I didn't even need to touch the stones or roots for the feeling of absolute fear to wash over me. I didn't think I would ever be afraid of a tree. I couldn't get to Whisper fast enough, but Anza could, rushing toward Tamaj, who was dancing in place, waiting for us. Like a mob of zombies from a bad movie, The Fallen rushed us all at once, and I wasn't fast enough.

25

———

"Run!" I screamed, Tamaj already moving as I spoke.

"We can't leave you!"

"Go!" I yelled, lashing out to throw up a barrier between myself and the onslaught behind me. I pulled a stone shield up to my side and reached out, imagining a wall for them to travel along, carving a wall, a beginning step to make a path for their safety.

Tamaj ran, Anza's hand still held out for me, Whisper tucked against him. The Fallen parted as the wall of stone sprang forth, falling to each side of the thick stone. I drew my feet together, pulling with every inch of my body. Using both hands, I split it down the middle, tearing a path into the earth, a path for them crafting an entrance in the side Tamaj was on just in time for her to slip in.

I started running for my friends again. Picking up my speed, I summoned a slab of earth beneath my feet to help launch me forward like a springboard, twisting my ankle as Anza's hand, which had barely been out of reach a moment ago, closed around my own.

"Gotcha," he said, pulling me onto Tamaj as I maintained the path before us. The path destined for us.

The Fallen had come up over the walls, the groaning still sounding behind us as I clung to Anza, settling behind him on Tamaj's back as she careened forward into the section of walls. I broke away ten-foot sections piece by piece as we passed them, dropping them back to crush The Fallen, rushing to try to awkwardly clamber over the walls. I struggled, fighting to keep the walls up as Tamaj ran. I barely saw the body of The Fallen heading for me. It crashed against us, the dead weight of a full-grown Echalon threatening to break us. Instead of breaking, Anza and I fell. My hand slipped from his as we tumbled.

I tried to roll, my twisted ankle shooting pain up my leg as I came to a stop, The Fallen upon us. I saw Anza on the ground, pinned down by a Fallen as another tried to grab his legs. Instinctively, without a second thought, I pulled a piece of stone out of the ground, wrapping it up and over Anza, giving him cover as one of them grabbed my leg. A giant fist came down on my head, leaving my ears ringing as pain erupted against my temple, darkness almost claiming me. At that moment, the sound fell away. I reached out, grabbing the egg bag at my side. Remembering why I was there. We were close. Whisper had said so herself. Tamaj had said so too. *Tamaj.*

The idea manifested as it hit my brain, pulling forth as I turned over, putting my stomach to the stone I was now pulling up from the depths of the ground, my head pounding, the taste of blood in my mouth as Anza made a break for me. I helped him up onto the growing mound I had made as I carefully crafted the stone creature. Somewhere in the distance, a shriek from a bird sounded as I quickly crafted the four legs, leveling out the form, seeing Tamaj in the distance before I willed the crudely crafted Barbarza-shaped stone forward. Anza clung tightly to me.

The form was a little wobbly, but as I willed it forward, I adjusted it for smoothness, noting how Tamaj ran, mimicking her gait. One, two three, four. One, two three, four. Anza lashed out at one of The Fallen, keeping them away from me, my head pounding as I desperately tried to keep the form moving, the bodies of The Fallen rushing past us now as we caught up to Tamaj's side.

"You've gotta be kidding me," Whisper said, her smile bright and awe filled, still clinging to the Barbarza's back.

"No way!" Tamaj exclaimed, almost jumping as she saw us beside her.

"We can freak out about it later!" I said, clinging to the stone Barbarza's back as I pushed it forward, finally bolting past the end of the path I had created, leaving The Fallen and the Shale Tree behind us. My head still pulsed with pain as we moved. It was only a few moments more though. I looked back and saw that The Fallen were no longer pursuing us. I slowed my Barbarza to a stop, Tamaj slowing beside me as I let the stone form sink back into the ground, Anza moving to keep me upright as it vanished. I could taste the blood thick in my mouth and turned to spit it out on the ground, shaking as I leaned heavily against him.

"Easy, I've got you, I've got you."

"Everything hurts," I said.

"Yeah, but you looked awesome." I couldn't help but smirk, looking up at him as he gently wiped my mouth with his sleeve. Sparking. I stepped back and swallowed hard to clear my throat.

"Please tell me there's a place we can rest nearby?"

"Oh, yes. The next town isn't far," Tamaj said, my head still ringing as Anza led me to her side.

"You okay?" Whisper asked.

"Yeah, I'll be alright," I said, clinging with one hand to Tamaj as she walked, leading us. Anza stayed by my side for a few minutes, but once it was clear, I wouldn't trip over myself, he moved to Tamaj's other side, keeping Whisper between us. His eyes kept flickering to me, though, and I did my best to pretend I didn't notice. The town came faster than I thought, but Whisper spoke as soon as we saw it coming.

"We really should try that spell, the one to hide us."

"Have you figured it out yet?"

"I think so. Should we try it?"

"Fuck yeah, we'd be way less of a target," I said as Whisper passed me a paper with the familiar sigil on it, Tamaj slowing to a stop to give us time to work it out.

"Think of your disguise, make it as detail-oriented as possible, and then activate the spell."

"Sweet deal," I said, breathing as I tried to settle the ache in my head. It took a few breaths before I could imagine what I wanted to be hidden as, a Maraung woman with dark hair; I imagined my brown skin a slightly different shade, closer to Anza's, with an olive undertone and a spattering of freckles. I activated the spell, running my fingers over the sigil, clinging to that image in my mind.

"Would you look at that…"

"It worked?"

"Oh, yes it did," Anza said, shaking his head as he looked me over. I pushed the sparking away as Whisper spoke.

"We could totally bind these to objects and use them whenever!"

"Really?"

"Yeah! You'd have to enchant the objects, but I can walk you through that, and we'd both be able to hide!"

"Let's try it."

"What would we bind it to?" she asked. I instinctively reached for the necklace hanging from my neck. Quickly, I took it off.

"Would this work?"

"Yeah, we would need something else too, and who would get what?"

"I'll give you the necklace and enchant a bracelet for myself?" I asked.

"Really? They're so cool. I don't want you to part with one if you don't wanna."

"Oh, little Moonbeam," I said. "I would part with everything to make sure you were okay."

"I promise the necklace is more than enough." I couldn't help but smile as she sketched out the sigil again. "Engrave it on the stone on the necklace, think about the intent you have, for me to disguise myself, and will it onto the stone, like you're pushing an idea into it."

"Alright," I said.

I focused on the necklace in my hand, carefully carved the sigil into it, small and easy to miss, imagining her hidden however she pleased, at her own will. It took time to get myself in the right mindset, but after a few moments, I felt the soft bubbling of the magic at work against my hands. I pulled my hands back, seeing the sigil flash with a weak light. Carefully, I passed it to Whisper.

"Think it worked?"

"Only one way to find out," I said, shrugging as she put the necklace on and adjusted it to a comfortable length. I stepped back to make sure that there was no way that I would accidentally activate anything.

"This is gonna be so cool! I've always wanted to do magic," she said, bouncing in her spot on Tamaj's back.

"Please do stop that," Tamaj laughed.

Whisper settled, closing her eyes as she focused. It was only a moment before her appearance started to shift. Her skin no longer caught the light as it faded to a pale color between green and brown. She had chosen dark hair, like mine, and kept her features very much the same otherwise, changing only what she needed to pass as a Maraung child.

"I can't believe that worked," I said, watching as she opened her eyes. She lifted her hands, seeing now the change of her skin.

"This is amazing!" she declared, throwing both fists in the air as she kicked her little feet.

The laughter was contagious through the group as we set off again toward the town.

I quietly thanked Flit for giving us a chance to hide in this last leg of our journey as we finally made our way into the village. There were people everywhere, Barbarza carrying different bags, some alone and others with Maraung and Photomyra; people bustled around, buying from merchants and drinking from taverns, tending to children they had. Anza and I stood on either side of Tamaj, Whisper still on her back. It was only a moment, though, before I heard it.

"Did you hear about that new Endering south of here?"

"The Mountain, right?"

"...and then she sent their own arrows back at them!"

"...wonder when she'll be through town..."

I couldn't help but smile, keeping my hands tangled into Tamaj's mane. Someone was spreading the story of The Mountain, and they had no idea I was right there.

"Don't let your ego go to your head," Tamaj's voice warned.

"Yeah, yeah," I said, patting her shoulder as we kept walking. It wasn't long before we found a tavern inn that didn't look like it was bustling to the brim.

"I'll get us a room," Anza said.

"Careful."

"I will be." He slid into the crowd, heading toward the inn while I stayed close to Whisper, who was at attention, looking all around us. She seemed tense.

"We're alright," I said, gently offering her my hand. She took it, holding it tightly until Anza returned to us a moment later.

"Alright, we have a room," he said.

"This is the last town before we get to the castle," Tamaj said.

"What's the castle like?" I asked.

"Well, there are three standing walls around it, the city lies outside them," she said, starting to follow Anza as he led us into toward the tavern inn.

"I bet it's gonna be really cool," Whisper said, reaching for me as we approached the tavern. I took her, settling her on my hip as we slid inside. I held her close, Anza sticking close to me.

She was heavy, still an Echalon tucked beneath that little Maraung disguise.

Anza led us upstairs to the room as the night threatened to descend upon us. Carefully, we settled into the beds once the door closed. We dropped the disguises, before lying down as the darkness cut light from the windows. I lay with my back to Anza, sleep having almost claimed me when I heard him speak.

"What do you think I should do?"

"That's up to you, young one."

"But she keeps—"

"I don't think she knows what she's doing."

"Maybe, and telling her would lead her to a conclusion she might not have found on her own, something she may not want."

"Right."

"Maybe it's a good thing it hasn't happened…we're close, right? We haven't talked about what it means to be who we are. A probable princess of Agrenon, he's probably going to crown her as soon as he can. We're just a raggedy Barbarza, a skittish stab-happy Echalon, and a lost Empathic Maraung."

"Oh, sweet one, I don't think you're lost."

"What I mean is…once we're there, who knows what rules will be in play, what they will expect from us…from her."

"I did spend quite some time in the castle, but not since Olaf became king. Anything could have changed."

"Exactly."

"You're not thinking of leaving, are you? Once we get there?"

"I don't know, our deal was to get her to the castle, but—"

"There's a chance there, Anza."

"A ghost of a chance."

"Still a chance," Tamaj said. *"Patience, young one, things like this can't be rushed."*

"If this becomes anything, will she even want me there once we get there? I mean, one day she'll probably be a queen."

"Whatever is to come is inevitable. All you can do is make the best choice for yourself."

"Right…thanks, Tamaj."

"Of course. Now rest, and don't let your mind wander too far or you'll be up all night."

"I won't, night."

"Night."

It hurt to breathe and move. I kept my mind blank so Anza didn't feel me responding to what he had said. It wasn't until after I heard those soft snores that my mind began to race. It didn't stop until I saw light kissing the horizon through the window of our room.

26

"Today is the day," Tamaj's words resonated deep in my chest. Anza and I lay close to one another. I couldn't believe it. We were getting to the castle today. We were gonna make it. We were gonna fucking make it. We got up quietly, preparing for the day.

Whisper was ready first, having already activated the necklace I had repurposed for her. I activated my bracelet, watching Anza pack the last of his stuff.

"Ready?"

"No," I said. "Yes, I don't know." The conversation they had the night before lingered on my mind. What was going to come of this? Was Anza going to stay? Were we going to be okay? What was I supposed to do once I got to the castle? Would there be expectations placed on me?

"Well, you better get ready," Tamaj said as Whisper opened the door, leading her out as she rubbed her little eyes.

"Right." We had been working so hard to get to the castle...

At least until we got you to the castle.

Anza's voice rang in my mind. That was our deal; until we got to the castle. Was Anza going to leave me once we got there? Once we were sure the eggs were safe? I swallowed hard and shoved the thoughts to the back of my mind as we slipped out onto the street. Whisper almost immediately reached up for me. I picked her up, holding her close as we stuck to Tamaj.

My mind raced. What would Olaf be like? Was he going to be accepting of my friends? Me? Was he expecting me? Would he not have sent someone to meet me at the portal if he had been? What was he doing to stop The Fever? The bandit issue? Where would I be expected to help? Would Anza stay near me to help me, or would he go his separate way? That thought alone made me feel sick. We were almost at the end of our journey, but I could feel the dread sinking into my bones.

We were almost at the end of our journey.

"Hey…" Anza said.

"Hm, yeah?"

"Breathe."

"Why do you think I need to breathe?"

"Because you jumped through like, eight different emotions there. Everything's going to be fine, even if you don't think it is, it is."

"How do you know?"

"Because we've gotten this far, and we're fine, and it has to be."

"If you would label the tiny fraction of time I've been with you as 'fine'…" Whisper started, yawning as she stretched in my arms. "You have a few bolts loose in that brain of yours," she finished, still mid-yawn.

"Oh, really? And you don't?" I tuned them out, passing Whisper to Anza, trying to breathe in time with Tamaj, my hand buried in her fur as we walked.

"He's right, you know."

"Yeah, worried."

"About?"

"With our luck, the castle will have been teleported into a different realm or some shit."

"Probably." Tamaj laughed. *"We'll be alright,"* she said.

Had she picked up that Anza had been worried about me? Was she going to leave too? She had been to the castle before, why would she not stay with me? My head was spinning, but it wasn't physically hard to keep going with her there to lean on.

The plains stretched out before us, but it was midday when a speck rose in the distance. I watched the speck grow and grow as we approached, Anza passing Whisper back onto Tamaj as we trekked toward it. At first, it was hard to make out the different sections of The City of Blood, but as we approached, it came into view. Houses and farmland spattered the city's outskirts. It was clear, even from farther away, that the houses became more and more dense the closer they were to the castle walls. Beyond those towering homes of different sizes and colored tan and white stone was a towering castle rising toward the sky. Built of well-placed white stone, ivy, ferns, and flowers spilled from every window I could see. Twin spires reached for the sky, each carrying a flag that danced in the wind. A green flag, on which the symbol of Agrenon flew; a flower bud woven in different hues of green to differentiate it from the darker green background of the flag. The center of the bud, what would eventually have been the flower if it wasn't a woven flag, was woven tight in an icy blue that stuck out against the darkening sky.

"Home," Tamaj whispered as we plodded down the path.

Gradually, it turned to cobblestones. People kept bustling around, moving around us as we marveled at the city's beauty on our approach, fooled by the illusion magic keeping Whisper and I hidden. The City of Blood had to be a name used to intimidate our foes. The pristine cobbled streets didn't have so much as a scrap of paper for litter. Children played tag with each other, some rushing after parents who called them to their side. As we saw the people come into view, though, laughter rose behind us as we stepped into the cobbled streets.

I turned in time to see the swath of dark browns and blacks heading for the outskirts of the city. For us. The castle rose far above us. We were this close, but it didn't matter how close we were. These people would fall into The Fever if we didn't react.

"Run!" Anza's voice sent people scattering as I prepared to fight, turning my back on the castle, so close but far out of reach. I focused on the pack heading for us, slamming a wall up between us and them. They hesitated for a moment before they parted, like a river around a rock.

"Guys!" I said, splitting the towering wall in half and dropping it on some of the Hazzal. Tamaj and Whisper backed up against me, grabbing at the back of a Hazzal's neck, Tamaj sent one flying. Quickly, I wrapped a thin layer of stone around her legs as Anza drew his sword, cutting Hazzal down. The beasts pulled people down as I pulled up small cobblestones, sending them like arrows through the creatures as fast as I could, trying to stop the carnage.

I heard the sound of a massive door opening and turned to look up. Seeing guards posted upon a tower, I lifted my hands, waving to them, and as they shifted what was likely a telescope to me, I dropped my disguise. I held my gaze on them for a heartbeat before turning and lashing back at the sea of Hazzal, Whisper lashing out at one that tried to go for Tamaj's shoulder. We were overwhelmed. They were everywhere. We were going to die here. We couldn't save the people. We couldn't stop them alone. We had gotten this close to the castle, and we were going to *fail.*

Ice leaped from the ground all around us as a thundering sound took over. Spearing into the sea of Hazzal, thousands of icicles rose thicker than my torso into the sky, skewering the pack members. One moment, everything was chaos. The next, there was eerie calm and the thundering behind me quieted. Anza and Tamaj turned to me but looked past me and quickly bowed. I flinched before turning around. King Olaf Hamilton, my uncle, sat atop a gray-streaked Barbarza, his dark tumble of hair swept back as if he had run his hand through his hair one too many times. Those eyes, as bright as the sky, were soft, kind as he dismounted. I quickly made a mess of a curtsy and he held back a laugh.

"None of that now," he said as he approached, waving at Anza and Tamaj before pulling me into a hug. He smelled of sword polish and peppermint, like a warm winter night in an armory. "Welcome home."

I wrapped my arms around him, burying my head in his shoulder, and sighed, feeling the tension I'd held since Arlo fell fall away from me.

"Finally," I said, and he stepped back, looking me over.

"I thought you had another month and a half before you were supposed to head in here. If I had known you'd be coming early, I would have sent an escort."

"Meh, we figured it out." I shrugged. "Ice?"

"Yeah, have you found yours yet?"

"Rocks. So many rocks." His smirk widened.

"That sounds amazing. I'd like to see what you could do in the sparring ring."

"Maybe once we're not exhausted, huh, Snowset?" Tamaj said, stepping to my side.

"Sunstorm? I didn't recognize you. You're so thin! What happened?"

"That story will take hours, and I swear if I don't get a bath soon —" Olaf lifted both hands as if he could physically ward off her irritation.

"Let's get you all a hot bath and a warm meal, no threats necessary," he said, hiding the laugh in his voice poorly as he looked at Anza and Whisper.

"Oh, these two are my friends as well. Anza here has been with me since the beginning, and we picked up Whisper along the way," I said. Olaf nodded along as I introduced them, reaching a hand to Anza, who shook it, both grabbing at the wrist.

"Thank you for watching over my niece."

"Oh, don't thank me yet. I'm not done," Anza said as they let go.

"I like this one," Olaf said before reaching a hand to Whisper. She took it similarly, but Olaf's face twisted in confusion at what his hand found.

"Should we tell him?" Whisper asked.

"Tell me what?" Olaf asked as he went back to his Barbarza's side.

"Not out here," I said, grabbing the egg bag. Olaf's eyes slid down to the bag before giving a knowing nod and gracefully getting onto his Barbarza mount's back.

"No one was bitten, right?" I looked at each of them, spotting the guards that must have come with Olaf as they helped the surrounding people. Each of my friends shook their heads.

"Miraculously, we're all good."

"Fantastic. It's Mira, right?" Olaf asked as we started walking back toward the castle together.

"Yeah, how did you know that?"

"Oh, I'll tell you all about it once we're inside the castle walls," he said. I nodded, keeping close to Whisper and Tamaj, Anza flanking Tamaj's other side as we padded through the empty streets.

The people must have been scared off by the fighting and Anza's warning. Slowly, they peeked their heads out of windows, watching as we walked through the castle's outskirts, up through the rings of The City of Blood, which were framed in layers of stone.

The first rose around thousands of merchant homes, some of which had closed their shops, ready to flee should they need to. Color and signs lit the place up, marking small wooden stations; some were designated for different vendors, and others were empty, open. We slid past the prying glances and toward the next ring. As we moved past the wall of stone, we saw battalions readying for battle before Olaf waved a hand to them.

"At ease." Relief flashed through them all and they

disbanded, returning to their duties. Finally, we rose past the last section of stone and into the castle grounds. Carefully crafted gardens framed the towering white castle, and light and dark blue flowers framed a balcony facing out toward the main road. Those same blue flowers draped from dozens of planters lining the castle's outside walls. A beautiful, elegant display that set me at ease.

We were finally safe.

We walked right through those massive heavy wooden doors, crafted to depict leaves of ivy and flowers in bloom, and into Castle Bloodthorn.

Like fucking idiots.

27

"Can I finally drop this?" Whisper said as soon as the heavy doors closed behind us. I looked around the space; it was quiet, warm, and comfortable. Home, it was *home*.

"Yeah, fuck it," I said, shrugging as Olaf looked her over, an eyebrow raised. I watched him, seeing the color drain from his face as Whisper dropped her Maraung disguise.

"What? Did one of them hatch?" he asked. "You couldn't have been here for that long! I—"

"Naw, we found her dicking around and stabbing things in Teramor," I said, watching relief wash through those blue eyes.

"I'm great at dicking around and stabbing things," Whisper said, shrugging before dismounting from Tamaj's back.

"Looks like you were in good hands."

"Meh, could have done with more blood on the way, but we're not dead," Whisper said, shrugging. Olaf cracked a smile, his amazement betrayed in those eyes.

"How about you all get a warm bath, a hot meal, and a soft bed?"

"That sounds amazing," Anza said, rubbing his temples.

"Tell me what god I have to fight. I'll fucking grow thumbs," Tamaj said.

"None of them, thankfully." Olaf laughed and gestured upward. I looked up, seeing the wrap-around banister traversing the entire room's perimeter.

Two figures moved quickly, their footsteps nearly silent even in the empty and echoing ballroom. Slowly, two Photomyra appeared, a man and a woman roughly my age. They walked in tandem, in sync with their movements, but their features drastically differed. The man had a well-defined jaw but hid those baby-blue eyes beneath a mess of his hair. Head turned down to watch his feet as he walked. Every inch of his being screamed that he was about to bolt, his orange blossom tucked deep into his hair, almost unnoticeable, arms rigid at his side as he moved with sharp, quick steps.

In sharp contrast, she was effervescent, her head held high, she easily made eye contact with us, every step made clear her magnetic personality. A small, polite smile danced upon her lips as she approached. Her features were sharp, with high cheekbones and a darker shade of green than the man, but only slightly so, and she walked with distinct poise.

"These two are Taryneer," Olaf said, the woman curtsying. "And Grazham." The man bowed. "Will you two please see our friends to the baths and their rooms? They'll need a hot meal brought to them so they can eat in peace."

"Of course. Please, call me Taryn," Taryn said, flashing us a bright smile. Her cohort didn't speak.

"Graz?" Olaf said.

"Right, yeah, I'd be happy to." Anza shifted beside me, but his eyes were locked on Grazham.

"You good?" I asked, and he nodded without looking at me.

"This way," Taryn said. "We have two separate bathing rooms so everyone can feel comfortable. There is nothing enforced so long as no one is hurt. We want you to feel safe wherever you go to bathe," Taryn explained as she started to lead us away.

"Like, for guys and girls?" I asked.

"Oh, no. It's a divided space in case some people prefer more privacy than others."

"I'll head to the other side," Anza said, and I nodded.

"Can I actually hang back and ask you a few questions?" I asked, looking at Olaf. I saw Taryn flash an alarmed look, but Olaf nodded to her. Anza gave me a quick hug.

"Be safe, Stone-Slinger."

"I'm not going to leave the castle. We're safe, Beetle-Brain."

"Safer."

"I will be, I promise." He nodded, looking at my face for a little too long, before slipping after them, Graz standing awkwardly as he waited for Anza.

"What's up?" Olaf asked as soon as they were out of sight, starting to climb one of the stairs toward the throne. I started to follow.

"Well, I have some questions about what is gonna be expected of me and what our plans are for some shit."

"Ah, of course you do," he said as we got to the top of the stairs before leaning on the balcony's railing overlooking the ballroom we had been standing in a moment ago. "Shoot"

"What are we doing about The Fever?"

"We're looking for a cure. We have a few promising options, but none of them have panned out yet. It'll be much faster now, though, if Whisper could focus on it."

"I'm sure she would; she's a bright one," I said.

"Real stabby though," he chuckled.

"You have no idea." I laughed, leaning on the banister with him and looking out at the empty ballroom.

"Any plans on the bandit issue?"

"We're spread pretty thin with The Fever right now. I'm trying to cover the country, but there's only so much we can do until this sickness settles."

"You aren't afraid of Korrewen getting ideas?"

"That's where the majority of the forces are, patrolling the border, making sure they don't."

"You're putting on a strong front."

"So they don't know how close to destruction we are," he said.

"That bad?"

"It's not good," he admitted, wringing his hands together. "I wasn't built for this."

"Fucking ditto," I said, and we laughed together. "What about my parents?"

He frowned, not looking at me, staring out at the double doors of the castle instead.

"Sorry, kiddo. They went out for a small mission together. They always had each other's backs. It wasn't supposed to be anything difficult; one day, in and out, but they came back in caskets."

"Damn, at least I've got you."

"Believe me, I'm not all I'm cracked up to be," he said, sarcasm dripping from him. We laughed together before he said, "I have a few questions for you, if you're up for them?"

"Hit me."

"Where's Arlo?" My stomach dropped, and I turned my eyes to my shoes.

"Hazzal, in the south wood." Silence stretched out, and I glanced up at him as he blinked tears away.

"He was a good friend."

"Yeah, he was. He died trying to save me."

"Well, he obviously succeeded."

"Yeah, my axe is his bone."

"Good, good."

"You did say questions, plural."

"One more, but I don't know if I should ask."

"I'm not gonna kill ya."

He smirked, breathing to steady himself.

"I wanted to ask you if I could declare you my heir. I have no children or partners, and I think under the right guidance.

Considering you made it here, you might be twice the leader I am."

"We were figuring you'd ask. Yeah, I can do that," Why had I said that? Could I actually do this? What if I fucked it up? I was totally going to fuck this up. "Wait, what do you mean, considering I made it? It almost sounds like you knew I was on my way."

"I didn't know it was you, but talk of a walking Mountain has made it to the castle."

"Yeah, that's the code name I chose."

"The Mountain, it's even better considering you're so damn short."

"Hey, I'm not short!" I said, reaching out to punch his shoulder. His slight smile widened into a grin.

"You certainly are. In fact, you might be the shortest Endering I've ever seen."

"You know I could probably bring this castle down, right?"

"Ahh, but would you? That'd be messy."

"I'm literally covered in weeks worth of blood and dirt; messy is kind of my thing right now."

"Not to mention that you smell terrible. Go on, I think I see Taryn waiting for you," he said, gesturing to an alcove where Taryn was patiently waiting, quieter than a mouse.

"Yeah, yeah, see you in the morning for that sparring match?"

"Bright and early, and be ready to get your ass handed to you!" he called after me.

"We'll see," I called back, smirking as I got to Taryn. She gave me a small curtsy before leading me down the hallway.

"Hey, you don't have to rush. You won't get in trouble if I'm late to the bath, right?" I asked.

"Well, no," she said, slowing her steps.

"Is Anza going to be alright? Your friend took him to the other side, right?"

"He did, and he will be. Graz isn't much of a fighter, quiet and reserved, at least until he gets to know you're safe to be around."

"So your friend isn't going to poison, or stab, or—"

"Oh no, no, the trouble we'd get in, even if we wanted to, it wouldn't be worth it," she assured me as we walked together.

"And you don't want to? Olaf treats you well?"

"Oh no, of course not. Olaf has been nothing but kind to us. Graz lost his parents when he was quite young. I did too. We met when we found employment here in the castle. Living here and working here is amazing; I don't think I'd ever want to leave," she said as she led me through an arch that acted as a doorway into a large bathing room. There were dozens of baths on the floor, curtains keeping them separate. Two were pulled closed.

"Sound off," I called.

"*I'm fine,*" Tamaj said.

"I'm clearly drowning, so much drowning," Whisper said, splashing in her bath, sarcasm dripping from every word.

"Can you fight the bath water?"

"I can try," Whisper said as I moved to an empty bath.

Taryn walked with me, showing me where the hot and cold water was and how to turn the water on before slipping away to stand near the door, her back to us. I pulled the curtain around, the only sounds Tamaj's soft sighs of contentment and Whisper playing in the water. I drew a hot bath, undressed, and sank into the water. Starting to wash away the dirt and grime from my skin. I scrubbed my hair with the provided soaps, unbraiding it and trying to get my tangle of curls together.

Once I got clean, I settled into the still-hot water and closed my eyes, my body aching as I lay there, reflecting on how far we had come. Once the tension in my muscles had eased enough that I could breathe comfortably again, I reached for my clothes and found that they had been replaced with clean clothes, but my bags were still there, including the egg bag. I dressed in clean pajamas and pulled my bags close, stepping out from behind my curtain as the bath drained.

"Wow…" I turned, seeing Tamaj standing there with Whisper, both of whom looked clean, and Whisper had a clean pair of pajamas on.

"What?" I asked. "Did I miss a spot?"

"You certainly didn't."

"Anza's gonna lose his shit."

"Oh hush, you two," I said, slipping my bags back on and heading toward the hallway again. I watched as Anza spoke to Graz, dressed in his own clean clothes, blood and dirt gone from his body. He was engaged in conversation and Graz had lifted his head a little, looking a little more relaxed, hands wrapping around his elbows, his crossed arms lax until I walked up.

He tensed, looking down and away, giving the slightest little hop that barely passed as a bow. I waved it away, the bowing and curtseying was already starting to feel weird. Anza turned to see what he was looking at and froze.

"Oh my god, what?" I asked, watching his mouth open a little, eyes wide as he took me in.

"Oh, um, I, nothing. You're-your hair is a little tangled," he said, stepping forward and reaching out. I closed my eyes, staying still as he gently worked through the tangles with his fingers, braiding it back again.

"Hey, Graz," I said as he got near the end of my tangles and the braid.

"Yes, Your Majesty?"

"I'm not going to beat you to death. You either, Taryn; breathe. You don't have to hide or put on a show. You're safe," I said, stealing a peak at Graz. His taut form slowly relaxed.

"Really?"

"Really, really. Don't worry about being overly formal with me, you don't have to bow or any of that shit."

"Sorry," Taryn started. "Sometimes some people can be—"

"Well, I'm not them, and if they want to be assholes, I will beat their asses. You're helping us, right?" I asked as Anza finished with my hair. Ignoring the sparking in my chest.

"Right," Graz confirmed.

"We've got you, right guys?" I asked, looking back at my friends.

"No matter what," Anza said, giving Graz a measured glance. He gave a small, sad smile in return.

"If we're gonna trust you to not murder us in our sleep, I think you can trust us to not murder you too," Whisper said.

She has a point, Tamaj followed up.

"Good," Taryn said in a hushed voice, the two simultaneously letting out a ragged sigh.

"It's been a while since we could be near people we can breathe near" Graz said, his voice cracking as he spoke, my uncle did seem ask a lot of them, especially if they didn't think they had the space to breathe. I needed to talk to him about that in the future.

"Let's get you guys to bed. I'm sure you're exhausted. I had the kitchen whip you up a meal, you'll find them in your rooms, ready to eat," Taryn said, gesturing for us to follow. Her shoulders had worn tension well, but now they were a little more relaxed, but only a little.

We followed her up a set of stairs and down a long hallway to the left. She stopped, gesturing toward a door. "This room was set aside for them," she said, gesturing to the egg bag at my side. I reached out and opened the door.

Inside was a simple nursery with a changing table and two bassinets. My heart dropped, grabbing the egg bag tightly as I struggled to breathe. A hand rested on my elbow and I turned to look at Anza standing there beside me. We had come all this way. The egg bag had been an extension of me, it was part of me now, but we were here. We were here.

"It's okay. They'll be alright; this is what we came here for," he said.

"Your room is right next to theirs," Taryn said. "You can see them whenever you want." I took a steadying breath and unzipped the bag, carefully resting each egg in its own little bassinet. It took a few deep breaths, and I still couldn't let go of their bassinet. I had protected and defended these two little lives with my own life, the lives of my friends, and now they were safe. They were finally in a home they could thrive in, finally in a place where they wouldn't be hunted for their hearts. Finally home.

"Whenever I want?" I asked without looking up from them.

"Whenever you want," she assured me.

"I can even sleep in here?" I heard her shifting where she stood and Anza slightly tensed beside me.

"No one would dare to stop you," Graz said.

"Damn straight they wouldn't," I said, running my fingers over each of them before taking a deep breath, sighing, and turning toward the door. "You said my room is right next door?"

"Ah, yes," Taryn started. "We've grouped your rooms near to one another, so you don't feel so far away."

"When people come in from even small quests, they're always uneasy." Graz's voice stayed quiet, and even as he spoke, he wouldn't look at me. His eyes darted along walls and the floor but never in my direction, shoulders still tucked in. I had a sneaking suspicion if I raised my voice, he might flinch. I didn't raise my voice.

"That's really thoughtful of you two," Anza assured.

Tamaj grumbled as Whisper patted her back with both hands.

"Aw, it's nothing," Taryn assured, gesturing to the next room. "As promised, right beside theirs."

I reached for the handle, looking back as Graz showed Anza to his room across the hall. He opened his door and left it open, Graz lingering in the hallway. I opened the door and stepped into the room, also leaving it open. I heard Taryn introducing Tamaj and Whisper to their rooms.

The room was cozy but not too small, with a single full-sized bed made of down and cotton-like material. Thick furs draped over the back of the bed, ready to be used. A small table and an even smaller wash table sat beside a prepared water jug, and a desk sat not too far from it. Underneath the bed, there were four drawers, empty and unused. A rug covered two-thirds of the floor, a simple pattern woven in greens and blues. I set my bag down at the end of the bed as I heard Taryn encourage Graz to leave us to it. A plate sat on the table, still hot from the kitchen.

"Wanna eat with The Two?" I looked up, seeing Whisper in my doorway.

"That sounds good; you don't wanna hang out in your room?"

"Naw, not right now; it feels lonely," she said as I dropped the now-empty egg bag on my bed and picked up my plate. "Tamaj and Anza are gonna eat in there too."

"Awesome, let's go," I said, putting my axe on the bed before following her to the nursery. Tamaj was already tucked into a large bowl of food, neatly gobbling up whatever it was, Anza sitting beside her, her tail wrapped around his back. I sat beside him, and Tamaj adjusted her tail, trying to include me in what served as a loose group hug.

"We did it," I said, tucking into my food as I looked at the bassinets.

"We sure did," Anza said before Whisper spoke, settling in on my lap.

"I never doubted us for a second."

28

"Get up!" I groaned and rolled over, pulling a pillow onto my head as Whisper shook me.

"What?"

"Get up," she growled, and I buried my head further under my pillow. "Mother!" she declared, climbing into bed before trying to pull me up by the arm.

"Oh no, my whole body, it's suddenly completely useless."

"Mira!"

"Totally limp."

"Tamaj has been talking about this library so much!"

"I can't...seem to find the will to get up."

"Ugh!" With one firm pull, she pulled me to the floor, trying to pull my blankets off me.

"Fine, fine, I'm awake, but food first."

"What? No!"

"Hey, do you know where this library is?"

"No..."

"Me either, and we'll probably find Tamaj where?"

"At breakfast."

"So, where are we going?"

"To get food first. I hate that you're right."

"Meh, hate it or not, I'm still right." I rubbed my eyes, untangling myself from the rest of the blanket. Seeing my axe propped against the desk, I hesitated before deciding I didn't need it. There was an entire metric shit-ton of soldiers in the second ring; we were okay. Whisper took my hand, quickly leading me out of the bedroom, down the stairs, and toward the ballroom.

As we descended the last few steps, I realized the ballroom had been turned into a dining hall for now. A few soldiers sat at different tables, chatting amongst themselves. Eyes flashed toward me and heat rushed to my face. I was still in my pajamas.

"Mira!" Anza's voice cut through the swelling embarrassment as I followed Whisper across the room toward Anza and Tamaj.

"Morning."

"You alright?" Anza asked.

"Yeah, I should have changed out of my pajamas first," I said.

"What are they gonna do that matters?" Anza asked. "You've literally dodged dragons and Nazzir; they probably can't say the same."

"Yeah, doesn't seem princess-like to me."

"You define what a princess is like," Tamaj said. *"Did he talk to you about that last night?"*

"Yeah," I said as a servant brought over a plate for me.

"Your Highness?" she asked, curtsying at me.

"Yeah?" I asked, waving her out of the curtsy with one hand. It was still weird, so many people bowing and curtsying.

"His Royal Highness has asked me to inform you and your friends of a feast he has arranged tonight for the people of Agrenon to come and bear witness to you formally becoming his heir. Taryn and Graz will assist you and your friends with preparations for the event."

"So fast?" I asked, and she nodded. "Formally?"

"He wants to make it an event, with a feast, to mark such a joyous occasion,"

"Great so there are going to be people there, like, lots of people,"

"I would hope so,"

"Sweet, awesome, I'm just going to go to my room and die," I said burying my head in my hands. I could almost hear the smirk in her voice as she spoke again.

"He is going to meet you in the sparring ring once you're ready for the day. He will tackle questions you may have."

"Awesome, thank you." I lifted my head as she nodded deeply, turning to leave, her billowing green skirt twirling as she started to sashay away. "Wait." She stopped.

"I didn't get your name."

"Oh, Naren," she said, tension in her shoulders as she turned back to me to answer.

"Thank you, Naren." A smile bloomed across her face and she gracefully curtsied again before gliding from the room. I tucked into the meal, listening to Anza and Whisper bicker about what to do today.

"Mira should go spar with the king."

"And I want to go to the library."

"He's the king."

"Only because he said so, I declare I'm a god. Am I a god now?"

"Whisper—"

"*Hush, you two,*" Tamaj said. "*We don't have to all go do one thing. I'll take Whisper to the library, and you and Mira head to the sparring ring,*" Tamaj suggested.

"You'll keep her safe?" Anza asked.

"*Of course, I will,*" Tamaj said.

"Alright," I said around some eggs I'd been given, swallowing before continuing. "We'll have Taryn show us the library after we're done sparring. Meet there?"

"Sounds like a plan," Whisper agreed, bouncing happily as Tamaj stood and scrambled to her feet. "This is gonna be so cool."

"Be careful," I said, watching Whisper dart between Tamaj's legs as she led her toward a staircase beneath the throne space. We finished eating quickly and went back upstairs and dressed before returning to the makeshift dining room. I expected to see Taryn or Graz waiting for us, but Olaf was there, waiting for us himself.

"Hey, shithead," I said, smirking as we approached.

"Oh, hello fuck face, we're doing affectionate name-calling now, are we? Well, you little fucker, let's see if you can live up to the name 'The Mountain of Agrenon'," he said, warmth and joy dancing in his eyes as he waved for us to follow him. Anza hung back, looking more confused with every word we spoke.

"Oh, I assure you, I live up to the hype."

"The self-declared and self-established hype. Oh yes, I totally believe that." Dripping with sarcasm, he led us through a set of double doors and down a long hallway lined with paintings of past kings and queens. I lingered on the painting closest to the door. A pretty Photomyran woman with bright green leaves, a kind face, striking eyes, and a harsh scar up the side of her face. Confidently poised, her deep sunset-orange bloom is on the opposite side of her badly scarred left cheek.

"Hey, cunt?"

"Yes, bitch?" I couldn't help but smirk at how effortless it was to relax into this back and forth.

"This was Saha, right?" He stopped, looking back at us.

"Yeah, that was her."

"What was she like?" I asked Olaf as I bounced forward to his side, Anza hanging behind us quietly.

"She was…" He sighed deeply before speaking again as he led me down the hall. "Stunning, vibrant, and so smart. She had her flaws, of course, everyone does, but she was an amazing queen." I heard Anza shift behind me a little and looked back to him, watching him look Olaf over, still confused. "Here we are."

I turned back around as I heard Olaf reach a second set of doors and fling them open. My breath caught in my throat. All thoughts vanished as I stepped into the sandy pit. A large green-house surrounded the massive training area shaped like a geodesic dome. Outside the transparent dome, plantain trees and other beautiful foliage rose, tucked into another, more enormous, secondary geodesic dome. Carefully placed between the trees in the secondary dome were seats resembling old wooden bleachers, a few were beaten up with burn stains and slashes, but most were crafted of well-made wood.

"I'm gonna sit over here out of the way," Anza said, pulling me into a soft hug. I hugged him back, drinking in his smell for a moment, that sparking getting louder before I pulled away.

"He's about to kick my ass, isn't he?"

"Eh, probably…be careful?"

"Careful is my middle name."

"I don't know your middle name, but 'careful' definitely isn't it," he laughed.

"I'll be careful," I said, smiling as he nodded and stepped toward the entrance to the bleachers. I turned to Olaf, waiting for me in the middle of the room.

"This place is pretty snazzy," I said as I approached.

"It was designed and imbued with magic to give us Endering a place to let loose without blowing up the castle. Both those domes are reinforced with magic."

"So I can throw rocks at them," I said, smiling wider at the thought of having a safe place to really test my powers.

"And they probably won't break."

"That's fucking awesome," I said as he walked a half circle around me. It wasn't until shards of ice danced across my feet that I remembered we were here to spar. I shook them off, sliding into a defensive position as he smirked, quickly slipping into a familiar stance. He advanced. I instinctively reached out for rocks beneath me, only to find none. We were standing on the sand. I dodged to the side as a spike of ice blasted past me.

"Oh, come now, you didn't start relying completely on your power as soon as it manifested, did you?"

"Naw," I said, trying to focus. The warmth was there, but he was already rushing me. I danced backward, dodging a flurry of blows as I tried to pull that warmth forward. It was there, but it was so fragile. The rocks were too small. They were small. I dropped my stance, throwing all of my focus into the sand.

"You should know better than to—" His voice cut off as I summoned the sand up and around his form, crashing in on him from all angles like a wave.

"Come on, it's everywhere!" I heard the onslaught of sand as I whirled it around him, feeling ice dart up my leg. I pulled the sand back as my vision froze over a sheet of ice, settling like goggles over my eyes.

"Hey!"

"Oh, come on, you weren't playing fair. I've got sand in my britches."

"You did not say 'britches'," I teased, pulling at the ice to get it off my eyes only to find him shaking the sand out of his hair.

"I did. What are you gonna do, call me old?"

"Try this on for size, you *old* fart!" I said, pulling another wave of sand up, focusing hard as I tried to sweep him off his feet. Adjusting my stance, my foot slipped. He had formed ice beneath me as I hit him and I didn't even know. Before I knew it, we were both on the ground. I struggled to get up, Olaf's laugh filling the space.

"What's so funny?"

"You are!" he said, still trying to dig himself from my swath of sand. His head and the ends of his limbs were the only things poking out. "Let me up?"

"Never!" I said, slipping again as I tried to stand, the ice beneath me bringing me to my knees as Olaf finally found enough of a foothold to break free from my sandy trap.

"Alas, it looks like ice wins," he laughed, reaching a hand for me.

As I took his hand, I knew the sparring match was over. It had been for good fun, but there was no way he had shown me everything. In fact, as he pulled me to my feet, knowing that if the display he had delivered when he came to help us was anything, he was holding back a considerable amount. While I'd been there giving it my all. He could ruin me if he wanted to, but he pulled me to my feet, the ice beneath me melting as quickly as it had formed.

"We have a feast to tend to later, and I'm sure you have things you want to do before Taryn steals you to get ready," he said.

"Yeah, Whisper really talked up that library, so I better look at what we're working with," I said, glancing up at Anza where he had sat, now standing, worry painting his gaze.

"You're going to love that library, it's beautiful and full of information. Whisper has to be buried beneath books by now."

"Yeah, she's a pretty big nerd," I said as he led us back toward the entrance to the training area. "Why did you really stop the match? Did you think I was going to beat you or something?"

He tossed his head back, laughing before ruffling my hair and waving Anza toward us.

"Oh sweet, sweet, summer child, you wouldn't stand a chance yet, but we can change that in time. Honestly, I was more worried about the people finding a bruised princess."

He said princess.

"Yeah, that'd make you look pretty bad," Anza said as he approached.

"It'd be bad for everyone, so let's not get to that point," Olaf said, leading us to the door together.

"Oh yeah, a believable cover for not wanting to get your ass beat."

"Oh yes, of course, you're terrifying. I was shaking in my boots out there," he said, rolling his eyes as we laughed, heading back to the ballroom.

29

"You had him."

"Because I'm amazing," I said, flipping my hair, watching Anza's cheeks darken from the corner of my eye as we got to the main room.

"The library's that way," Olaf said, pointing to the staircase that wove out of sight below the throne.

"Hey, I'll beat your ass tomorrow," I said, firing finger guns at Olaf as I moved toward the staircase.

"Challenge accepted!" Olaf called after me as Anza and I slid into the winding staircase, moving down and down and down.

"He's pretty nice."

"Yeah, it's good to have someone who can match my me-ness."

"For sure. Being able to flip someone off as you beat their asses in tandem would be amazing." He laughed.

"Yeah, hopefully we kick some metaphorical infected ass, get the bandits out of here, and bring Agrenon back to a better place."

"Hopefully."

"Hey, I didn't get to ask you something," I said, feeling the lightheartedness of the previous sparring match begin to wane.

"What is it?" he asked as we stopped in the darkened stairway together at the same time.

"Our deal was that you would get me here, and don't get me wrong, I want you to stay, but I want you to…want to, I guess? I don't want to hold you back from doing something else if you thought up other plans and—" A finger found my lips and I let the sentence die in my throat.

"I'm not going anywhere." I found his eyes in the darkness and he found mine. Sparking.

"Yeah?" I said as he pulled his hand away from my face.

"Yeah."

"G-good," I said, feeling my face growing hot as he lingered for another moment before starting to lead the way back down the stairs toward the library at its base. "Guess who's here?" I asked as we rounded yet another bookshelf, finally spotting Whisper at the end of the massive stack of books.

The library more than lived up to the hype. The rows of books stretched on beyond sight, the intricately designed shelves rising repeatedly, each stuffed with well-managed, clean, and efficiently kept books. I could tell there was some order to them, but I did not recognize the order. Tables were settled between the widely set shelves, giving people plenty of places to sit and read.

Whisper popped her head out of the book she was reading, settled in a haphazardly arranged nest of books piled around her on the table and adjacent seats. Tamaj sat closer to us, quietly reading an open book, but looked up as we walked in.

"Mira, Anza!" Whisper yelled getting up and running to us. I scooped up her heavy form, drawing her close and hugging her tightly.

"Huh, almost like we didn't see you at breakfast this morning," Anza said, ruffling her hair.

"Well, I missed you already." She pulled away from the hug and reached out to him. He carefully took her from me, holding her propped on one arm.

"Well, will you tell me what you've been reading?" he asked.

"Oh yeah, for sure!" she said. "So far, it's a book of legends right now, lots of cool stuff in it…"

I wandered over to Tamaj as they spoke to each other.

"How are you doing?" she asked. *"Get your butt handed to you?"*

"Completely and utterly." She laughed as I spoke, finding a place between books to sit down. "He didn't want to beat me up too bad."

"Good call, honestly."

"It's weird. He called me Princess."

"Well, you are a princess, so get used to it, Princess," Tamaj said, nudging me with her snout.

"Great, I'll try," I said, nudging her back before I looked up at the shelves that surrounded us, what must have been a history section, and the rows and rows of books I could see from this seat. Whisper was in her element. Just sitting with access to this library, she suddenly became the most dangerous being in Agrenon, maybe in even all five kingdoms. I listened to her stories, stories of a home I had barely known, stories of a world I didn't get to see, for a few hours, thankful that the worlds were separate before Tamaj spoke again.

"It's getting a little late. If we don't go start getting ready, Olaf might come looking for us."

"You're not wrong," Whisper grumbled and put a bookmark into the book she was reading. Carefully, we got up together. "No one's gonna touch all this?" she asked Tamaj.

"No one would dare," Tamaj said before leading the way up the stairs and back to the ballroom.

"There you are!" Olaf said. Taryn and Graz were not far from him. "I was about to ask these two to come and fetch you."

"We're masters of timing," I said.

"Yeah, bad timing," Whisper said.

"No, no, it's perfect timing to get ready for tonight. Taryn will take special care of you, Mira. Graz will ensure that the rest of you are dressed properly and ready to mingle with the people."

"This is gonna be stuffy, isn't it?" Whisper grumbled.

"Probably at least a little," Olaf said as Taryn reached a hand for me. My face flushed, her bright eyes glancing to meet my own. I gently took her hand.

"We won't be terribly long," she said.

"Hey," Anza said, and I turned to him to feel his hands wrap around me, gently hugging me.

"You've got this." I wasn't sure if it was the beautiful Photo-myran woman standing before me, Anza, the fact that I was about to accept a royal title, or the idea of dealing with a bunch of people, but between those options, I hadn't noticed how much tension was in my body. At his hug, it melted away.

"Of course I do. I've got you." He pulled back, gently brushing a hair out of my face as he smiled.

"I'll be waiting down here when you're ready."

"Alright, Beetle-Brain, see you soon."

"You too, Stone-Slinger. You too."

I let Taryn lead me away and back upstairs, past the bedrooms, and toward a room at the end of the hallway. I stepped into the room and the doors closed behind me and the dread and fear crept in. I was in danger for a moment, surrounded by so many pieces of fabric. I was in a new room with someone I barely knew. I took a few deep breaths, trying not to think of the times we were stuck finding the caves we had stayed in for shelter. This room looked nothing like a cave and we were far from getting frostbite. Rows of racks stood with dresses and what seemed to pass as a version of a suit in damn near every inch of the place. I was alone with a beautiful woman I didn't know, and there were dresses fucking everywhere.

"Hey, are you alright?"

"Wh-why wouldn't I be alright?"

"Well, for starters, all the color drained from your face."

"Great, awesome, love it," I said.

"Overwhelmed?"

"Very."

Her laugh was like a first snowfall; warm in a way you didn't expect snow to be.

"Well, you have to choose one. It's your choice, one huge day for a princess."

"I don't want to look like...a pile of flashy vomit." I grumbled as I started to pick through the dresses, bright and vibrant and glorious as they hung from their places. Some were too large for me, others too small and dainty. Some were clearly for children, and by the time I got to the second rack of dresses, I was confident that I would have a headache by the time I was done.

"Weird question?"

"Weirder answer?" I couldn't help but smirk as I met her eyes again.

"Help? I don't know what I'm doing and you look like you've got your shit together."

"Aww, what a wonderful compliment. I assure you I don't," she said.

"But seriously, I don't know what I'm doing, and I want to make a fantastic first impression."

"Do you trust me?"

"Eh, fifty-fifty?" I said as she extended her hand to me again, eyes bright.

"I can work with that."

I took her hand and let her lead me into the mass of dresses. It wasn't long before she left me standing in the middle of the room, returning a few moments later with an armful of dresses. She stepped back away from me, holding each up before picking up a gray dress with dappled diamond patterns in different hues of gray that faded as they reached the waste. She set it aside on an empty rack and pulled up a chair for me. "Sit down for me?"

"I'm trusting you with a lot right now," I said, sitting down, my back to her as she played with my hair.

"Believe me, I know. I've got you. Breathe. We can do this."

"We can do this."

There was one mirror turned away from us so I couldn't

watch her as she worked, carefully playing with my hair, different products coming out at different times. She let me move my head about before wrapping my hair in a tight towel. I had no idea what the vision was, but she helped me slip out of my clothes, feeling far too vulnerable as I stood there naked, but it was only for a moment before she helped me into the dress.

I expected to feel weird in it. I hadn't worn a dress before, but it was flowy, comfortable, and rested well against my form. Almost like it was made for me. My shoulder itched a little as Taryn situated it and I reached up to satisfy the feeling, spotting a tiny letter stitched into the inside of the cap sleeve. A small *E* stared back at me, and I couldn't help but smirk as I ran my fingers over the flowy dress. It went past my knees, making it perfect for spinning and dancing in; it was gorgeous, but it wasn't until Taryn settled a necklace of dark stones on my neck, paired with earrings, that I realized what was about to happen. She spun the mirror around to face us and took down my hair.

"Well, what do you think?" Taryn asked.

Upon taking one look at the girl looking back at me, I knew one thing for sure: I was gonna make Anza shit his pants.

30

"Breathe, breathe."

"Is it weird that I'm nervous?" I asked Taryn as she escorted me back out of the room and down the hall toward the stairs again.

"No, not at all. People can be so aggravating to deal with. Be on your best behavior and you'll be fine. You're second in command; *they* need to be polite to *you*," she reminded me as I stopped in front of the door to the nursery, slipping in quickly.

"I'm not worried about people," I said as she slipped behind me, quietly waiting by the door as I moved between The Two. Neither of them had hatched yet and still rested snugly in their blanketed bassinets.

"He's going to be a tremble-vine watching you walk down those stairs." My face flushed again, turning to look at her.

"You think?"

"Yes. A million times, yes."

"But what if that's a bad thing? What if he reacts badly?"

"You'll know if he's a real friend or not. Mira, if he doesn't look at you like you're literally the sun, he's not worth the time of day."

"We're talking about...like, *friends*, right?"

239

"Right." Taryn didn't miss a beat, keeping up.

"But if he doesn't, it might make him distant. I'm already worried about him maybe leaving, what happens if he does?"

"You go on thrilling, wonderful, vibrant, exciting adventures without him. Sure, at first it'd suck, but you are your own person, with or without those that stand by your side. Some people stand with you that you don't even know."

"How did you get so wise?" I asked as she moved to my side.

She pulled me away from the eggs and close to her, my face growing hotter as she tucked me into her side, my face an inch from hers.

"People are all a little deeper, smarter, and stronger than they seem; I am not an exception." I could feel my heartbeat in my damn eyes as she took my hand and dragged me to the nursery door.

I closed it behind me as she led me toward the main room, curtsying deeply to me before pointing down the stairs at the three standing at the bottom. "Don't fall."

With that, she walked away as I turned to look at Whisper, Tamaj, and Anza. They were whispering with one another and hadn't noticed me yet. Whisper was in a pretty blue dress that rivaled her blue-gray moonlight color. Tamaj's mane was brushed out and woven with tiny flowers. Anza stood in a sleek dark pair of pants and a long-sleeved white shirt that buttoned on one side, a matching coat draped over the back of his shoulders. I took a steadying breath, hoped I wasn't too red, and centered myself on the staircase, carefully descending toward my friends.

"I don't believe in goddesses, but whoa," Whisper said. "Helloooo."

I couldn't help but laugh at her reaction as she turned to me. Anza turned after hearing her and froze in place. I prayed the flats I was wearing didn't slip out from my feet, that my dress didn't get caught, and that catastrophe didn't strike as the only part of him that moved was his eyes as I descended to the main floor.

"Someones been reading too many books," I said to Whisper.

"There is no such thing as too many books," Whisper said.

"You look fabulous, Mira," Tamaj said, padding forward to give me a gentle hug. My curls tumbled around as she moved them.

"Aww, thanks. You guys look amazing too," I said, moving to hug Whisper, who hugged the bottom of my dress and my legs. "Anza?"

"Hmm?"

"Hi."

"What?" Tamaj and Whisper laughed as I stepped forward to hug him, the sparking brighter than usual, but it died as I pulled back.

"You look great."

"You don't look so bad yourself," I said, hearing movement behind me. Graz, Taryn, and Naren were moving about, helping many other servants to get the space ready. Still, the movement I heard was my uncle, wearing a suit similar to Anza's, woven with accents of light blue along the hems.

"Whoa, kiddo, look at you."

"Do I look like I'm at least half a princess?"

"You look like all you need is a crown," he said. "Come on, we're about set up. Let's greet some fancy assholes."

I couldn't help but laugh, hugging Anza again before following him to the front door. I tried to be as graceful as I could, trying to embody the way Taryn walked as I met dozens and dozens of people and their families. It passed like a blur and I almost immediately forgot their names, different species inter-mingling there in front of me. Some couples were both men, some both women, others were a man and woman, some didn't present with a gender at all.

Some came with their older children, talking about them inheriting something essential and being delighted to work with me. Someone asked me if courtship had started and Olaf chastised them, sending them scurrying inside. Before I knew it, we were settling at the head of a table, Olaf on my right, at the head of the main table. Across from me, Anza sat, eyes bright, with Whisper to his side, Tamaj beside her.

"You alright?" I asked him.

"Yeah, keeping close to the little moonbeam."

"There are a lot of people here. Sorry if it's a little—"

"Much. Don't worry about it. Olaf is right, you know."

"About what?"

"All you need is a crown."

I smirked as a Maraung, older, with more scars than I could count, settled in his place at my left.

"How are you fairing, Mountain?" he asked, and my brain scrambled for his name. He must have seen the panic on my face. "You haven't met me yet." He laughed as my shoulders sagged with relief.

"Oh, I'm doing the best I can. Please, it's Mira," I said, extending my hand to him.

"Titanys," he said. "Military advisor to your uncle."

"He put you beside me on purpose, didn't he?"

"I would if I were him," he said. "I won't let anyone bother you. Enjoy your special day."

"Thanks, Titanys."

"No problem at all."

"*What in the stars do you think you're doing, T, trying to get out of your pet names?*" Tamaj said, snorting, a smugness glittering in her eyes.

"Oh no, not you." 'T' laughed as plates were served. "You haven't diffused any magical bombs or frozen over the sun in the last few years, have ya?"

"*Oh yes, it's me,*" Tamaj said. "*Meh, haven't really felt the need to in my bones.*"

I turned my attention to the food, tucking into the delicious meal of roast bird. I ate quickly, knowing I needed to be available soon. Making sure not to get any food on my dress, face, or hands was a difficult feat. We ate, Anza helping Whisper with her food while Tamaj and Titanys bantered. I sat, trying to relax, catching Taryn and Graz glancing at me from afar as I ate and letting the moment settle in.

"How are you feeling about this?" Olaf asked from his place at the table. His eyes didn't watch me but wandered about the room. I followed his gaze, seeing the king's guard posted around the room, hidden behind the shadows of the columns to stay out of sight.

"Nervous, but excited. I came through the portal thinking about bowing to a queen. I never thought I would stand as a princess."

"You've got this. You were a natural with all those stuffy people."

"What was their deal, anyway?"

"Gotta get on the good side of the future Queen of Agrenon; flattery is an easy way to do that."

"So that guy that asked about courting?"

"Really fucked up," he said, a smirk coming to his face.

"Right. Remind me of who he is again if we see him?"

"Will do, but I already threw him out. People who act inappropriately toward you won't be tolerated. Why? What were you going to do?"

"Treat him…appropriately," I said, flashing a devilish grin.

Olaf chuckled, glancing at me as he scanned the room.

"No killing people."

"I didn't say anything about killing, and you didn't say anything about maiming," I clarified.

"Stars save me."

"The stars aren't out right now." I popped the last of my meal in my mouth, trying to hide my smile. He rolled his eyes, finishing his own meal. I glanced around again, seeing that most of the guests had also cleared their plates. Olaf rose, lifting a glass and gently tapping on it with a piece of silverware. The ballroom-turned-dining-hall went silent, the conversations dying in the throats of those having them.

"Tonight is a night I've hoped for, wished for, for nearly two decades. Everyone here knows this old dog isn't exactly the best with the ladies," he started, his voice projecting around the room with grace, bouncing off the walls. Laughter spattered across the room. However, they were trying to stay quiet. "Thankfully, I don't have to be because my niece has finally come home for the first time!" Subdued applause sounded as I watched him from my seat, glass held high, shoulders back, chin lifted. He was proud. Proud to call me family. He was proud to do what he was about to do. "It is an honor to welcome the Mountain of Agrenon, Mira Hamilton, to our beautiful halls. It is an even higher honor to announce that such an intelligent, strategic, wise, and capable woman has agreed to be my heir, so please join me in welcoming Princess Mira Hamilton, The Mountain of Agrenon!" Applause erupted in the room as Olaf gestured for me to stand, Taryn stepping close with a tiara resting on a small pillow. Olaf lifted it as I kneeled and gently nestled it into my well-crafted curls before leaning in close to my ear.

"There's that crown," he said, before he stood fully, gesturing for me to stand up.

I stood, turning to wave at the still-seated people in the room as they applauded, a few whooping out with joy. I tried to imagine how hard it must have been, being in charge of a kingdom without an heir for so long. Different nations had probably tested Agrenon's boundaries. They had probably tried to overthrow the beautiful place I loved and lovingly hate. How hard had it been defending such a beautiful place from bandits, The Fever, and regular attempts at an overthrow? How many assassination attempts had he endured and survived? I pushed all this out of my mind as people got up from their seats, servants quickly stealing away plates, tables, and chairs as the dining hall transitioned to an open ballroom once more.

"Come," Olaf said, holding his arm out to me. I glanced at

Anza; that dazed and star-struck look hadn't left him since I walked down those stairs.

"I'll be back in a bit," I promised, linking my arm to my uncle's and letting him lead me up the stairs to the throne space. A throne space that now had two chairs, a large one centered and a smaller one off to the right. Carefully, we settled in our respective seats.

"That was awesome," I said.

"An awesome moment for an awesome day," he said. "How was Titanys?"

"He was fine. He and Tamaj talked a lot. Why?"

"Eh, no real reason. He's up there in age and I wanted to make sure he didn't say anything strange."

"Strange how?"

"He has his...opinions on how things should be run, and though I trust his military advice, he worked closely with Saha before she passed, so he's a bit set in the old ways."

"Ah, gotcha. Yeah, he badgered Tamaj a lot; something about a magic bomb?"

Olaf chuckled.

"You know about the magic bomb?"

"That's a story for a different day," he said, gesturing to a small band that had finally set up.

"Can I dance then? I got all dressed up, it would be a shame for this fantastic look to go to waste."

"Eh, I don't know; we did paint a target on your back, making you my heir and all."

"But we're here with people. You know these people, right?"

"Yes...I suppose it wouldn't hurt. If anything bad happens though, either use your power safely so no one innocent gets hurt, or get a guard, alright?"

"Deal," I said, standing up. I gave him what was probably the most haphazard curtsy of my life before I moved back toward the stairs.

31

I stuck to the side of the dance floor, trying to find Anza, Tamaj, or Whisper in the crowd. I didn't think it'd be challenging, but there were more Barbarza than I expected. Finally, I spotted them and Tamaj nudged Anza in my direction. He looked at me, face flushed, eyes wide. I raised an eyebrow as Whisper said something to him, and he retorted with something before starting in my direction. Whisper had always been a girl of intellect, but she crossed her fingers as she watched him approach me.

"Hey…"

"Hi, what was all that about?" I asked.

"Oh, I just-she just-they just-ugh…" I couldn't help but laugh.

"Spit it out."

"I wanna ask you a question, but I don't know if I can."

"Well, what was the question?" I asked.

He took a slow breath, tension in every inch of his body as he slowly held a hand out to me, terror in his eyes. I took his hand, surprise flashing across his face as the song shifted to a more upbeat dance. He didn't hesitate to lead me to the center of the dance floor.

"Did you really think I wouldn't dance with you?"

"Maybe a little?" he said, leading me in a simple swing number. I let him lead, keeping up, paying attention to him, how he moved, and each step he made so I could move in tandem.

"Are you okay?" I asked, looking at his flushed face and slight smile. The sparking in my chest was back, but it was hard to focus on when he was there in front of me, putty at the ends of my fingers.

"Ooh, I am so much more than okay," he said, taking my hand and spinning me away. I spun, stopping as I came to the end of his reach, my hand still in his as he pulled me back to him. My right shoulder was at his left as we moved around each other. The sparking became louder, brighter, more robust, almost feverish.

There he was.

The man who had scrambled for my hand even after I killed his sister, the man who had untangled my hair when I got overwhelmed, the man who had fought through a dozen bandits to get to me, the man who had stared death in the face, time and time again for me, who had braved a dragon, an Echalon ghost city, and the Shale Tree with me. For me. We had saved each other more times than I could count. Back to back, night and day. With gilded brown eyes locked on mine, I realized like a wave crashing on the shore that this was the bright, capable, strong man that had, and still was, ready to rip both our worlds apart for me. He had killed for me, reached for me, covered me in a hundred little ways, but it wasn't because he had to. No, he never *had* to do any of it. In that single, crashing moment, one word took over my mind.

Love.

The moment I knew I loved him, the sparking cooled to a thin, delicate, steady thread within me. No, us. Within us. Surprise. Fear. Not my own, though. No. Anza's. I somehow knew exactly what had happened as he scanned my face, almost panicked. As if he had known and hadn't wanted to tell me, in fear of forcing it into place. A complete understanding of him burned through me.

I grabbed him by his collar as he realized I wasn't angry and leaned my face closer to his. He took the hint, leaning down ever so slightly. His lips pressed against mine, soft, kissing me deeply, his hands slowly moving up to my neck and cheeks as we stopped in the middle of the dance floor. Relief and deep love, like a thunderous rain, bounded down the newly formed bond. I could feel him there, and he could feel me. We didn't need words. As far as we were concerned, we didn't need words to define what we were now.

"Fucking finally." I broke the kiss at Whisper's voice, looking up into those gilded eyes as he leaned in to kiss my forehead. I closed my eyes, draping my hands across his shoulders as his arms found a place around my waist. I tried not to smile too wide as the disbelief hit him. Knowing he could feel the coy triumph that ran from me. The raw, giddy joy.

"Did you know about bonds?" he asked.

"No, but it almost feels like I did, maybe because you did?" I had known. It was almost as if I had simply not let myself think of the idea of loving him. We had been through so much. Had I not wanted to muddy the waters of survival with this feeling? This heated and untapped need?

"Maybe…are you alright?" he asked.

"I am more than alright."

"I'm sorry I didn't tell you earlier."

"I'm not mad."

"I know," he said. "I didn't want it to form unless you came to this conclusion yourself."

"You could feel it though, couldn't you, every time it sparked?"

"Yeah."

"That must have been hard, loving me and feeling the reciprocity flutter."

"It was," he said, a slight twinge of pain in him, but it slid away quickly. "Doesn't matter now."

"Right. Can anyone do this?"

"They usually don't form unless someone in the dynamic has the whole empathic skill thing, but yes."

"Oh, gotcha," I said, leaning my head on his shoulder as he planted soft kisses against my neck. It was right, having him so close to me.

Taryn was gorgeous for sure; the way she walked and spoke, the raw confidence in her being, how she was unafraid of pulling me close. She was beautiful, but she was not Anza. Anza was everything. He made every movement with a slight hesitation, asking for consent without words. We had both flipped off those bandits simultaneously when we ducked into the tunnel. Hell, even before we met Tamaj, we had both moved as one to help that little Photomyran girl. We had been moving in sync since we had met. This was fate, raw, honest, and trustworthy. "We're safe now, Beetle-Brain."

"Safer, Stone-Slinger, safer," he said, swaying with me in the middle of the floor.

"You're really not going anywhere, are you?" I asked, and amusement fluttered through him.

"No, especially not now," he said.

That thread was already growing more robust.

I don't know how long we stayed in the middle of that dance floor, arms wrapped around each other, gently swaying, but I didn't care. I didn't care what Olaf may have thought or what all those stuffy people may think. They had all fallen away. As far as we were concerned, only two people danced on that dance floor that night, joy bounding through us on both sides, compounding on one another.

He gripped my hand tighter, spinning me outward before drawing me back to him. His strong arms wrapped around me tightly. I didn't have to ask anything. We didn't have to speak. I knew. I knew he would be there for me, knew that he wouldn't stop me from chasing whatever I decided, and would stand by any decision I made. I knew he would catch me any time I fell and do everything he could for me. I was there with him, and he was there with me. It felt like it had only been a few minutes, but I heard my uncle clear his throat before I knew it.

"Hmm, oh, sorry," I said, pulling Anza to a stop.

"You're good, you're fine, don't worry," he said. "Letting you two love birds know I'm off to settle in for the night, don't stab anyone or get in too much trouble by morning."

"No promises," we retorted, and he shook his head.

"I guess that's the best I could hope for, night."

"Night," I said, watching him head toward the stairs. Whisper was asleep on Tamaj's back, Tamaj watching us intently as we moved.

"Hey."

"It's about time, Princess Clueless."

"Oh, come on. You're never gonna let me live this down, are you?"

"Absolutely not," Anza said, kissing my forehead, a hand still wrapped across my back and around my waist.

"Great," I said, rolling my eyes at him.

Tamaj got up, came over to us, and gently nuzzled my hand as Whisper stirred on her back. I stroked her head, itching behind an ear.

"Hey, library," Whisper said.

"You're exhausted."

"Library," she insisted again, and Tamaj looked at Anza and me.

"Fine," I said, watching the little Echalon perk up. "Not all night, alright?"

"As you like to say, 'no promises'," Whisper declared as Tamaj laughed, padding toward the library.

"I think you have a few shadows, Mira," Tamaj warned as they left. I glanced over my shoulder, spotting Taryn leaning against a column, Graz tucked behind it, peeking out.

"You two are amazing together," Taryn said.

"Aww, thanks," I said. "You two aren't too bad yourselves." Graz's face went a dark green as Taryn laughed.

"Well, if you want a romantic evening, stroll around the market ring. This late, all the markets are closed up, and there aren't any clouds anymore, the stars are out."

"That sounds like a great idea," Anza said, and the unsureness fluttered within him, giving away his desire for a chaperone.

"Why don't you two come with us?" I asked her.

"I don't want people to talk," he whispered.

I didn't take my eyes off Taryn as I nodded in response, my hand finding his.

"I'd love that," Taryn said. "Graz?"

"Eh, I don't know..."

"Come on, the fresh air would be good for you," Taryn insisted.

"Alright, but not too long," he agreed, coming out from behind the column.

"It's a double date," I said, the two Photomyra blushing deeply as Taryn led the way toward the castle's front door. Anza and I followed, still riding the high of feeling each other's emotions. For a moment, I could almost see how he could so often predict how I felt, my moods, and how he seemed to read my thoughts. Doing this over time would mean you're good at reading people.

"Whoa."

Lost in thought and letting Anza lead me, I had forgotten to look up, but as Anza spoke, I looked up, seeing the thick spattering of stars across the sky. I could hear the wildlife outside the castle walls as we followed Taryn and Graz toward the market ring. As we walked, I heard the familiar sounds of the rustling trees, the cricket-like noises, and a bird of prey crying into the night. The cool night air wove around us, but even Graz seemed more relaxed.

"Come on, I'll race you to the next set of stalls," Taryn said, patting Graz's arm.

"Oh, you're on," he said as they both took off, two green blurs in the night. The following section wasn't too far off and they were still in our line of sight when they stopped. I wasn't sure who had won, but that didn't matter. Their conversation wasn't close enough to hear. For a moment, I thought I saw something standing near one of the fluttering banners, a dark cloak and a bundle of green, but as I blinked, it was gone, only the dark banner of Agrenon there.

"Are you alright?"

"I think the journey is getting to me. I'm seeing people where people aren't."

"We went through a lot; I think I see people too sometimes, in my peripheral."

"Exactly. Do you think it'll ever slow down, stop?"

"No clue. I hope so, though. What do you think about those two?" Anza asked, pointing toward Taryn and Graz.

"They're different, alright. She seems confident enough in what she's doing, but he seems, well…"

"Awkward."

"Yeah."

"I've felt like something's up since we met them."

"What do you mean?"

"They feel nervous, even more so around us, around you."

"Nervous, how?"

"Nervous like something big is coming, but I can't think of what it is."

"Maybe they're nervous about change. I mean, having a new person around is always taxing, and it's probably even more taxing if that person is declared an heir."

"Right, that could be it," he said, gently twirling me before I went back to his side, our shoulders softly bumping together.

"It probably is. Don't worry about it. They'll settle down once they learn I'm not going to bite their heads off."

"Good, I hope they settle down soon."

"Me too."

The night continued silently, and before I knew it we were carefully ascending the stairs side by side. Taryn and Graz had gone off to their rooms, and Anza was gently leading me toward our own, my hand in his as we padded quietly down the hallway toward the bedrooms. What if he kissed me that deeply again? I hadn't let myself feel many needs when we were out in the thick of our journey. Now here we were, safe, freshly bonded, and I was trying to smother the buzzing need to be kissed like I was the whole night sky again. I had never felt such an unquestionable love before. As we got to our rooms, he kissed me goodnight, soft and sweet. I grabbed him by his collar, knowing down the bond he felt the same want I did and backed up into my bedroom. He followed, closing the door behind us.

32

"Stupid sun," I grumbled, burying my head under my pillow. Anza stirred beside me, burying his head under our shared pillow on the small bed with me. Naturally, the fiery ball of Hell spilled its morning blood through my window and I groaned. Carefully, I sat up, trying to get the audacity to fight the sun.

"Morning, Stone-Slinger," he said, his arms finding their way around my waist.

"Morning, Beetle-Brain," I grumbled, lying back down and resting my head on his shoulder.

"You're a sleepy little princess."

"I'm gonna fight the sun."

"Good luck with that." He laughed as my stomach growled. "Let's at least get you some breakfast so you *can* fight the sun."

"Gotta have the energy to tackle those solar flares."

"Not sure what you said, but yes, that," he said as I pulled back, rubbing my eyes.

We got up, carefully dressing, and I let him lead me downstairs toward the ballroom, which had already been converted back to a dining room. Anza flagged down a servant, asked for breakfast to be brought to us, and got me to a table. I promptly buried my head in my arms on the table and cursed the sun again. Anza took one of my hands, drawing little swirls on it happily as we waited for our food.

"Morning, Princess," I heard from a familiar voice

"Titanys," I grumbled before looking up. "Why?" That was all I asked.

"I won't bother you too much. I just have to let you know that last night your uncle had a bit of an emergency to attend to. He should be back in a few days, so you are technically in charge, but I'm here if you need me."

"I'm not gonna have to attend meetings or anything like that, right? I haven't even been a princess a whole day."

"No, no, it's a formality."

"Alright, cool, I'm going back to bed," I said, burying my head back in my arms.

"Goodnight."

"Night," I said, waving at him with my free hand as he left, only to hear a more familiar sound approach.

"Is she dead?"

"Naw, but she might wish she was," Anza said as Tamaj settled at the end of the table.

"Do you know of any way to defeat the sun?" I grumbled before looking up at the equally sleepy Barbarza.

"Unfortunately, no. Have you seen your little Moonbeam?"

"No, why?"

"I put her to bed last night, but knowing her, she probably snuck back down to that library."

"I bet you everything I own that she's under a pile of books," Anza said to me.

"I'm not taking that bet because I'd lose," I said. "Let her have her fun. She doesn't need to eat much and she can stay up way longer than us anyway," I said.

"I'll check on her in a while, make sure she didn't get trapped under one of those treacherous book columns she's building," Tamaj said, and I pointed at her.

"That's a good idea."

"You know what was also a good idea?" Tamaj asked, turning to stare firmly at Anza.

"Hey, I couldn't have known she'd dance with me. She'd just become a princess."

"Oh, come on. It's Mira, and look where it went."

"You really were scared of asking me to dance?" I asked as our plates came out, another carefully resting in front of Tamaj. "Thank you."

"Thanks, and yes, I was terrified, but I'm so happy I did it *now*." I couldn't help but blush as he spoke, lifting his eyebrows at me. Thankfully, Tamaj didn't seem to notice.

"Also, the fact that you've been so clueless was painful. I wanted to tell you so many times," Tamaj said.

"Why didn't you?" I asked, trying to ignore the sharp, coy triumph at getting me to blush that was rumbling from his side of the bond.

"Because someone had asked me not to," she said, glaring at Anza again.

"I didn't want to worry about if you actually liked me or if the bond formed because you learned about me liking you."

"Well, thankfully, I was a little focused on breathing, but I kind of knew I was in love with you without letting myself admit it."

"Love is funny that way. It creeps in slowly, then all at once," Tamaj said as I tried to pick up my breakfast sandwich, Anza kissing my fingers.

"Eat your food."

"Naw," he said, kissing my hand a few more times before letting it go, turning his attention to his plate.

"I could go on all day about how this man tensed up every once in a while, probably when he felt that reciprocity flutter."

"It wasn't that obvious."

"Even I noticed a few times, I just didn't know what it was about," I said as Anza brushed his foot against mine.

"Well, now we all know."

"Even Whisper picked up on it faster than you, Mira," Tamaj said, nudging me before finally turning to her food. I couldn't help but roll my eyes, finally tucking firmly into our meals.

"Do you want to go to the markets today? I'm sure I can rustle up some coin, and it'd be nice to get a lay of the land out there," I asked as we finished.

"I'd love to look at it," Anza said, returning to playing with my hand.

"I'm gonna go wrangle the Moonbeam. You two have fun," Tamaj said as Anza got up. I didn't want to fight the sun now that I had eaten and let him lead me out of the castle and down toward the markets again. Hand in hand.

"I do feel kind of embarrassed for not picking up on how you felt sooner."

"Don't, we were dealing with a lot, and like you said, you kind of knew but didn't know, you know?"

"Yeah, thanks for not giving up on me."

"I would never give up on you," he said, his thumb still rubbing against my hand as he led me to the market.

The stalls, which had been closed up and tucked away the night before, were all open and adorned with vibrant things, from armorers and weapon smiths to jewelers and embroiderers and everyone in between. People bustled from vendor to vendor, getting food and other staples for the day.

Many people recognized me, whispering about the new heir, curtsying as we walked past. I waved away their curtsies and bows and, after a few times, they stopped curtsying at me when they saw me. Their whispers were like wildfire; hushed, excited voices. It wasn't long before a Maraung child tip-toed toward me. As she revealed a flower, I dropped Anza's hand to get on the little one's level. Carefully, I took it.

"What a most precious gift. Thank you, little one," I said, gently tucking it behind my ear. "You have a parent nearby, right?" The little one nodded and pointed to a woman not far from us, watching intently, proudly.

"Good, thank you so much for the gift. You've got a good, strong heart," I said, and the little one giggled before bounding on their toes and quickly scrambling back to their mother, who nodded her thanks to me. I nodded back in understanding as Anza's hand found mine again.

We spent the day like that, weaving back and forth through the crowds, Anza keeping close, keeping an eye out. People were patient, loving, and kind. Word spread quickly about the benevolent heir to the throne of Agrenon. The Mountain that saw and knew all, the woman who would fix everything for them. I had been taught that there were a million things I had to be to be an Endering. The expectations of being a queen, though, were clearly much bigger.

My legs trembled as we returned to the castle as the sun flirted with the horizon line, my feet aching. My shoulders were tired, flowers woven into my locks of hair like a makeshift crown. Anza looked just as tired, with a few flowers tucked behind his ears. He, too, had gotten the seal of approval from the people in the market ring. He had always been good with kids and they seemed to catch on to that quickly. As we stepped off the streets and back into the castle, we walked into pure pandemonium. Guards rushed back and forth, searching for something.

"Hey, what's wrong? What's happened?" I asked, Tamaj appearing from one of the hallways and rushing to our side.

"There you are! I couldn't find you in the crowds," she said quickly, panic in her eyes. *"We're looking everywhere, to be sure so we don't cause a panic throughout the rings too, but I can't think of another place to look."*

"What happened?" Anza repeated, Tamaj still shaking from shock as she looked us over, as if she didn't want to say what she was about to say. As if she wished she could take the truth from us. As if she could save us from the pain she was about to inflict upon us.

"Whisper's missing."

My blood ran cold.

"Where have you looked?"

"The library, her room, my room, your rooms, the ballroom, and even the training room. She knows better than to have run off."

"Listen to me very closely, Tamaj; this is very important. When, exactly, was the last time you saw her?"

"When I put her to bed last night," Tamaj said.

Whisper hadn't joined us for breakfast. We all assumed she was asleep in the library.

"She wasn't upset, right? Like, not enough to take off?"

"No, a little upset that she had to get some sleep, but she probably would have snuck down to the library if she was going to defy me."

"And she's not there," Anza said. "Wait, what about the nursery? Did you check there?"

"No, I don't think I did," Tamaj said, a little hope flashing in her eyes.

"Breathe. She probably went there to check on The Two," I said, trying to smooth over Tamaj's mane. She nodded, taking a few deep breaths.

"I've got her. Go check for them, Mira?" Anza asked, and I nodded, turning and bounding up the stairs. She had to be in that nursery, she probably slept the day away on the floor near them. She had to be in there. I got to the door quickly, my heart slamming in my chest as I moved, but as I opened the door, my stomach twisted.

Whisper wasn't there, but that wasn't what made my heart stop. It wasn't what made me feel sick and dizzy at the same time.

The bassinets were empty.

33

"They're gone, they're all gone!" I said as I rushed back into the ballroom, the color draining from Anza's face. I could feel my blood in my ears. We had no leads, no evidence of where they had gone, no clues, nothing, and my uncle was nowhere near us. He did not know they were gone. He did not know we needed his help. This was on me.

"Okay, was there anything at all that we have? Any note, a ransom, anything?"

"There was nothing in the bedrooms or the library," Tamaj said. Anza's gaze had torn off toward a small doorway and fury and suspicion rattled across the bond as I traced his gaze, catching sight of Graz and Taryn slipping out of sight.

"You don't think…?"

"They feel guilty, like they're up to something."

"I can't follow up those stairs; they're too narrow," Tamaj said.

"You wait down here, make sure they don't double back," I said, shaking my wrists. "Anza, you and I are going to get our weapons." Tamaj nodded and headed for the small door as Anza and I quickly rushed upstairs.

"Why not tell the guards?" Anza asked.

"It might be a coincidence. Maybe they're sneaking away for some alone time."

"This feels bigger than alone time," he said.

"If they have them, if they know what happened…"

"I'm going to fucking kill them."

"Good to know we're on the same page," I said as we finally got to our rooms and I grabbed my axe.

Anza and I got back to the hall at the same time and together, we rushed back to Tamaj.

"Did they come down yet?" I asked.

"No."

"Good," I said as we slid through the narrow doorway.

"Yell if you need help," she said as we climbed.

I hoped this was a misunderstanding, hoped that we weren't right, hoped that they were being silly up here together. I even hoped we'd see something we didn't want to see for a moment before stepping out onto the roof of one tower. The night air spilled in from the open-windowed design. The center of the room was piled high with wood from broken chairs, sticks, and other debris, the smell of fuel rancid in the air. The only light that danced around the room was from a torch resting firmly in Taryn's hand.

"You stop right there," I said firmly, looking into those beautiful orbs.

"This…isn't as bad as it looks."

"Naw, it's worse," Graz said.

"Shut up," Taryn hissed.

"What is going on? Where are the Echalon?"

"We don't know where the Echalon are."

"It's really suspicious that you two, feeling defiant, sneak your butts up here right after they go missing," Anza said. Taryn hadn't moved, still holding the torch tightly. She looked at the pile of wood then up at us.

"Don't even try it," I said. "What's this for, anyway? Are you some kind of spy? Working for another kingdom? Trying to signal them? Let them know we're vulnerable?" I asked, starting to approach, Anza moving in tandem with me.

"No, no, none of that."

"What the fuck are you doing?" I asked.

"I can't tell you."

"Why the hell not?"

"Because you won't believe us," Graz said, and as he spoke, Taryn moved. I was close enough to move between her and the pile of wood they had made and snatched away the torch, twisting her around and throwing her back to Graz. Torch in one hand, axe in the other, I watched as Anza stepped forward to keep them down together, his sword ready in case he needed to kill them.

"I highly suggest you talk," he said, eyes flashing in the low light.

"Alright, fine, fine."

"Taryn!" Graz warned.

"We have to, okay?"

"They're gonna kill us, anyway," he said.

"We don't know that," she countered, glaring at him.

"Talk," I said, louder.

"Olaf's been lying to you," Taryn said, looking at me, her eyes alight with fear. "About everything. About Saha, about your parents, about everything. We think he took Whisper and The Two, but we don't know why he would do that."

"Sounds like you're trying to blame someone who's not here to get out of having to answer for the extinction of a species."

"I'm not lying!" she said.

Anza was tense, his glance bouncing between her and me.

"What do you have?"

"She's not lying," he confirmed.

"She really believes this shit?"

"It's not shit, it's the truth, but you're so blinded that you won't accept it!" Graz snarled, his voice lifting far more anger than I had ever expected it to.

"Prove it. You think he took them? You think he's lying to us?"

"We know it," Taryn said.

"Prove it."

"How do we—" Graz cut Taryn off.

"The dungeon," he said quickly.

"If we take her down there and she's loyal to him—" Taryn started.

"What choice do we have?"

"What's in the dungeon?" Silence.

Graz slowly, carefully stood, Anza's blade trained on him.

"I'll show you."

"I don't know if that's a good idea," Anza said.

"You can feel me still, right?" I asked, and he nodded. "If I'm in pain, if the bond breaks, kill her," I said, nodding to Taryn. "I'll take him down to the dungeon."

"Got it, but hurry, and be safe," he said.

"Safer," I said with a nod as he shifted his blade to Taryn, who still sat on the ground, her back pressed close to one of the few walls in the small space. I tucked my axe away, shaking my bracelets to remind me they were there, and gestured for the door, sending him down first. It didn't take long until we got to the bottom of the space, Graz moving carefully, his face turned down as we stepped into the main room.

"What's going on? Did they have them?" Tamaj asked.

"No, they don't have them, but they're telling some bullshit story. They say they have proof though."

"Don't believe them for a second."

"I don't. Anza has Taryn up there, we're heading to the dungeon to see this 'proof'."

"And when there isn't any?" Tamaj asked.

"We get to the bottom of where the kids are, one way or another," I said sternly, keeping the torch close in case I needed to use it against Graz. Tamaj quickly took up my rear as Graz led us to another staircase downward. I assumed it was the right one to the dungeon because Tamaj didn't correct us. The darkness engulfed us, stopped short only by the torch's light. Graz moved carefully, working slowly.

"He has lied to you, you know."

"Yeah, as you keep saying," I said as we finally got to the bottom of the winding stairs. He started forward, moving toward a set of carved metal cells. "Where's this 'proof'?" I asked, and Graz stopped before pointing into a small cell in the wall. I turned, looking into the small, damp space.

It wasn't a considerable cell. It had a bucket, a cot, and a window, but not much else except for a thin, emaciated form in the corner. His clothes hung from his frame, eyes as green as moss watched me, unfocused and distant, a scraggly beard and matted hair as dark as the night sky hung from his head, but those features were unmistakable. I remembered them from the dozens of pictures Sil had back home. Remembered from how she had described him in the stories. From the way, those mossy eyes lit up in the low light. I felt the world shift. Everything was suddenly sideways, and I was still trying to live right side up. Everything was wrong. My stomach turned and my eyes started to burn…*one day, in and out, and they came back in caskets…*

Taryn and Graz were right: Olaf had lied to me.

"Do you have a key?" I asked without taking my eyes off the figure in the cell.

"Only Olaf does." My heart dropped.

Think. Think.

"Is that Brian?"

"Tamaj?" His voice was weak, crackling, broken. He was alive.

"Oh my stars, that's Brian."

"We don't need a key," I said firmly, doubling back to where the start of the cells was, reaching for the rock in the wall and pushing it back.

"He's down three, and please try to stay calm so your partner doesn't murder Taryn."

I took a steady breath, trying to keep as calm as I could, passing Graz the torch before forcing the side of the walls away. Each cell was framed in stone, the bars at the front. It was easy enough to tear through them and get to him. I rushed to his side, brushing some matted strands from his face.

"Hey, hey…"

"Mira?" I could see the tears forming in his eyes as they finally focused on me.

"Hey, Dad." The tears spilled over as I pulled him into my arms. He was far taller than me, but his lack of weight made him easy to carry. "I don't think I can get him up the stairs."

"*I can. Get him to me,*" Tamaj said, Graz holding the torch up so we could see. I carried him carefully back the way I had come and to Tamaj. He winced with every step I took and stifled a noise of pain as I helped him onto Tamaj's back.

"Where? Where does it hurt?"

"Everywhere," he said, his voice even more distant.

"*We have to move,*" Tamaj said as I turned to Graz.

"Lead the way."

He rushed toward the entrance, leading the way up toward the ballroom again.

"You said he lied about Saha too?" I asked.

"That's what Taryn, and I were doing. Olaf tried to commit regicide, but he failed. She's out there, waiting for our signal." I didn't think I could feel more shock. My dad was alive. So was Saha.

"He's gone. He took the eggs and Whisper," I said.

"And she can help get them back," he said as we rushed toward the infirmary.

"Hey!" I called out, seeing nurses and doctors in the room. At my voice, they rushed to me. I reached out, trying to take the torch from him, but he held on, both of us holding it now.

"Olaf couldn't have done this alone, right?"

"Right, and if you try to go after him with anyone in this castle—"

"They'll ignore me or stop me because they're loyal to him."

"Save for a few of us. We've been informants for the queen for a while now," he confessed.

"Do you know anything about medicines?"

"I have to," he said, nodding.

"Stay with him; make sure they don't try to kill him," I ordered.

"What are you going to do?"

"I'm going to finish what you started," I said as he met my eyes before nodding and letting the torch go.

"Tamaj, we need to be ready to leave!" I said as the nurses and doctors got my father from her back and onto a bed. Graz rushed to his side to keep an eye on the doctors.

"*On it,*" she said as I scrambled on, keeping the torch from her as she rushed back to the door. I quickly slipped off and climbed the narrow stairs to the roof to find Anza and Taryn right where I had left them.

"Well?" Anza asked, looking at me, Taryn still at the end of his sword.

"Let her go," I said, tossing the torch on the pile. Hope flashed in Taryn's eyes.

"What?"

"I'll fill you in on the way down," I said. "We have a queen to go meet."

Looking out at the edge of the nearby forest, one, then two, then four, then eight, torches slowly sparked to life until dozens of them dotted the forest's edge, moving toward the castle walls. I led the way to the stairs, rushing downward. I filled Anza in by the time we hit the ground floor.

"Where's Graz?" Taryn asked.

"Infirmary, I'll get Saha, you make sure no one messes with them," I said, and she nodded, breaking away from us as Anza and I scrambled onto Tamaj's back. She started toward the door, slamming it open. We burst into the night and Tamaj rushed through the rings of the inner City of Blood, to the outer ring, past the outskirts of the town without hesitation. Slowing to a stop as we approached the cloaked figures, their torches held high.

There was a long pause before one figure stepped forward, drawing an elegant rapier from its hilt. The guard looked like leaves as it wove around her dark green hand. The other hand lifted up, and she dropped the hood. The scar on her left cheek blazed a trail of truth up the side of her head, her hair was woven back and tied in a thick, loose bun at the base of her neck, and a bloom of orange flowers sat across the back of her head, small and dainty, but as elegant as ever. Those eyes, as bright and blue as the clearest lake, narrowed on us as we stopped. She was ready to fight for her crown and throne and did not know if we were friends or foes.

"My queen," Tamaj said as we slid off her back, bowing deeply. Anza and I both bowed, and I glanced up, watching her face soften slightly.

"It's nice to see you again, Tamaj. Rise." We rose. "Names." Her voice was stern but measured, careful, her weapon still drawn.

"Anza."

"Mira."

"Mira? Brians's girl?"

"Yes."

"She did say you'd be here."

"What?"

"It doesn't matter. Is your uncle here?"

"No, he took the Echalon. He doesn't know you're here."

"Does he have an heir?"

"He declared me his heir late last night."

"Do you, Mira Hamilton, revoke your claim on my throne?" she asked, her grip tightening on her hilt.

"I, Mira Hamilton, revoke all claims I made to the throne of Agrenon, if you help me get my kids back."

"Your kids?"

"The Echalon."

She hesitated, her eyes looking between us, but she wasn't looking at us. I could tell by how she didn't meet our faces. She was playing chess.

"Go," she finally said.

I didn't hesitate to get back on Tamaj, Anza scrambling on with me. "Once we've reclaimed the castle, I'll send some of my most trusted after you. Do not engage!" she called after us as Tamaj bolted over the ground.

"Did you hear that last part?" Anza asked.

"Nope."

"Hear who?" Tamaj said as we moved, putting her head down to search for Olaf's scent. *"Got him."*

"Good, let's go get our fucking kids."

34

My heart slammed in my chest, giving me strength as Tamaj navigated the rolling plains northward. North. Toward Korrewen. *Leaders will rip their kingdoms apart to get their hands on an Echalon's heart.*

I didn't know why he wanted to bring them there, but he wouldn't get my kids killed. He wasn't going to use them or sell them or let them go for any sort of fucking deal with another kingdom. I wouldn't let him. They were too precious for that. I didn't lose Arlo and cross an infection-filled nation for some fake king to kill the one thing I almost died keeping safe. Fuck that.

I ran through all the bright spots in my mind, asking myself repeatedly if he had been lying. Tamaj didn't stop as the night continued, fueled by pure spite. I could feel Anza through the bond, his fury swirling with my own. He was ready to commit as many acts of violence as I was and his grip kept tightening and loosening on his sword. Clenching and releasing. Itching for blood.

I remembered the ring. Remembered that he had beaten me. It wasn't just me, though. I had them with me. We had something to lose.

The sun had crested over the horizon, spilling over the rolling plains as the Barbarza came into view in the distance. As we approached, the light hit the back of it for a moment and light spiraled outward through the shadows.

"*There,*" Tamaj said, picking up more speed. I reached out, finding the strength to grab hold of the ground they were passing over. I pulled it up and through the chest of the Barbarza. It collapsed, sliding down the spire it was now impaled upon as Whisper fell off. I summoned a smaller spike near her head, sharpening the sides.

"Run!" I shrieked as Tamaj ran as fast as her legs would carry her toward them. Whisper immediately worked at the ropes with the sharp stone I had provided as Olaf tried to get his bearings. Turning, he saw us. There, hanging from his side, was the egg bag. I reached out, trying to find the purchase to spear him through right there, but as I did, Tamaj's legs gave out and she collapsed onto the sheet of ice beneath us, expansive and never-ending. Anza made a sharp noise as I was pitched from Tamaj's back skittering like a rock on ice for a few yards. Looking up, I saw Anza's leg pinned beneath Tamaj as she struggled to get up. I found my feet first, several yards from them now. It was only a moment before a thick sheet of ice obscured them from my view as a small dome of ice wrapped around Olaf and I.

"I think there's been a misunderstanding," he said, eyes as hard as ice. I readied my axe.

"Careful, Mira, we're coming!" Anza said as I heard Tamaj slam herself into the thick ice.

I kept my eyes on Olaf. Carefully, he stepped to the left, and I stepped to the right, noting where Whisper lay, still working on her restraints, without looking at her. I was moving toward her.

"I think there certainly has been."

"Oh, so we're on the same page still?"

"Oh no, we're not," I started. *Buy time, buy time.* "You see, you seem to think I would willingly let you endanger their lives," I said, pointing to the egg bag on his shoulder. *Don't bring attention to Whisper.* "You misunderstood what I would put myself through, the pains I would endure, for them. You seem to think I will let you do whatever you want with them because you dared to put a crown on your head this morning." *Keep it moving. What else can I say?* "You stood at that throne thinking making me some princess would be enough to placate me, but it isn't; it never was."

"You seem to misunderstand the intent of the mission. They were never meant to be brought back to keep alive. Even Saha was going to use them in time," he said, circling around me, hands sliding into a defensive stance. He was ready for me. I was ready for him.

"Interesting," I said. "It's so smooth how you lie."

"It's not a lie."

"How would I know?" I said, keeping his gaze unblinking. "Not like I knew when you lied about my parents, huh? What exactly was hiding in that dungeon again?" His eyes flashed, and he lunged. I felt a hand wrap around the handle of the sharp dagger I had pulled up. The thudding from Tamaj, the slamming of walls, the flash of spiraling light. A simple flick of the wrist and Whisper, now free, had cut the strap on the egg bag, sliding it neatly away from Olaf as he lunged for me.

I stepped backward, my feet slipping on the ice. A pressure pushed from behind me in the soft bend of my knee and pain laced up my leg. I looked down where my leg was, blood dripping slowly onto the icy ground beneath me as I landed hard. Tamaj broke through. I blinked and Olaf was gone, but I couldn't tear my eyes from the icicle that had torn completely through my leg at my knee. My vision was blurry already, tunneling. I wasn't losing too much blood. Yet. But even I knew it was only a matter of seconds.

"No!" Whisper was at the wound, trying to press against it. Anza and Tamaj were there a moment later.

"We have to move her."

"If we move her, she dies."

"If we don't move her, she dies!" I don't remember being moved, only my stomach pitching itself sideways. I tried to steady my breathing.

"The ice is melting."

My heart slammed in my throat, the pain threatening my consciousness. Anza's turmoil and panic ran down the bond as he tried to brush my hair out of my face.

"You're alright. It's not as bad as it looks. Hey, look at me, look at me."

"That ice is going to melt," I said.

"Yeah."

"When it does…" I finally looked up at him, those gilded eyes framed with tears.

"Yeah." We didn't have to say it out loud. We both knew that my hot blood would melt the ice. Sure, the cold would slow the bleeding, but a wound that bad, that clear through. Soon enough, nothing would keep pressure. We had run all night to get here. We were hours from an infirmary.

"Where did Olaf go? Did you get The Two?" Tamaj's voice asked.

"I don't know where he went, but I've got The Two," Whisper said.

"I'm sorry," I said, reaching up to Anza's face as he rested his forehead on mine. "I tried."

"Don't you ever apologize," he said, feeling the hot tears slide out of my eyes. Trying not to think about my leg or how mangled it was, I could feel the tendrils of the bond growing weaker as I lost blood.

"Is that Saha?"

"She'll have supplies we can use, and I have an idea," Whisper said. I heard Tamaj rush away, but Anza stayed right there. I could feel myself being pulled away, the darkness creeping inward.

"Stay with me Mira. Please. Please, I can't do this again, I can't lose you," he begged, his hand on my cheek, brushing away my tears as his own slid down his face. I was dying. We both knew it.

"Stay safe, Beetle-Brain."

"I will, Stone-Slinger, I will." His eyes stayed locked on mine, tears flowing as he clung to me.

He was the last thing I saw as darkness flooded my senses.

35

The room was dark when I opened my eyes again. I almost instantly recognized the infirmary back at the castle. The one we had left my father in. *My father.* I turned, trying to spot him, but instead spotted Anza tucked into a chair, his head on the edge of my cot. Asleep.

"Dedicated, that one," I turned to the voice, seeing Saha sitting at a makeshift desk in the corner, her eyes spilling over papers, her voice as soft as the candlelight that lit the room.

"Where are the Echalon?" I asked, and she gestured to a small cot nearby. Whisper lay on it, wrapped tightly around the egg bag. Tamaj lay at her feet, asleep. I sighed, relaxing back against the soft bed.

"They're okay," she assured me. "They're safe here."

"Olaf said you were going to use them."

"Not how he was going to."

"So you are?"

"No, not necessarily. Echalon are very capable and bright people, they are an asset wherever they are, but they are children; they should be allowed to be children. Allowed to have a say in the life they want for themselves, not ransacked for their hearts."

"That's what Sil told me."

"Good."

"My leg?" I asked as she stood, coming closer to sit on the edge of the bed.

"Whisper found a way to save it. A healing spell, I think? It stopped the bleeding temporarily. It was a long shot; I believe some of you Endering might have even called it a 'Hail Mary.' You're going to need a brace, but you'll be able to use it."

"Good, good," I said, laying back, taking deep breaths. I had thought my leg was gone, but it wasn't, I still had a leg.

"How was the whole getting-the-castle-back thing?" I asked.

"Messy, but coming back from the dead always is, I guess," she said.

There wasn't a single thing out of place about her. She looked like her painting, but she had been *dead*. Olaf had convinced the kingdom she was dead.

"You have a lot of experience with that?" I asked, raising an eyebrow at her.

"I wouldn't say a lot, but far more than I would like to," she said, a smile playing across those lips, reaching her eyes.

"What has happened since I got knocked out? How the hell did Olaf get your throne from you? I have a million questions."

"And I have a million answers," she said. "Olaf took advantage of my vulnerability after I gave birth to my heir. Birth for a Photomyra is perilous, and though it went well, he, um..." She hesitated. "He hit me with a candlestick over the back of the head and paid some goons to take me out into the woods. He didn't seem to care what their plan for me was so long as they killed me before they left me there, but they didn't get as far as they wanted before I woke up."

"I'm so sorry. Your heir?"

"I'm still looking for them," she said. "Whisper has decided to help me."

"Do you think they're alive?"

"Yes, and I think Olaf would have kept them close. Can't have potential enemies being out of arm's reach."

"He wouldn't have killed the baby?"

"Could he kill you?"

"He could have."

"But he didn't. Your Uncle's fatal flaw is that he hates seeing life leave people's eyes. He doesn't mind the idea of them dying, but he can't help but want them to die at someone else's hands, especially his potential enemies. Your father nearly starved to death, he sent me away, he even left you to bleed to death."

"Potential enemies. Graz said something about people being with you on the inside."

"Yes, I had a handful of undercover aides in the castle when you first showed up."

"Who?"

"Well, Graz and Taryn for sure; Titanys has been feeding me information since I was overthrown; Naren, and a few others." Her eyes were still on me, a hand picking at the blanket draped over me.

"Did you catch him?" I asked.

"No." She sighed, closing her eyes to take a steady breath, as if settling the disappointment in herself. "But everyone in the kingdom knows his face. He won't get far in Agrenon."

"Good, he can go fuck himself."

"He tricked you too, huh?" she asked, and I tried to swallow the lump in my throat.

"I trusted him."

"You and me both. He was my Royal Endering, Second in Command, my dearest friend."

"And then he clocked you in the head with a candlestick and promptly shoved the kingdom down the fucking toilet."

"Yeah, it still throws me off, the whole indoor plumbing thing."

"Indoor plumbing?"

"Ah yes, didn't have it as a child. It was all added after my father got an Echalon advisor; it was a whole thing."

"Still shakes me that some people still fight with bone weapons and some poop in a toilet."

"It's a weird time." She laughed. I liked her laugh; it reached her eyes. The way she tilted her head and looked away, as if embarrassed, it was genuine. "Listen, Mira, I do want to ask you something important, if I may?"

"Ask away."

"I need to have a Royal Endering to ensure that Agrenon does not look like it's an easy target, but it can't be your father. And I've already heard the word of The Mountain of Agrenon in port towns. Other kingdoms will know of your prowess soon enough."

"You want me to be your Royal Endering?"

"I would be honored if you would, but I understand if this has been too much."

"I'm in, but I have one question."

"Ask away."

I couldn't help but smile as she repeated my comment.

"Why not my dad?"

"Well," she said. "What do you know about your father?"

"Jack and shit."

"Excuse me?"

"Absolutely nothing but his name and his face."

"Ah, not even his power?"

"No, not even his power. Wait, what's his power?" I asked, watching her shift slightly in her seat.

"Remind me that if I ever see Sil again, to give her a piece of my mind?"

"You're gonna have to get in line, but yeah, his power?"

"He can cure and create illnesses."

"Like…plagues? Like The Fever?"

"Yes."

"Did he?"

She pressed her lips together, her eyes finally pulling from mine.

"He admitted to it, so I can't trust him. He has his reasonings, but they're not reasons that would support him being Royal Endering and—"

"Arlo died because of him. Rania, Anza's sister, and his parents *died*."

"I am so sorry," she said, looking back at me. "I tried so hard to stop it, but he was locked in these walls and any attempt to get in with Olaf around was—"

"Impossible."

"Indeed. He could freeze me on sight. I even had your mother try, but that went awry as well."

"My mother? You knew her." It wasn't a question.

"Don't tell me. Sil told you nothing about her?"

"Not even her name. She wouldn't talk about her."

"I'm going to burn her alive from across realms." Saha said, her jaw cracking with the tension as she wrung at her wrists.

"Can you do that?"

"No, but I fucking wish I could," she said, standing and striding over to her makeshift desk and pulling through what seemed to be a pile of pictures. It was only a moment before she padded back over to my side, sitting now at the side of my bed instead of the foot.

"This is your mother." She passed me the picture. I stared at it, my heart slamming in my chest as I looked at that familiar face. The brown skin, shorter but still neatly prepared locks, wide nose, the light in her too-familiar stone-gray eyes. My eyes. A small bundle of a child in her arms.

"What's her name?" I asked, knowing that the answer would push the tears in my eyes over the edge. I knew what the answer to my question was. I knew, but I needed to hear her say it. I knew why she had set me on edge so much, why I had felt both secure and unsure of her. When I met her eyes, I was looking at my own.

Saha shuddered, seeing the emotion on my face, knowing that the next thing she said would break my trust in so many people. She had been right there, right there in front of me. Tamaj had known my parents, so had Sil. Why had they kept this from me? Why hadn't Tamaj said something?

"Emai."